D0093135

THE FIFTH ELEMENT

ALSO BY JØRGEN BREKKE

Where Monsters Dwell

Dreamless

THE FIFTH ELEMENT

Jørgen Brekke

MINOTAUR BOOKS
NEW YORK

This is a work of fiction. All of the characters, organizations, and events portrayed in this novel are either products of the author's imagination or are used fictitiously.

www.minotaurbooks.com

The Library of Congress Cataloging-in-Publication Data is available upon request.

ISBN 978-1-250-07391-4 (hardcover)
ISBN 978-1-4668-8541-7 (e-book)

First published in Norway as *Menneskets natur* by Gyldendal Norsk Forlag, 2013

First U.S. Edition: February 2017

10 9 8 7 6 5 4 3 2 1

The human body contains blood, phlegm, yellow bile, and black bile. These things make up the nature of the body, and because of them a human being either feels pain or is in good health.

—Hippocrates (ca. 460–377 BCE)

Life consists partly of what you yourself do, and partly of what others do to you.

—Aristotle

PROLOGUE

"*This is no mystery.*" The voice came from the burned-out sofa. "It's a thriller. I don't watch thrillers. I like mysteries. They have a meditative calm about them. But this has been too much of a thriller. Don't you agree?"

The rest of the room was completely destroyed after the explosion. All the windows were blown out. The wind coming from the sea was saturated with moisture and salt, and everything smelled scorched. Behind the pistol that was pointed at him, Detective Inspector Odd Singsaker saw a smile that seemed distant, as if nothing of what had happened were real.

"It's a mystery to me," replied Singsaker.

At first the pistol had been pointed in his general direction, not directly at him. On the floor between them lay the shotgun and the body. Singsaker thought about what had happened as though it were a scene in a film. How was it possible to distance oneself like that?

"I know you want to shoot me, but as a police officer there are certain rules you have to follow. So let me make it easy for you: Pick up the shotgun!"

Singsaker remained calm and didn't move. Now he could almost see right down the barrel of the gun, which was six or seven yards away from him.

"Pick up the shotgun, or I'll shoot you." The voice did not waver. The tone was expressionless.

Singsaker took two steps forward, still unsure what to do. Now he stood with the shotgun between his feet. His heart was pounding.

I

Two weeks after it happened . . .

O*dd Singsaker opened* his eyes. He'd shut them to try to visualize the scene. Time seemed to have stopped ever since he'd stood in that house with the shotgun at his feet. Now he was sitting in an interrogation room along with Kurt Melhus, an investigator from Internal Affairs.

"Can you describe how you felt when you stood there?" said Melhus.

"I don't know what I felt," replied Singsaker.

"Was it hate?"

"I don't know what hate is, to tell you the truth. That's too abstract for me."

"Haven't you ever hated anyone?"

"I'm not sure."

"What about love, then? In this very room, you told me about your love for Felicia Stone."

"Yes," said Singsaker, suddenly claustrophobic in the cramped interrogation room.

"Hate is the opposite of love, isn't it?" Melhus seemed genuinely interested in this topic.

"Nothing is the opposite of love. When you love someone, there's no opposite to it. Well, sorrow, maybe," said Singsaker, looking down at the table between them.

"Is that what you really think? Well, they do say that love does not know its adversary," said Melhus.

"I don't know if hate exists. But never mind. I was angry, furious, I think."

"So you picked up the shotgun?"

"Yes, I picked it up and took aim," said Singsaker.

"And then what happened?"

"Then I said: *You know I'm never going to kill you. Not as long as you haven't told me where Felicia is and what you've done with her.*"

PART I

PHLEGM

Winter fills the body with phlegm.

—Hippocrates

2

The day before it happened . . .

L*ook carefully at the* boy. Is he eleven? Thirteen? A confusing age.

When he's asleep, his face looks like a little child's. His head rests on the desk in the back room of the shop, with a trickle of saliva running down his chin. On the screen in front of him the game he fell asleep playing is still flickering. He must have gotten bored with it. Maybe he hoped he would dream about something more exciting. You have no idea what's going on inside his head. Now and then he twitches, like a dreaming dog. Under his head of wispy dark hair there's a book. A rare Spanish edition of *Don Quixote and Other Works* by Pierre Menard. The saliva has made a spot on the dust jacket; it looks like a thought, a question that's sinking in through the cover. What will his father say?

In the kitchen the man looked to see whether there were any glasses left, but the cupboard was bare. Nothing but dust and grease spots. The faucet coughed hoarsely when he turned it on. After a moment the water ran free of rust. He bent down and took a drink. When he had quenched his thirst, he spat in the sink and watched the phlegm wash down the drain. Then he opened the cupboard again. He'd noticed something inside.

A children's book lay on the bottom shelf, *Charlie the Choo-Choo*. Something the previous tenants had left behind. He took it out and brushed off the dust, the rubber gloves he wore making a rustling sound. He leafed through the book, and found an old faded photo that had been used as a bookmark. It was a picture of a girl with braids. She was standing in the living room of the apartment, smiling confidently. The girl was slightly blurry. The photographer had focused instead on the easy chair behind her, where a wineglass lay tipped over on the seat. It was a bad photograph, the kind that would be deleted from the camera nowadays. But in the old days that sort of image occasionally got caught on film. He folded the photo of the girl and put her in his pocket.

In the living room he stepped over the pump-action shotgun and went over to the telescope on the windowsill, a Zeiss Victory Dia-Scope 85 T FL—2011, the latest model. He reached up to brush back his hair. It was still thick and dark, with a light sprinkling of gray. Then he took one last look at the shop on the corner down below before he stowed the sawed-off shotgun, the scope, and the collapsible tripod in the duffel bag and left the apartment as empty as when he'd arrived.

The snow was blowing horizontally. The storm that had raged earlier in the week had started again this morning, but wasn't supposed to last long. After he crossed the street he stopped outside the door of the shop and shook off the snow that had settled on his shoulders and the hood of his all-weather jacket. He wasn't that happy with the jacket. On a hike in the mountains last fall he'd ended up soaked through.

There was a stained cardboard sign hanging in the window inside the door. CLOSED it said, in handwritten letters that sloped down to the right.

He went inside.

The owner, Isaac Casaubon, looked up at him sleepily.

He set his duffel bag down on the floor.

"Didn't you see the sign?"

"Yeah, I saw it."

"I'm not sure you get it. We're not open for business today."

"I know. But I'm not a customer." He turned, shook off his hood, and locked the door. "Now no one else will bother us," he said, picking up the duffel bag and striding to the cash register.

"Who are you?" The shop owner didn't look sleepy anymore.

The man was sitting on a high stool behind the counter. Then he leaned forward, and their breaths mingled invisibly in the air between them.

"Come here, over to the window," he said, placing his hand on Casaubon's shoulder.

The shop owner got up, moving as though he were lifting weights. "What do you want?"

"Just come over here."

Reluctantly, he obeyed.

"Awful weather," the man said. "You can hardly see the building across the street."

"What the hell do you want from me?" Casaubon's eyes shifted nervously.

"Do you know who lives in the corner apartment on the fourth floor?"

"How would I know? Why are you asking me this? I want you to leave." Casaubon straightened up, succeeding in making his small body look bigger, but he still looked scared.

"No one is living in that apartment on the fourth floor. It's empty at the moment."

"And what does that have to do with me?"

"The police have rented the place."

Now Casaubon looked him in the eye for the first time.

"What are you talking about?"

"We were supposed to start the stakeout last week. But we've been dragging our feet, and the apartment is still empty, unused."

"Are you a cop?"

He didn't answer.

"This isn't how the police work. Where's your ID badge?"

"I'm not on duty." He picked up the duffel bag and unzipped it.

Casaubon took two steps back toward the cash register.

"I'm actually on vacation. I've been spending it with a telescope up in that empty apartment. You've had two visitors today, even though it's Sunday and the shop is closed. Both of them brought some items in with them."

He rummaged around in the duffel bag for a moment. Then he took out the shotgun. It was an old Browning he'd inherited from his father, a classic, worth a lot to collectors before he'd sawed off the barrel the night before. The gun was unregistered. He'd never used it himself. He straightened up.

Casaubon took two more steps toward the cash register.

"Stay where you are," he said, holding the shotgun loosely in one hand without aiming it at anything in particular.

Casaubon stood still.

He walked past the shop owner and went behind the counter. A pistol lay on the shelf right below the cash register. He removed the magazine, checking that it was full, and shoved it back in. He stuck the pistol in his belt.

"Please go back behind the counter and sit down," he said calmly, looking at the shop owner. He returned to the middle of the room and took up position with his legs spaced wide apart. He whistled something that was almost a melody as Casaubon sat down. He set the butt of the shotgun on the linoleum floor.

"Do you think I'm going to shoot you?"

Casaubon was silent.

"Are you afraid to die?" He raised the shotgun and aimed it at the shop owner. "Fear makes you stupid, my father always said."

Casaubon's hands were shaking like an old man's.

"He was a smart guy, but I'm going to give you a chance to prove him wrong." From his duffel bag he took out a toiletry kit and flung it onto the counter.

"Open it!"

Casaubon managed to pull the zipper open only partway before he gasped. He reached in and took out an unused syringe, a small plastic bottle of liquid, and a teaspoon.

"What am I supposed to do with these?"

"Don't give me that."

"But these are for a junkie."

"Right. And the raw material is your livelihood."

"I run a shop." Casaubon stared at him, his eyes wild. Looking for something that might give him hope.

The man went over to the shop owner, swinging the barrel of the sawed-off shotgun lightly through the air, as if it were weightless, like a baton. He placed the muzzle almost hesitantly against the shop owner's sweaty brow.

"The cranium isn't very thick," he said.

Casaubon's lips moved, but no words came out.

"Some of the thinnest bones in the body protect its most important organs. What do you think? Is the brain the most important organ in the body? Or are you a heart man?" He pointed the shotgun at Casaubon's chest before moving it back to his forehead. "If I pull the trigger, your head will be filled with buckshot," he explained. "The alternative is to use this paraphernalia here. Do you know how to shoot up?"

Casaubon shook his head.

"Right. You're just a middleman. You barely even know how your product is used or what it does to people. Is that what you're trying to tell me?"

Casaubon nodded like a little boy.

"What do you know about the dosage?"

"The dosage?"

"You heard me. How large do you think a user's dose should be?"

Casaubon didn't answer. Snot was running from his nose down into his beard.

"Let's see the goods!" he said.

Casaubon stared at him for a long time before he began to rummage through his pockets. He fished out a key ring and unlocked the steel cabinet under the counter. He bent down and then came up with a package wrapped in see-through plastic, which he placed on the counter.

"Step away, please." He took out his pocketknife and punctured the package. He moistened his little finger with spit and stuck it in the hole. Dabbed it on his tongue. Heroin. Pretty good quality, he thought. He spat it out on the floor. Then he took the spoon and filled it. "What do you say? Is this an overdose?"

Casaubon didn't utter a word.

"If you had to choose between shooting up this dose or me pulling the trigger, which would it be? If you ask me, I think you'd survive with the heroin." He began to whistle again, those disjointed notes that didn't quite come together in a melody. "I'll give you ten minutes to decide." He looked at the heart rate monitor on his left wrist, which also showed the time. "No, forget it, let's make it five."

Casaubon studied the spoon closely before he picked it up and held it in his trembling hands.

"Careful not to spill it. Do you know how to do it?"

Casaubon nodded and took the bottle and a lighter from the rack next to the register. It took him almost two minutes to prepare the shot. His coordination was clumsy.

The man leaned down and took a length of rubber tubing out of the bag, which he handed to Casaubon.

Casaubon took it, and as he began to roll up the sleeve on his left arm, he gazed out over the store, as if searching for salvation among the shelves of canned goods.

It was over in a matter of minutes. First the silent injection. Then the tourniquet was loosened. His muscles relaxed. The trembling slowed, and his body left time behind. The world went on without it.

A few final spasms with his head resting on the counter, drool running from his mouth, his gaze turned inward, until at last the pupils of his eyes were swallowed by the darkness that came from within.

The end.

He put the muzzle of the shotgun to Casaubon's head one last time. This time he pulled the trigger. There was no sound apart from an apologetic click from the unloaded gun.

Then he stood there thinking. He had no idea what it meant that Casaubon had died from such a low dose, but it wasn't good. Mistakes had a tendency to multiply. Once a plan had gone wrong, it was hard to get back on track. But he couldn't let this unnerve him. All he could do was go on.

So he walked around the counter to the steel cabinet. He'd kept an eye on the shop all week, and he knew what went on in here, who delivered the goods, and who showed up to pay. What made it a little confusing was that Casaubon was the middleman for more than one customer. Which meant that every so often there might be both money and dope in the shop at the same time, because a customer had picked up his goods and paid, while another package was waiting to be delivered. That was the case today. He took a fanny pack out of the cabinet and placed it on the counter. Unzipped it and saw that it was stuffed with thousand-krone bills. How many? Maybe five hundred. So he strapped it around his waist over the pistol, put the shotgun back in the bag, cleared off the counter, and left the shop. Outside he paused in the blowing snow to think.

The rubber tubing. He'd forgotten it inside. Had it fallen on the floor when Casaubon loosened it? Back inside the shop, he saw that the tubing had rolled under the counter. He picked it up and put it in the duffel bag with everything else.

When he straightened up, he caught sight of the boy. He was standing between the shelves, staring at him. His cap was way too big. Why was he wearing a cap indoors? And what was that old book in his hand? The boy stood there motionless except for the blinking of his eyes, as if his eyelids were counting out a beat that moved slower than the earth's rotation. The boy stared at the dead man. Behind him the door to the back room stood open. On a desk was a PC with Angry Birds on the screen. Had the boy been there the whole time, waiting for him to leave? Why hadn't he seen the boy enter the shop along with his father? The kid must have arrived when he went to the toilet to take a leak. That was the reason cops never did stakeouts alone.

He stood there looking into those brown eyes. Looking at the boy. So often it's impossible to tell what a child is thinking.

Back in his car, he once again pulled on the rubber gloves and glanced at the heart rate monitor. It displayed his pulse in both percentages and whole numbers, along with the maximum rate and the average. It also had foot pods, a watch, and a fitness test. It was PC compatible, with a timer, a lap recorder, and a target zone indicator with an alarm. Even though it was almost three years old, it still worked fine. He was pleased with it.

His pulse was thirty-nine.

Before he left the shop he had decided to take some of the dope. He had filled a small, watertight cylinder with several doses of heroin. The cylinder was meant to store small things when he went swimming or diving. He'd bought it in Thailand. He normally wore it on a cord around his neck when he was on various assignments, and he'd often found a use for it. Now he removed the cylinder from the cord and stuck it in his duffel bag.

Then he drove off to work.

"Aren't you on vacation?"

Eriksen glanced up from the papers he was reading. It was Sunday, and there weren't many people in the office.

"Yup. Just had to come in and get a few things." He pulled out a drawer and took out a Mammut X-Zoom and a Panasonic LX5. He stuffed both the headlamp and the camera in his jacket pocket.

"Are you taking a trip somewhere?"

"Yeah."

"How's the wife?"

"Fine. Why do you ask?"

"Just wondered whether you were going on vacation together."

He stared at Eriksen, whose desk was across from his.

"Don't mean to be nosy, but we do share this office, and I actually thought we shared a little more than that. I ran into one of your wife's friends the other day. She said your wife left you."

Fagerhus glanced at his heart rate monitor. Still thirty-nine.

"That's why I'm taking my vacation in the wintertime," he said. "Trying to work things out."

"I heard she'd moved out of town. Where'd she go?"

"She hasn't moved. We're just taking a break. That's all."

"How long have you and I shared this office, Fagerhus?"

"Two years."

"And how many years before that did we work together? Sitting with the scope in empty apartments on Akerselva, chatting with each other?"

"A long time."

"You know I've got your back, right? You can always talk to me."

"It'll work out, Eriksen."

"I hope so. That would be best for your little girl too."

"I know. She's more important than anything else. Listen, have you seen my handheld GPS anywhere? Didn't you borrow it from me? Is it in your locker?"

"Oh, right. Just a sec." Eriksen got up and left the room.

Fagerhus went over to the key cupboard, opened it, and put back the key to the vacant surveillance apartment.

A couple of minutes later Eriksen returned.

"Here. So where are you headed? You're not going out in the woods in this weather, I hope."

"No. But it's a good thing to have along. See you in a few weeks, Eriksen."

Eriksen nodded.

"By the way, I heard some news from the top brass. We're starting surveillance of the Casaubon Fruit & Vegetable shop next week. Rumor has it that he's been getting in some insanely pure heroin lately. There's going to be lots of overdose cases in the spring. It'll be good to put that bastard out of business. You're going to miss all the fun."

"I'll survive."

Fagerhus got onto the E6 and drove the speed limit, heading for Hamar. Before getting that far, he turned off and pulled into a gas station. The snow had stopped, but the wind ripped at his jacket as he filled up the gas tank. Afterward, he opened the duffel bag and got rid of the things he no longer needed, like the rubber gloves, the boy's cap, and the used syringe. He threw everything in the garbage can next to the gas pumps. Then he backed the car into a parking place, grabbed the bag from the backseat, and placed it next to him. He set the shotgun on the floor and got out the fanny pack. Finally, he had time to count the cash. Four hundred and fifty thousand Norwegian kroner. A little less than he'd expected. He took out the counterfeit passports and studied them. One for him, one for his daughter. Stenersen was the name they'd been given. Vidar and Kristine Stenersen. Then he looked through the travel documents. The plane left Stockholm in four days.

Finally, he took out the brief letter and read it again:

I now realize that I've been putting up with things for too long. I've taken Tina with me. The only reason I'm even writing to you is that I want to ask you to get help. There's no hope for you and me anymore. But maybe you can save yourself. You need to talk to someone, Rolf. Not for my sake, but for your own.

A.

P.S. Don't even think about trying to find us.

His pulse was now forty.

He studied the blotch on the top of the page. Oil from her fingers? A tear? Saliva?

"And why a letter?" he mumbled. Who writes letters anymore? He could understand why she wouldn't risk sending him a text message. He was a police officer, and he had contacts. But why hadn't she just sent him an e-mail? Did she think it would be easier for him to trace an e-mail than a letter? But she was wrong. A letter was more dangerous than an e-mail sent from an anonymous address or a message sent via Facebook. She'd never been smart like that. He'd tried so many times to explain to her how the world worked, but she'd never listened.

He put everything back in the duffel and put it on the backseat. Then he reached for the glove compartment. Along with a book, a bag of plastic zip ties, and a pack of gum, the gun he'd taken from Casaubon was in it. He took out the book. It'd been in the glove compartment for a long time. A lousy novel written by an author Eriksen had recommended. An American named Aaron Klopstein. Not exactly the sort of book to get a reader's pulse racing. The best thing about it was what it said on the back cover. The author had killed himself at the age of thirty-three by shooting himself in the thigh with a poisoned arrow with a blowpipe from the Amazon.

He sat there reading until ten minutes to midnight. For a few more minutes he stayed where he was, staring at the middle-aged man who was preparing to close up the gas station. There were two teenagers inside the store. He waited until they'd gone. At exactly one minute to twelve, he got out of the car, took the duffel bag from the backseat, and went inside the store. He was hungry and needed a bite to eat.

"We're closing," said the man.

"I thought so," he replied, setting the duffel on the counter. "A hot dog with bacon, please."

"I haven't got any left."

"No?"

"I just took the last hot dog off the grill to throw it out. It's over there." On the bench behind him was something that looked like a dead, shriveled-up finger.

"Don't you have time to grill another one?"

"Sorry. I need to get home."

"What's the rush?"

Then their eyes met. The first real connection. It didn't last long. The man turned off the radio.

"So what do you think?"

The gas station attendant turned to look at Fagerhus, confused by the question.

He clarified. "So what do you think about the story on the radio? About that boy in Oslo? And his father who committed suicide?"

"That guy in the shop? Fucking awful business."

"Fucking awful?" He smacked his lips.

The man behind the counter didn't reply. He could no longer hide his uneasiness.

"What are you going home to?" Fagerhus went on. "Who's waiting for you at home? A wife who tries to stay awake until you get there but who usually has fallen asleep by now, her snoring keeping you awake into the night? Or an empty bed? An old, slow computer to keep you company until you fall asleep at the keyboard?"

The man stared at Fagerhus for a long moment before he said:

"They didn't say anything on the radio about a suicide. They just said that a man had been found dead in the shop."

"Do you believe in the Devil?"

"Like I told you before, we're closed."

"Fix me a hot dog with bacon. Then I'll go."

"I could call . . ." He put his hand on the phone and fell silent.

"Who are you going to call?" He left the question hanging in the air for a moment. Then he said:

"Let's not make things difficult. I need a hot dog. I've driven a long way. And the next place to get any food is miles from here."

The man looked down at the counter. Then he went over to the freezer and got out a frozen hot dog. He put it on the grill and turned up the heat.

"You didn't answer my question," said Fagerhus. "Do you believe in the Devil?"

"Why are you asking me?"

"Don't you think it's an important question?"

"I don't know."

"Neither do I. But my father used to say that some people believe in the Devil, while other people believe that evil is something innate. So how a man answers the question says a lot about him."

The gas station attendant glanced up abruptly from the hot dog he was cooking. It was slowly browning.

"Did you just spit on the floor?" he asked, but Fagerhus didn't answer.

"You do believe in the Devil. I can tell. I bet you think it was the Devil who took that boy in Oslo today."

Drops of sweat. A hand wiping his brow. The same hand reaching for a package of hot dog buns.

"It doesn't look like it's done yet."

Silence. Fumbling to insert the sausage into the round hole in the hot dog bun.

"Aren't you going to warm up the bun first?"

The man dropped the hot dog on the counter and hastily picked it up.

"You always warm up the bun. Isn't it strange how little it takes to change our routines? Just a few minutes past closing time, and that's enough to do it. I've seen it happen so often. I seldom change my own routines." He smiled and glanced at his heart rate monitor.

The man turned around and put the bun in the toaster oven.

"It's all in the breathing," Fagerhus said. "Breathe deep from your abdomen, faster in than out. But never too fast."

"I don't know what you're getting at with all this. I'm fixing you a hot dog. Can't you be satisfied with that?"

"Do I look dissatisfied?"

The man didn't answer. After a moment he opened the toaster oven and put the semi-grilled sausage in the bun.

"Catsup and mustard are over there."

Fagerhus took a bite without adding any condiments.

"What about you? Are you dissatisfied?"

"I just want to go home."

"I can help you with that," said Fagerhus, picking up the duffel bag. Then he paused, considering different ways he could help this poor guy. The simplest would be to leave him alone.

"Thanks for the hot dog," he said. Then he turned on his heel and left.

He sat in the car watching the man as he locked up the gas station and then drove off in an old Volvo, going home to a silent house somewhere.

After that, he took a nap. Two hours later he continued on, driving through the snow.

The night before it happened . . .

Østerdalen. This was where they'd gone hunting.

Even though there was no one on the road, it wasn't possible to use his brights. The snowflakes danced toward the windshield like the splintered souls of dead animals. Some struck the warm glass and melted, while others whirled onward, disappearing into the pitch-black night behind him.

The heater was turned up full blast. He'd stripped to the waist. A film of sweat covered his skin. He was focusing all his attention on specific points on his body. His wrists, his calves, his throat. He couldn't feel his pulse anywhere. He imagined the blood coursing through him like spring water through pipes, steadily, evenly.

Fagerhus thought about his father and the hunting trips here in Østerdalen. Back then there was no snow here. He was only a boy when his father was alive. That was before everything—marriage, the child, his job.

They had taken more breaks as they got closer to the car. His father was moving slowly at the end of the hunting expedition. Something inside of him longed to go back to the woods. He wanted to stay there.

Then he'd stopped, breathing hard.

Whenever his father leaned against a tree, he always gave the impression that it was actually the tree that was leaning against him. The sun was low in the sky, lighting him from behind. Night was preparing to take over the world, already creeping in as scattered patches of shade. His father was a stout man with a full beard. He was outfitted in green clothing, a creature of the woods. Something from a mythology written for the two of them alone.

"Shall we give it one more try? Didn't you want to take a shot?"

His father had promised to let him shoot. It would be his first time. He had only fired a gun at the shooting range; he'd never killed. He thought he was looking forward to it. He'd been waiting for just such an invitation. Now he looked at the rifle slung over his father's shoulder, almost as if it were a part of the big man, and he felt uncertain.

But he nodded.

"Come on," said his father. "Follow me."

They turned around and went back into the woods, his father soundlessly leading the way. He followed, hungry and worn out after days of little sleep. His feet hurt. He had no idea what was drawing him forward—a question he needed to answer, his father's swaying gait, an inherited force that was neither dark nor light, that was just as much outside as inside of his body. He thought it was something they shared, he and his father.

Finally, they came to a clearing in the forest where a hill sloped down toward a meadow. The shadows hadn't yet reached this far. He thought they'd been here before, on a previous hunting trip when he was even younger.

"Deer often come here in the night," whispered his father as he squatted down near a tussock in the ground.

He stood still, looking at the moss that spread softly around his feet, as if it had settled there and instantly began to creep under his clothing.

"We always get something here. It's just a question of waiting. Silence. And patience." His father looked at him and held out the rifle. "Only when the hunt is over do you use it. There's only one reason for you to shoot."

He looked into the exhausted eyes of the big man. Sometimes he tried to see if he could catch a glimpse of the strange thoughts in his father's mind. But all he saw was gray.

"So what's the reason?' he asked.

"The reason may be the only thing, deep inside, that we can agree on."

"What is it?"

"That everything comes to an end."

"I thought we shot to get food," he said.

His father looked at him and laughed. The boy liked him better when he didn't laugh.

"That too," he said. "But a meal is also a form of ending. Everything is. Except the hunt, the silence, and the hunter's pulse."

His father handed him the rifle. He took it, holding it for a long time in both hands. He'd held it many times before, but now it felt unpleasant in his grip.

They sat there in the dripping moss, looking out across the meadow. He'd grown used to having damp clothes and constantly wet feet, but now it felt as if the groundwater soaking through his pants was warm and soothing, something he could fall asleep in, an unmoving moisture, a floating cocoon made of fluid and the microscopic life-forms that lived in the woods.

A couple of big birds danced past below them in the tall grass and then vanished into the forest as abruptly as they had appeared. The lingering autumn twilight was fading, and soon it would be too dark to see anything.

All of a sudden it was there. It looked around a few times, blinking, indifferent. The evening hour and the strange beauty of the dark trees made no impression on the deer. It was young. With slender horns, a mere inkling of antlers. There was much about the deer that had not yet grown.

He turned to look at his father, who sat in silence, meeting his eye. Then he calmly nodded. The boy put on the ear protectors, raised the rifle, and aimed it at the young buck. He pressed his cheek against the butt. Then he looked through the sight, searching the plain until he again found the deer. The buck was still there. It had begun to graze with the wariness all deer possessed, its own mortality reflected in every movement and hesitation. Slowly he squeezed the trigger.

That was when he felt it. A sensation that seemed to come from the air hovering between him and the deer. Something tough, like the moss he was sitting on, filled his whole head. He noticed his hands were shaking. He was a sensible boy who never had a hard time making a decision. Something was pounding inside of him. He was breathing hard. His eyes were swimming, and he could no longer see the deer clearly.

Then he fired without taking aim. The bang never came. Only a brief click. Like a pinprick in the air. He lowered the rifle and took off the ear protectors. Below he saw the young buck disappear into the woods, vanishing in the dark.

The memory of that hunting expedition still got to Fagerhus, more than anything else. It always made his pulse quicken, so he didn't look at the heart rate monitor.

"I don't know what's more scary about you," she'd once told him. "The fact that you have the resting pulse of a frozen toad, or that your pulse is always a resting pulse."

She'd meant it as a joke. That was before he started frightening her. Before he'd started to say things she didn't like. Back when she still felt safe with him. His calm rubbed off on her, taming her own restlessness. She didn't know there were certain things that could shake him up. Not many. But there were some.

Now he began thinking about the girl. "I'll just take Tina with me. Then I'll leave, and you won't ever have to see me again," he muttered.

He tried to remember what she looked like. His daughter. But for some strange reason his thoughts veered to the boy he had in the trunk of his car. That was a real slipup. He hadn't foreseen that the boy would be in the shop. With those eyes of his. First the mistake with the father. Then the boy.

Fagerhus had only planned to take some money from the guy's rotten business, to let a cynical criminal get a taste of his own medicine. He'd been working in the narcotics division for years. He knew the junkies, and from them he'd learned what the proper dose should be. The amount that Casaubon had shot up shouldn't have killed him. It wasn't an overdose, at least not under normal circumstances. Of course, the shop owner had never used heroin before, but still it must have been some of the pure stuff that Eriksen had mentioned. Why hadn't he heard about it earlier? What a mess he was in. He'd only intended to drug the shop owner for a while so he could get out of town before the bastard had time to talk to any of his friends.

Fagerhus knew that the police would come after him when he took off with his daughter. But he'd been prepared for that. He had a good plan. Two sets of passports, so they could switch identities halfway to their destination. The route he'd chosen was complicated, involving a long stretch of traveling by train across the continent before flying the last part of the way. He'd also decided on the right country in Central America. A place where no one would bother looking for a father who'd run off with his own child, and where none of Casaubon's cronies could reach him. But if the police came after him for murder, it was a different story. He had no plan B for that scenario. And he also had a witness. What was he going to do with the boy?

While he was thinking about this, Fagerhus lost control of the car. He was driving on a fairly straight road, feeling confident and in command, until there was an unexpected curve in the highway. He tried to slow down too abruptly, and the brakes locked and the car began to skid. Before he could recover he was crossing at full speed into the oncoming lane. The snowbank left by the plows on the other side of the road rose seemed to grow to the size of a glacier in the headlights. Automatically, as if driving a car were a primeval instinct, he took his foot off the brake and threw himself over the steering wheel. The car doors scraped against the snowbank on the shoulder of the road. He saw the side mirror get smashed against the windowpane next to him, but he managed to get the car back on the highway.

He was still speeding along as he returned to the proper lane.

That was when it appeared. He saw it in the distance, where the beams of his headlights met the darkness. A deer. A creature magnified by the lights into something unreal, something that had wandered out of one of his father's stories, something recounted at a campfire, back when stories had made a strong impression on him. A wild thought flew through Fagerhus's head. It was the young buck from that time out in the meadow, come back as a king, with an enormous rack of antlers gleaming brighter than the snow.

Then the car swerved.

It skidded onto the edge of the road, the right front headlight taking the brunt of the blow. This time the car plowed right into the snowbank. He was thrown forward, feeling the seat belt pull taut across his shoulder. The air bag embraced him like a maternal gust of air and synthetic fibers.

Dazed, he sat still, listening to the front tires spinning crazily in the loose snow beneath him. The driver's-side window was a web of cracks, but the piles of snow hadn't shattered the glass. He turned off the ignition and took several deep breaths. When he looked around, he could see that more than half the car was buried in snow.

But the back window and the left rear door were still free, sticking out into the winter darkness under clouds heavy with snow.

Fagerhus crawled into the backseat and then climbed out of the car. Once outside, he inhaled and then watched the frosty vapor billow as he exhaled. He examined his arms and legs, his slender fingers which she had once loved, his face and ears, his nose, which had ended up askew after an involuntary brawl in a bar in Belize many years ago. Nothing was broken, nothing had been wrecked that couldn't be replaced.

He didn't bother with the clothes he'd taken off inside the car. Wearing around his torso only the strap of the heart monitor, he walked down the road to the spot where the deer had stood, but he couldn't find a single trace of it in the snowdrift. Slowly he made his way back to the car, looking over his shoulder. He saw no sign of any traffic coming from either direction. No sounds other than those made by nature on a winter night. But that wouldn't last forever. It was now three thirty, though that didn't mean the road would remain deserted until dawn. He had to consider the possible appearance of some nocturnal truck driver, jacked up on caffeine, dance music, and stored-up cholesterol. Guys like that could be way too helpful. And the last thing he needed was someone stopping to help him.

When Fagerhus got back to the car, he leaned inside and took out the sweater and jacket he'd tossed onto the backseat. He put them on and checked his pulse monitor. Thirty-nine beats per minute. As usual, his heart ticked slower than time. On that score, everything was as it should be. Then he got out the duffel bag and went around to open the trunk.

The boy lay very still. He wasn't even shaking, even though it had to be fucking cold in there. The only signs that he was still alive were the fact that his eyes were open, cautiously scrutinizing Fagerhus, and the vapor coming from his nostrils. He was bleeding from a cut on his forehead. It must have happened when the car crashed.

He took a knife out of the duffel bag and cut the plastic ties binding the boy's legs together. He didn't touch the ones around his wrists. Or remove the gag. Then he lugged the boy out of the trunk and ordered him to stand up. He exchanged the knife for the shotgun, slung the duffel bag over his shoulder, and gave the boy a light shove between the shoulder blades with the sawed-off muzzle. He didn't have to say anything, he just pointed. With the boy walking in front, the two of them walked along the road to a spot where the hill sloped downward, away from the asphalt, and the drifts weren't as high.

There he led the boy out into the snow toward a grove of trees below. Before they reached the trees, he took a look around. In the distance, on the other side of the valley, he could see lights shining from a few remote farms and houses. He saw headlights as a car drove along a narrow road up on the slope, and he could just make out the sound of an engine. Otherwise nothing but darkness and silence. Only the snow gave off a faint glow, as did the moon when it appeared for brief moments from behind the drifting clouds.

The wind subsided as they entered the forest, and the snow floated almost straight down. He kept on walking as he listened to the boy breathing hard and gasping now and then. He sounded like he was crying. Then the boy stumbled in a deep snowdrift and plunged forward without being able to use his hands to stop his fall. His face was covered with snow, and more snow had probably gone down his neck and under his sweater. He turned over. His face was red above the gag as he shook off the snow, as if after a fierce snowball fight on some playground far from here. The boy got up without any help and stood still, staring wide-eyed. Again those eyes. Fagerhus tried to decipher his expression, but couldn't. Had the boy given up? Had he lost hope? Or was he planning to take off suddenly? The gasping sound grew louder, less controlled, less comprehensible.

"Calm down," he said, his tone both soothing and commanding at the same time.

He kept on talking as they started walking again.

"It's important to breathe calmly. Concentrate on the here and now. The next step you take. What comes after that, neither you nor I can tell. The important thing is to breathe."

He spoke more and more quietly, and he didn't think the boy was listening any longer. His voice faded to a whisper, merging with the wind.

"Breathe in and out, in and out," he whispered, now mostly to himself.

Fagerhus thought: *What the hell were you doing in the back room? You shouldn't have been there.*

After about a kilometer they stopped. They were in dense forest and could no longer see beyond the trees. At one place they'd crossed a ski trail. At another spot they'd passed a dark cabin, maybe a hunter's cabin or a summer vacation home, now merely a frozen smudge in the woods, a mausoleum to dead memories. Otherwise they'd seen little trace of any people.

He caught sight of a hill not far from where they stood. The incline was steep, and only a single lonely birch stood at the top. He ordered the boy to go up the hill. When they reached the top, he stopped and looked around.

The birch trunk was thin enough that he could tie the boy to it. He put the shotgun down in the snow, dropped the duffel bag beside it, and got out the knife. He'd bought it on Crete last summer, during the vacation that really tore them apart. It was handmade. It took five different craftsmen to make a Cretan knife. No better knife could be found south of the Arctic Circle. It was a showpiece that had cost him more than a thousand euros. His father would have liked this knife.

"If you even think about running, I'll cut you to pieces," Fagerhus said, placing the blade against the boy's skinny throat.

He sliced through the ties around his wrists. In a flash he switched the knife to his left hand and used his right hand to grab the boy's upper arm. Maybe he gripped him too hard. The boy gasped louder than ever. It was almost a scream. But Fagerhus didn't understand what this half scream meant. Was it despair or hatred he heard? Or something else altogether? Hope? A survival instinct that had no other means of expression?

"You weren't supposed to be in the shop," Fagerhus said. His voice was calm. But inside he was beginning to feel something he'd felt only a few times before; that strange swimming sensation he'd had that time in the woods with his father. The first and only time his father had ever invited him to take the life of a deer. It had been a phony invitation, a test.

Now he tied the boy to the trunk of the birch.

Then he went over and picked up the shotgun. He made sure it was loaded before he raised it and took aim. The boy started to shake. He suddenly noticed how skimpy the boy's clothes were. He was dressed for the indoors. Again he wondered what the boy had been doing in the back room. What was that book he'd been holding? Where did it come from? Fagerhus vaguely recalled something from the prep work of the investigative team, something about Casaubon being a book collector. In addition to his legal and illegal shop activities, he frequently trolled through used bookstores and went to London and Madrid to attend book auctions. Was he genuinely interested in old books, or was it only for money-laundering purposes? Did the boy share his father's interest in books? Was the boy old enough to care? The only thing Fagerhus knew was that the kid wasn't dressed for winter nights in Østerdalen. He was freezing. His head had started to droop, and he was shaking terribly.

"Do you realize that we're at the edge of the taiga? Behind you is an enormous expanse of forest that covers vast parts of Sweden, Finland, and Russia. It stretches all the way to Siberia. Just think of all those trees. At this time of year, their roots are frost-bound deep in the earth. In permafrost. Frozen decay, the remains of animals and trees that once lived in the forest, life that has perished and revived, either unchanged or changed."

Fagerhus had a faint memory of his father once saying something like that. Maybe the words would offer the boy some comfort. He aimed at his head. Then he was seized by nausea, dizziness, a trembling in his legs. Sensations that were foreign to him.

"Pull the trigger, you ice-cold bastard," he whispered to himself.

But he knew he couldn't do it. He took a step closer. Then a bigger step back. Then he lowered the gun, only to raise it again. This time he placed his finger firmly on the trigger.

"Breathe calmly," he told himself. "Very calmly," he went on, in a voice that quavered for the first time in his life.

Only much later when he once again stood next to his car in the gray light of dawn did his pulse return to what it should be. Fagerhus thought about everything that had gone wrong. As soon as he solved the problem of the boy and gone back to the car, the American woman showed up, coming around the curve. If she hadn't been so damned quick and well trained, he would have handled things. But she was as slippery as one of his fucking colleagues. She almost got away. He didn't dare think about what the consequences might have been. But in the end he'd managed to limit the damage here too. At least he hoped so.

Now he got out his cell and called the emergency number for Viking road service. He couldn't leave his car here. It was registered in his name. That would connect him too closely to this place and the forest where someone might eventually find something of interest to the police.

"Call 06000 night or day—from anywhere in Norway," he murmured to himself as he tapped in the number. He chuckled and glanced at his heart rate monitor. Thirty-eight regular beats.

They had a tow truck available in Åsta. It would take half an hour, the woman on the phone told him. He killed those thirty minutes, which stretched into a whole hour, by jogging back and forth along the road to stay warm. Big semis had begun roaring past. Only three of the drivers stopped to ask if he needed a hand. Now that he cleared away the buckshot and all the bloodstains in the snow, he had no trouble convincing them that everything was fine, and the help he needed would soon arrive.

The man who climbed with surprising grace out of the tow truck was over forty. He had lips that were stained with snuff but otherwise seemed energetic.

"Jeez, looks like you took quite a hit. Is the injury serious?"

"What do you mean?"

"Your arm."

Fagerhus looked down at both arms. That was when he noticed the bloodstains on the right sleeve of his jacket. He'd been so preoccupied with getting rid of all traces on the road and snowbank that he hadn't paid any attention to his clothes.

"It's nothing. Just a superficial cut."

"I've got a first-aid kit in the truck."

"No, that's okay. I put a bandage on it."

"You should have a doctor take a look at that. After a crash like this, you never know. Internal bleeding. Shock."

"Thanks, but I think I'm fine. My pulse is normal."

"Christ, look at that. A heart rate monitor. Not bad. I've heard about people who wear that sort of thing when they go skiing. But when you're driving a car? That's a new one on me."

"Let's just say that I have some particular habits."

"So tell me this. Were there two vehicles involved in this accident? I only heard about one car being stuck in the snow. And I assume that's the one."

He pointed at the one car buried in the snowbank and then turned to look at the other vehicle that was parked neatly at the side of the road.

"That one's a rental. I need to get going."

"A rental? You managed to get a rental car out here even before a tow truck? This early?"

"I've got connections." He held his breath. Glanced surreptitiously at his Polar RS. Thirty-nine. It was going up.

"Connections? Don't tell me you know Fredriksen in Koppang. I wouldn't rent a car from him even if it were free." The tow truck driver bellowed with laughter, a frosty vapor gusting from his mouth.

"Okay, well, I can get your car out of the snowbank. Do you want me to take it all the way to Elverum? They have the best mechanics."

"That sounds good to me," Fagerhus said. "But tell them I won't be able to pick it up for a couple of weeks."

"They're not going to be happy about that. Give me your phone number so they can get in touch with you."

3

In the morning, the day it happened . . .

It *really was a* rental car. That much was true. A discreet tag from Hertz was on the key ring that he'd taken out of her pocket. He got behind the wheel and glanced in the rearview mirror, watching the taillights of the tow truck vanish around the curve. Then he turned around and placed the duffel bag with all the essential equipment on the backseat.

Fagerhus started the car.

What was a woman who spoke Norwegian with an American accent doing in a rental car driving up through Østerdalen? He wondered where she'd been headed. To Trøndelag, which was where he was planning to go, or even farther north? Why hadn't she seen him and kept driving? How had she almost been able to get away after he'd overpowered her? He had a strange feeling that she was a cop. Something about the way she fought back to the very end. But there was nothing on her to prove that. She wasn't on duty, that much was clear. If she was, she'd have had her ID with her.

None of that matters anymore, he thought as he put the car in gear. The storm was letting up. Now it was only a light snowfall, with sporadic gusts of wind. He looked at his watch. Even if he didn't drive fast, he could make it there early in the day, while there was still daylight. He didn't know whether that was an advantage or not.

As Fagerhus drove, he thought about his father. In the car on the way back to Oslo after that hunting expedition so long ago, he'd asked his father:

"Did you know the rifle wasn't loaded?"

His father didn't answer for a moment. Then he said:

"You don't know whether you really want to kill. You won't know that until you've pulled the trigger. And now you have. Now you know."

"So it was a test to see if I could shoot?"

"No, not to see whether you could do it. I knew you were capable of bringing down a deer. What neither of us knew was how you would feel about it. Whether you really wanted to pull the trigger. What if at the decisive moment you realized that you didn't want the deer to die, but you shot it anyway?"

"Do I know now? Do I know if I really wanted to do it?"

"Yes. Now you know."

"So will the gun be loaded next time?"

"If there is a next time," said his father.

The following year his father went hunting alone. He never returned. He disappeared into the forest for good.

The weather and the road conditions continued to improve. He could drive faster, even though he wasn't very happy with the car. A Subaru, probably a 2010, not much pep. He thought it felt tinny, too lightweight for the road, not suited to winter driving in spite of the four-wheel drive.

The letter had been postmarked in Trondheim. Before it arrived he'd already called her sister, who lived on the island of Hitra. At the time, he didn't think it could really be that easy. And her sister had said that she hadn't seen her. But the whole time they talked, he felt she was lying. So when the letter came, he phoned Eirik. That was a good place to start. Eirik was a former colleague who was now on the Trondheim police force. He'd been friends with both Fagerhus and his wife, and he'd had dinner at their place on numerous occasions. He told Eirik a story about her being in Trondheim on vacation, and he was driving up there to join her. He suggested they meet.

"In Trondheim?" Eirik had said. "I just ran into her on the street today, and she said she was in town for a little while, and that she came in on the Fast Boat. But she's staying on Hitra. Borrowed her sister's house over there. Isn't that right?"

"Yeah. She's supposed to be on Hitra this week," he'd replied. "But next week, when I'm there, we'll be staying in Trondheim."

As he'd hoped, his wife hadn't said anything about them to Eirik, who invited both of them over for a dinner of bacalao.

He'd accepted.

That's how simple it had been.

They had stayed in her sister's house once before. It was late summer, a year ago. They went diving and fished for crab, which they ate out on the veranda, which was on the wrong side of the house, the only side without a view of the sea. His sister-in-law had two houses—the one on Olderøya, an island northwest of Hitra, where she had her workshop; and the house on the main island, right near Kvenvær. It was a ramshackle old place. Once upon a time she'd planned to fix it up and turn it into a shop so she could sell the pots and cups that she made. But the place had ended up being a dilapidated vacation cabin for friends and family. She had a lot of friends, so it was always occupied. He guessed that was where his wife would go. How could she be so predictable?

On the early morning news on the radio, Fagerhus heard that the Hitra tunnel was closed due to an accident, but by the time he got there, it had been cleared. Out here on the coast the snow hadn't settled on the roads, and the storm, which had raged over large parts of Norway, had begun to move off. It didn't take him long to reach the small gravel road that led up to his sister-in-law's house by the shore. He thought about parking the car and walking the last part of the way, but the house was hidden from the road by two huge glacial boulders, so he could drive quite close without arousing suspicion. If she happened to look out the window just as he pulled into the front yard, she wouldn't recognize the car, so she wouldn't try to run or send Tina away before he was standing at their front door. Not that there was anywhere to go. He just wanted his daughter. That was all. Everything would go nice and smoothly. No more mistakes. No more surprises. It would all go according to plan.

As he drove around the boulders, he noticed at once that the door to the house was open. It had blown open and shut twice in the brisk breeze by the time he got out of the car and took the duffel bag with the gear from the backseat. He caught a glimpse of the sea beyond the veranda stairs. There were whitecaps, as if the water were still shaking from the storm. Then he entered the cabin. The floor creaked, just as it always had. The only difference was that the place looked even more decrepit. There were black patches on the ceiling. In the hallway the wallpaper was peeling. He noticed a moldy smell as he went into the living room.

Why would she want to stay here? he thought. Why would she rather live here than back home in their apartment in Homansbyen, where everything was nice and clean? Where they had a new ventilation system and probably the best heating system in town. What did it say about her that she'd rather hide out in this place? What did it say about him? Had he really been so impossible? Was it that difficult to put up with him? One thing was clear: This was no place for his daughter.

He stopped in the middle of the room and looked out the windows at the view. The water, the whitecaps, the birds. They'd had a good time here that summer. Was it the year before Tina was born? He'd fucked her here on the table after pulling off her wet swimsuit. A bucket of crabs stood next to the table, and they'd heard them rattling around. What a body she'd had back then. Drops of water glittering on her skin; invisible, downy hair on her stomach; eyes that promised to liberate him, promised him life—if only he would feel something in return.

He had tried. All these years he'd tried but never got any closer than on this table. He'd almost felt it, the way he thought it should feel. Almost intimacy, almost love.

Back in those days, down at the dock there'd been a boat that guests could use to go out and visit her sister in the archipelago. He saw the boat was still there, moored, with the canopy down, as if it'd been used recently. There were also two other boats. But he noticed that the boat belonging to the old man they'd met last time was gone. The man used to live in Trondheim and would come out here on weekends to fish. He'd seemed ancient back then and must be dead by now.

"Where have the two of you gone?" he murmured.

From where Fagerhus was standing, he could look into the kitchen. Other than the toilet out in the hall, there were no other rooms on the ground floor. He wondered if they were hiding in the bedrooms upstairs, but decided that his daughter would never hide from him, no matter what her mother said. That was when he noticed the piece of paper on the dining table. He reached out to pick it up. As his fingers touched the note, he noticed a tiny red laser dot dance over his hand. Instinctively he turned around and caught sight of a gray box attached to the wall above the sofa at the end of the room.

He grabbed the note and read what it said:

Look under the table!

Quickly he leaned down to look. Between the table legs he saw a wooden crate. It was filled with sticks of dynamite, and attached to them was a blasting cap with a digital timer. The numbers on the display were red. It said:

04.

It must have started counting down from ten when his hand

interrupted the laser beam. That set off the remote control on the wall, which sent a radio signal to the unit under the table, which began the countdown. Quite a sophisticated setup, designed to start the second he picked up the note. Not before, and not after.

03.

He tried counting the dynamite sticks, realizing there was enough to blow up the entire ground floor. Who the hell used dynamite these days?

02.

He straightened up, looking for a way out. He didn't need to look at his heart monitor. His pulse was racing faster than the timer under the table; he could feel it pounding. He took two swift steps back and stared out the window at the sea.

01.

I should have realized it was way too easy to find you, he thought. *Who the hell helped you with this? Who do you know?*

00.

The table was lifted off the floor when the explosion came.

4

Two weeks after it happened . . .

Y*ou're a cliché,* Odd Singsaker." Felicia Stone looked at him and laughed.

What did she mean by that?

"I'm old," he said.

She sat on the kitchen counter and tossed her hair back.

"Old?"

"I'm a policeman."

"You're a cliché."

"I am who I am. A man of habit. An aging policeman. I don't want to be anything else."

"Come on, let's do something crazy."

"You don't like doing crazy things either."

"I've never tried it."

"Yes, you have. You left me. You ran off to Oslo. I thought you'd gone home to Richmond. For a while I thought you were dead."

"Maybe I was." She jumped down from the counter and went over to him to put her arms around his neck. "Maybe I was dead."

Odd Singsaker woke up. The bed was empty except for him. He felt his back. No sweat on his shirt or on the sheet. Again he had dreamed about talking to Felicia. They had long discussions about who they were and what they wanted. He didn't understand these dreams.

Then he got up. Went straight to the kitchen wearing his shirt and underwear. He looked for his pants, but he couldn't remember where he'd tossed them. There was no time to take a shower.

"I put them in the washing machine. Time for a change, Odd." She was standing next to the kitchen counter. The same place as in his dream.

It took him a few moments to realize that she was really there. He'd been through so much. It hadn't helped his memory any.

"It's going to be a long day," he said tersely.

"A tough day," she said.

"A day. Just a day that I have to get through. But it'll be a long one."

"When's your doctor's appointment?"

"In twenty minutes."

He got out a bottle of Red Aalborg aquavit from the kitchen cupboard and filled a glass half full. He downed it in one gulp.

"No herring today?"

"I don't feel like eating anything," he said.

"You have to eat," she said. "Not eating isn't going to make anything better."

"It's just a doctor's appointment and an interview," he said.

"Oh, sure. An interview with Internal Affairs. And you're the one being questioned."

"I know that. I'll grab a roll at the station."

"It's up to you."

He went into the bedroom and put on clean clothes. On his way out, she handed him coffee in a paper cup.

"Drink this on your way. At least you'll be awake."

The sun was shining for the first time in weeks, or so he imagined. They'd had one snowstorm after another this winter. And it had been bitterly cold for a long time. Today he was almost too warm in his wool coat as he headed down the road. Or maybe it was because he was walking so fast. He was in a hurry, and there were beads of sweat on his forehead. He felt even hotter because of the heavy leather shoulder bag he was carrying, which was filled with documents.

Well, there's really no rush, he thought, mostly to calm himself down.

At the medical center, they were always running half an hour behind schedule, even in the morning. So an eight o'clock appointment meant in reality eight thirty. These delays were so consistent that, in Singsaker's opinion, they could just factor them in when they made their schedules. It would save the patients a lot of unnecessary time spent in the waiting room. And it would spare him from feeling like he was late, when he probably wasn't. But then it might not be such a bad thing to feel a little stressed. Maybe it was a good sign that he cared about such trivial matters. That he was able to think about something other than what had happened after Felicia disappeared when he was working on the music-box homicide case, and then what happened later on Hitra, when he saw her again.

Odd Singsaker had been through a lot in life, many tough murder cases, a divorce, and surgery for a brain tumor. But he had no idea how he was ever going to get over what happened on Hitra on that windy winter day two weeks ago. It would haunt him to his grave, like some incurable growth on the anatomy of his psyche, a second brain tumor, one that never grew any bigger, never shrunk, and could never be cut out by a surgeon. Not lethal, and yet not something he could live with.

At the 7-Eleven nearby he tossed out the coffee even though the cup was still half-full. Then he headed for Vollabakken at a relatively calm pace.

"You're not well."

Dr. Barth was Odd Singsaker's primary care physician. A patient man around fifty with permanently rosy cheeks, the doctor was fond of repeating himself.

"And you know it. I've explained it all to you before. The tumor we found in 2009, an astrocytoma, as we call it, was malignant. The operation was successful, but we couldn't remove all of it. That's not possible with that sort of tumor. Sooner or later, it's going to start growing again."

Singsaker listened without fully taking in what the doctor was saying. He'd heard it all before. The first time, he'd made a vow not to let this news affect his life. His estimated life expectancy was about ten more years, give or take. He knew that, but he didn't think it was all that bad. Not really much shorter a life span than any man of his age and in his profession could expect.

"The good news is that you're shamelessly healthy for a man who's sick. All the test results are good. I've sent the latest images over to St. Olav's. The tumor is still in stage two. That's what it should be, and it may stay that way for a long time. Physically it shouldn't give you any problems, unless the attacks start up again."

Dr. Barth was referring to the hallucinations and other ill effects that had occurred when the tumor was discovered. A couple of years back, Singsaker had suddenly collapsed at the police Christmas party.

"I feel fine," he said.

He wasn't lying. His head felt heavy, but that was not due to any pathological cause.

"I think you're doing as well as you possibly could," said Barth. "And I see that the cognitive test you took for Dr. Nordraak is okay too."

Singsaker nodded. He had to take these memory tests at regular intervals for as long as he stayed on the job. Lately the problem was that he wasn't on the job. Officially he was on sick leave. He'd been taken off active duty ever since he'd suffered an ax blow to his leg during the last homicide case. That was one of the reasons he was in trouble now. He was still on sick leave when he'd joined the action out on Hitra.

"So let's take a look at your leg," said Barth.

Singsaker pulled up the leg of his pants and his long underwear to bare his calf. The stitches had come out a week ago.

Barth lifted Singsaker's heel and did a halfhearted examination of the dark red stripe that was in the process of becoming a permanent but not too disfiguring scar.

"Good," he said. "Looks like both your physical and invisible injuries are healing nicely."

Singsaker nodded silently.

"But something is bothering you," said Barth. "Want to talk about it?"

"No."

"Is it about what I've been reading in the papers?"

"I don't want to talk about it."

"Is it true what they're saying? That your wife . . ."

"It'll pass," said Singsaker. "I really don't want to talk about it."

He walked down the street and continued on to the restaurant Baklandet Skydsstation. The ocher-colored building presented a cheerful façade to the street, as always. Icicles hanging from the eaves glittered in the sunshine. He went inside and claimed his usual table closest to the door. He went over to the counter to order his food, then sat back down at the table and stared at the door. He liked to look at the people as they came and went. He could study them without seeming too intrusive. He found it relaxing. It let his mind wander.

His food arrived. He ate the herring, drinking coffee and a glass of water. The one shot of aquavit he'd had earlier that morning would have to do. He had a long day with a difficult interview ahead of him. Singsaker glanced at his watch. It was almost nine thirty. They'd agreed to start late today, not until noon.

He leaned down and took a stack of documents out of his bag. He placed them on the table next to the platter of herring. These were the transcripts from yesterday's interview, forty single-spaced pages with everything that had been said during the first interview regarding the Hitra affair.

He thought back to his meeting yesterday with the chief investigator for Internal Affairs. He and Kurt Melhus were old acquaintances. In his younger days, Singsaker had spent a year working in Horten. It was his first full-time job on the Trondheim police force. In Horten he and Melhus had been colleagues. He remembered that they'd gotten on well together. Melhus had studied logic at the same time as he attended the police academy. That was enough for the younger police officers in Horten to give him the nickname "the Philosopher." He didn't make it any easier for himself by quoting words of wisdom from classical philosophers. Singsaker had liked that about him. Melhus had a genuine depth of character. He often came up with surprising ideas.

These days, it seemed like an eternity between occasions when they saw each other. Melhus was a special investigator, not someone any active police officer wanted to encounter. Their first meeting yesterday outside the interview room had been unsettling because of the unusual situation in which they found themselves. Melhus had wasted no time addressing the difficult matter, and Singsaker couldn't tell whether that was a sign of friendship or simply a good interviewing technique.

In his mind, Singsaker again heard Melhus saying:

"*Life consists partly of what you yourself do, and partly of what others do to you*. That's what my aunt used to say. I think she got it from Aristotle. Plus illnesses, she used to add, and those were her own words. She knew what she was talking about. She lost both of her parents to cancer. As did her sister, who was my mother. She died when I was five. Have I ever told you this?"

Singsaker shook his head.

"I was really upset when I heard that you were sick. I should have sent you a card," said Melhus.

"That's okay. I'm doing better now," said Singsaker.

"No, you're not. At least not after what you've just been through. But let's put that aside for the moment. We have a lot of ground to cover. We're not such close friends that this should be a problem from a legal standpoint. We had dinner together a few times when we lived in Horten. But that was a long time ago. Now we have a job to do. Let's stick to that."

And with that, the tone for the interview had been set. It was the only appropriate course. This was a serious matter, and Melhus might have to make a difficult choice. He couldn't allow personal considerations to come into play.

As an investigator, Singsaker usually prepared himself between interview sessions by reading through the transcripts and carefully studying everything that had already been said. Sometimes a close read could lead to unexpected breakthroughs. But now that he wasn't the one conducting the interviews and was, in fact, the one being questioned, he just wanted to forget everything that had been said on the previous day. Repress all of it. Pretend that it'd never taken place. Yet the policeman in him knew how important it was to be prepared.

He finished his coffee, which was now lukewarm. Then he leafed through the first pages of the document, in which he and the chief investigator, Kurt Melhus, from Internal Affairs, Central Norway Division, went over the formal aspects of the case. He came to the page where his chronological account of the events began, and he read:

Page 5 of 48

Melhus: When exactly did you arrive at the station that day?

Singsaker: I don't remember. It was in the morning.
Melhus: On the morning of Saturday, February 19?
Singsaker: Yes.
Melhus: On February 17 you were discharged from the hospital after suffering a stab wound to your calf during the Music Box case. Is that right?
Singsaker: Yes, that's right. I helped to apprehend a murderer who kidnapped and killed young women. The media dubbed it the Music Box murders because the perp repaired a music box and placed it near one of his victims. During the apprehension, the perp attacked me with an ax. The injury was not life-threatening, but it did put me out of action for a while.
Melhus: And you were still on sick leave when you were discharged from the hospital?
Singsaker: That's correct.
Melhus: Would you say that you were feeling weak? Was the wound bothering you at that point?
Singsaker: I was aware of it. But it wasn't hampering my mobility.
Melhus: Perhaps there were other things that were bothering you more?
Singsaker: What do you mean?
Melhus: While you were still in the hospital, you received a phone call from your wife, Felicia Stone. Isn't that right?
Singsaker: Yes.
Melhus: What was the phone call about?
Singsaker: She told me that she was in Oslo but she was coming home. She was going to catch a flight on Wednesday, February 16.

Melhus: And you didn't know she was in Oslo before she called that day, did you?

Singsaker: We'd had a fight during the Music Box investigation. She'd gone away, I guess to take a breather. I don't really know. She didn't tell me why she left.

Melhus: Can you tell us what the fight was about?

Singsaker: It's a private matter. I'm not sure it's important.

Melhus: Singsaker, you know as well as I do how things work. You have to tell us everything, and I'll decide whether it's important or not.

Singsaker: It had to do with the fact that on one occasion I'd had a--what shall I call it? An intimate relationship with a friend of hers. But it happened before Felicia and I were together. Actually, before I'd even met her. Felicia and the person in question weren't friends at the time. So I guess we were fighting about the fact that I hadn't told Felicia about this.

Melhus: Who was the person you had this relationship with?

Singsaker: Her name is Siri Holm. She's a librarian at the Gunnerus Library.

Melhus: I see. So you and Felicia had a falling out because of this Siri Holm, or rather because of something you and Siri had done before Felicia knew either of you. So she went to Oslo and was gone for several days while you were working on the murder case. How did you feel when your wife finally called and told you where she was?

Singsaker: I was relieved. The fight hadn't done any damage that couldn't be repaired. I was sure about that. We just needed to talk to each other.

Melhus: What happened after she called?

Singsaker: She wasn't on the plane she said she was taking.

Melhus: I see. And three days later you went to the police station, even though you weren't supposed to be working, even though you were still on sick leave. Would it be correct to say that you were worried about your wife at that point?

Singsaker: Of course I was worried. But I thought it had something to do with us. With the fight we'd had. That she'd decided to stay away.

Melhus: But isn't it also correct that one of the reasons you went to the station that day was because you were hoping to find out more about what had happened to her?

Singsaker: I can't deny that.

Melhus: So what did you do when you got there?

Singsaker: I talked to Jensen.

Melhus: Chief Inspector Thorvald Jensen?

Singsaker: Yes.

Melhus: He's a close colleague of yours, right?

Singsaker: Without a doubt.

Melhus: Also a good friend?

Singsaker: Yes, a good friend.

Melhus: And you asked him for a favor, between friends?

Singsaker: I asked him to check the passenger list of the plane Felicia was supposed to take.

Melhus: And what did he find out?

Singsaker: That she'd checked in for the flight, but never showed up at the boarding gate. So she'd gone to the airport, but didn't board the plane.

Melhus: What did you think about that?

Singsaker: I thought maybe she'd gotten cold feet.

Melhus: Is that all?

Singsaker: To be perfectly honest, I feared something worse.

Melhus: Like what?

Singsaker: To be blunt: I thought she'd fallen off the wagon.

Melhus: Did you have reason to think that?

Singsaker: She'd been sober for a long time. I've never seen her touch a drop in the time we've been married. She wasn't tempted at all. But she told me that when she was young, she'd been in rehab, and she considered herself a recovering alcoholic ever since. I also thought about something my son said.

Melhus: What was that?

Singsaker: When she called me from Oslo, that's where she was. At my son's place. Felicia got along well with him and my daughter-in-law. He said something to me after I talked to Felicia. He mentioned that he could smell booze on her when she arrived.

Melhus: I understand. When you say she was in rehab in her younger days, are we talking about just alcohol? I have to ask because the blood tests showed that she . . .

Singsaker: I know what they showed. Apparently she'd also taken a lot of pills back then. I don't know what kind.

Melhus: What about heroin?

Singsaker: Only once, as far as I know. I think it was a suicide attempt. As I understand it, that was the incident that made her parents intervene and send her to rehab.

Melhus: For the record: How much time did Chief Inspector Jensen spend finding out that she wasn't on the plane?

Singsaker: I'm not sure exactly. He told me the day after I'd asked him to check on it.

Melhus: So that was on Sunday, February 20?

Singsaker: That's right.

Melhus: And it was on that day that you decided to report her missing?

Singsaker: Yes.

Melhus: And you were still on sick leave, which meant this was a matter for your colleagues to handle, right?

Singsaker: Initially, yes. But of course it wasn't a high priority. There was nothing to indicate that she wasn't acting of her own free will.

Melhus: So everyone continued to view this as a private matter, between you and your wife? Yet that didn't prevent the police department from devoting resources to finding her. I'm thinking in particular about the rental car. Which ended up playing a crucial role, not only in her case but in the whole tragic story. Do you agree?

Singsaker: Unfortunately, that's all too true.

PART II

BLACK BILE

If the human being were one, he would
no longer feel pain.

—Hippocrates

5

The day before it happened . . .

F*elicia Stone's thoughts* were dark and muddy.

She was afraid to open her eyes. When she finally realized where she was and who she was, she wished she'd never have to look at the world again. She especially didn't want to see the room where she'd spent the night. She remembered the black-and-white bedding and the mirror. What kind of person had a mirror on the wall over their bed? The mere thought of that mirror made her sick to her stomach. Not to mention the smell in the room. The stench of suffocating desperation. He'd released something inside of her last night. At first she'd thought it was desire. But that wasn't it. It was something else, a dark insanity. *Will I ever know myself again, after this?* she thought, burrowing her head into the pillow.

She could hear him whistling in the bathroom. Then he came into the bedroom, stinking of aftershave. She heard him set something on the nightstand next to her. Finally, he left the apartment. She lay still for a long time, listening to make sure he'd gone. Then she rolled onto her back and took a couple of deep breaths before opening her eyes. The ceiling was painted gray. What was she doing here?

She threw off the covers and was struck by a terrible realization: *It's the same smell. I smell the same right now.* This mixture of male and female scent she always awoke to the next day. The one she knew from up in Trondheim after Odd left for work, while some of his smell still clung to her skin. A scent she thought of as the fragrance of love. Right now the smell was the same. *Is this how it always smells?* She had so little experience. She was in her mid-thirties, but she hadn't had enough sexual partners to know whether it always smelled like this after every man. Her thoughts involuntarily drifted back to her youth, to Richmond, to that time in her life when everything fell apart. Had it smelled like this back then too?

She reached out to pick up the note and read what it said. As she'd hoped, he'd gone to the office. Felicia had a vague sense that it was Sunday, but she didn't think it was unusual for a defense attorney to work on the weekend. That gave her time. She went straight to the bathroom to take a shower. Afterward, she looked for her clothes. Her panties and top were lying next to the bed, the rest strewn about on the cherrywood floor in what was a combination living room and kitchen. Strangely enough, this small two-room apartment reminded her of a spiffier version of her own place back in Richmond. The apartment she'd owned for only six months before she moved to Trondheim.

She got dressed and made herself a cup of strong black coffee.

Then she found the old red bag made of Italian leather that her father bought for her years ago. She pulled out a pack of Camels. It was hiding under the printout she'd made at Lars and Eline's apartment in Oslo. She'd slept on the sofa belonging to Odd's son for several days after that stupid fight they'd had. The printout was her e-ticket for the flight back to Trondheim.

Felicia lit a cigarette. The first puff made her cough.

Her plane ticket was dated Wednesday, February 16, which was four days ago. On that day Odd was still in the hospital and expecting her to come visit him. After that she'd turned off her cell. What had gone wrong? Why had she done it? If only she could answer those questions.

Don't I love him? she asked herself.

She sat at the kitchen counter in front of a bay window. From there she looked down on the quiet street in what she assumed was central Oslo, trying to recall as many details as possible from the preceding days.

She remembered a baby crying.

6

Five days before it happened . . .

F*or some reason* she stayed where she was, studying the tiny, angry face, the baby's lips losing all color when he opened his mouth for each new shriek. His slender, taut neck. The wrinkles on his forehead, like on the face of an old man, merely painted with a softer brush. His eyes, which looked like they would never close, never blink. The crimson flush on his skin that ebbed and waned.

You can say that again, Felicia thought as she listened to his angry cries.

The mother tried to get the baby to nurse, but it didn't do much good. She took off the knitted sweater, which the child had probably worn all the way through security. The sweater had to be way too hot. Even though she could see the snowstorm raging outside all the huge windows at Gardermoen airport, it was warm indoors. Too warm, in Felicia's opinion, feeling an urge to take off a layer of clothing too. But she simply sat where she was, looking at the desperate mother, who now put the baby back in the stroller. She wasn't sure what she felt. It couldn't be envy. Yet there was something about the situation that was strangely compelling. Trying to lull a baby to sleep was an all-consuming task, but it seldom took very long. The mother began moving the stroller back and forth. The intervals between cries grew longer, until the child finally stopped, sleepily smacking his lips and then falling asleep. The mother, who looked a little too young for the role, sat down across from Felicia to read a romance novel. She now seemed completely calm.

Very little that goes on outside has any significance for an airport. Except the weather. There was a long wait between departures on that day. In spite of the thundering, circuitous dance of the snowplows out on the runways and the gallons of de-icing fluid sprayed on the snow-covered airplane wings, there were long delays. It didn't help matters that weather conditions were the same in all of northern Europe, so the delays were also the result of planes that hadn't yet arrived from other airports.

The departure for Trondheim had been delayed by half an hour when she decided to have a beer. It was not a carefully considered decision. More of an impulse. She hesitated only long enough to persuade herself that there was nothing wrong with such an idea. Besides, she wouldn't have time to drink enough to get drunk before the plane left. And she was on her way home. It seemed safe to have a beer.

After she finished it, she went over to check the departure screen. Another half-hour delay. Time enough to have another drink. And then one more, since there was another thirty-five-minute delay. As she sat with her third beer, she fell into conversation with an elderly man who was going to London to sell a book at an auction. He'd inherited a small library of rare British first editions from his mother, and every year he went to London to sell one of them. Apparently that brought in enough money to finance several days of drinking in pubs and going to Queens Park Rangers football matches.

"This book was written by a nineteenth-century scientist who was apparently brilliant. Professor James Moriarty may not have won the place in the history of science that he deserves, but his book *The Dynamics of an Asteroid* is actually one of the few scientific works from the Victorian era in England that is still referenced today," said the elderly man. "You see, I take the trouble to study the books carefully before I sell them. Makes as much sense to preserve all that knowledge in this old noggin of mine as it does between the covers of dusty old tomes that are much too valuable."

The London flight was delayed even more than the plane to Trondheim, and Felicia had two beers with the old man. After yet another glass she suddenly realized that she'd forgotten to pay attention to her watch and the departure times.

There were no further delays for the Trondheim flight that day. It departed at 4:35 P.M., about five minutes before Felicia Stone got up from her chair at the bar for the last time.

When she made it over to the departure screen, she stood there staring at the words GATE CLOSED, which were flashing next to the departure time for the flight she was supposed to be on.

She started to laugh.

Then she cried.

And then she simply left the airport.

The next thing she remembered, she was sitting in a bar in central Oslo. She might have ended up there by chance. Or maybe she liked the name: Teddy's Soft Bar. There were hardly any other customers. The place had a jukebox. She put on "When the Music's Over" by the Doors. Ray Manzarek's hypnotic keyboard tones resonated inside her as she went over to order eggs, bacon, and a beer. She drank the beer but didn't touch the food. Then she played more gloomy music before stepping outside to smoke three cigarettes in a row. When she came back in, she ordered another beer, but was refused service.

"I think you've had enough," the bartender told her.

"I'm American," she heard herself say.

"What does that have to do with anything?"

She switched to English:

"That's why I talk like this. I'm not slurring my words. I have an accent."

"You could be the goddess Freyja, for all I care. I'm not serving you any more drinks."

She had a few more somewhere else, but she couldn't recall the name of the place.

At some point she found her way to Lars's apartment and fell asleep on the sofa. She had a key. Lars had given one to Odd and one to her. Odd had never used his. It wasn't his style to arrive somewhere unannounced. This was the first time she'd ever used her key. The whole family was out. At the movies? At a café? She couldn't remember what they'd said they were going to do that evening. If they had been home, they could have stopped her. Then everything would have ended there. Maybe they would have let her sleep it off and then helped her to buy a new plane ticket to Trondheim. As it was, she took a shower and went into town again before they returned home. She had sobered up a little, and she left no visible trace of her visit to their apartment.

She went out drinking again.

Some instinct, or simply sheer good sense, made her find a hotel room sometime during the course of the night.

The next day she was at it again.

She went on like that for several days, new bars, new hotel rooms, until things went truly wrong.

7

Two days before it happened . . .

B*ad day* at work?"

She was sitting in a bar somewhere in Norway's tiny capital. The guy who sat down at her table was about her age. His head was shaved, and he looked like he'd just changed his clothes in the men's room on the other side of the bar. His shirt seemed to cry out for the return of his jacket and tie. He dropped his bulging leather shoulder bag onto the floor and undid the top button of his shirt.

Felicia gave him a long look before she replied.

"I don't know if a job exists that could give somebody days as bad as the ones I've just been through," she said, unable to muster even a smile.

"You haven't tried my job."

"And what's that?"

"Defense attorney."

"High profile?" she said in English.

"No."

"Okay. Maybe you've had a worse day than I've had. But I still doubt it. And I really don't know whether my day is going to improve any by meeting a defense attorney. That's a professional group that specializes in tearing apart the work I do."

"Ah. A prosecuting attorney with an accent?"

"No, police detective. Or, at least I was, in a former life. It's a long story."

"Where in the States are you from? Somewhere in the south?"

"Virginia."

"Does this long story of yours include falling in love and moving to Norway?"

"Why should I tell you about it?"

"Because I'm a good listener. You police folks think that defense lawyers like me do nothing but talk. But most of my job involves listening. Anyone who can't stand to listen to all the shit doesn't belong in my job."

"It sounds to me like you've had enough of it yourself."

He looked at her and laughed.

"I thought we were talking about you and your problems."

There was something about his laugh, something that provoked her, aroused her, made her scared.

"So are you going to buy me a beer, or what?" she said.

She'd switched to English by now. It made her relax, feel like a foreigner.

"I like your eyes," he said. "It's like you're looking inward. Gives you a melancholy air."

"I am melancholy."

"Really? Well, I guess I was right." He laughed again. "I think you're the kind of person who's always evaluating yourself, never taking a break from your thoughts. Am I right?"

"I was described in almost those exact words once before."

"Let's hear it."

"It's a story I've actually been trying to suppress. It says way too much about my profession and way too much about the sort of people I meet on the job."

"Don't tell me you're one of those officers who's seen so much shit that you've lost all faith in people."

"When I was young, I was in rehab."

"Rehab? Maybe it's not such a good idea for me to be buying you a drink."

"Are you going to let me tell my story or not?"

"Sure. Go ahead."

"I was only nineteen. Had just graduated from high school. Was about to go to college and study literature. Instead my parents ended up taking me with them to Alaska for a whole year. I guess they wanted to get me away from Richmond and make sure I didn't have a relapse. My father, who was a police officer and grew up in Alaska, got a temporary position as a sheriff in Barrow, the northernmost town in the States. On the North Slope, Iñupiat country. I was allowed to go along and help him with his work. He often gave me more responsibility than a teenager ought to have. I think it was his way of building my self-esteem. And I guess it worked. He always understood me better than my mother did.

"One day I got permission to drive out of town to visit an Iñupiat family who lived on the coast. Every morning, all the children in that family were picked up in cars and driven to Barrow Elementary School. But the school reported that one of the pupils, a young boy, hadn't shown up for a long time. The boy's name was Adlartok. This was in early October and the middle of the whaling season, so school attendance fluctuated a lot more than at other times of the year. It wasn't unusual for children to be absent from school. But this boy lived with his grandfather, and everyone knew that the old man didn't go out whaling. And the boy had never before missed a single day of school. So when the teacher hadn't seen him in almost two weeks, she phoned my father and asked him to go over there and see if the boy was okay. It seemed routine, so my father passed it on to me.

"The little shack was built on stilts, which was customary up there. Not, as many people think, to keep the polar bears away at night but to make sure the heat inside the house didn't melt the permafrost, because then the house would sink into the ground. That ramshackle house didn't look like it had enough weight to sink into anything at all. I climbed up the ladder, which had a broken rung, and knocked on the sheet-metal wall next to the doorway. No answer. Three layers of walrus hide covered the door opening. Finally, I pushed them aside and went into the dark room. The grandfather was sitting at the hearth in the middle of the room. A cooking pot hung over the flames, and I could see meat boiling in the water. There was no electricity, which was unusual, even out there.

"The old man looked up at me when I came in. I sat down next to him and explained that the sheriff had sent me. Then I asked if it would be all right if we had a chat.

" 'You are welcome to chat,' he replied in hesitant English.

"I told him I'd come to see Adlartok.

"He said, 'Adlartok is in here,' and he pointed to his chest.

"Then he looked at me, and I looked into his eyes. They were gray, as if their original color had long ago faded into his bloodstream, and I saw nothing. People always say that the eyes are the windows to the soul. I've been a police officer long enough to know they're actually the window shutters of the soul. But I'd never seen eyes like that before, or since. It was like I could see right through them, all the way through the man and the wall behind him, out into the gray, twilight landscape.

"I got worried and asked him what he meant.

" 'Don't ask me what I mean,' he said, and he stared at me for a long time with those squinting gray eyes of his. 'We are alike and not alike, the two of us,' he said. 'We look inward. But I see a desolate landscape, while you see a stormy sea. You are trying to quiet a sea with questions. You will never succeed.'

"When I got up, I thought what he'd said might be some pearl of wisdom. Had he told me something important? Something that might change me? I was nineteen, and I thought there was some truth that defined me. Something that others could see but I couldn't. I also thought that old folks could see things more clearly than most people.

"I also understood that I wasn't going to get anything more out of the old man. So I drove around to ask the neighbors about the boy. No one had seen him in a long time. Either him or his grandfather.

"On my way back to town something suddenly occurred to me. The thought was monstrous, but I was sure I was right." Here Felicia fell silent. "So what's happening with that beer?" she asked.

"Aren't you going to finish the story?"

"I don't much care for the ending."

"You can't just stop like that."

"The point was that the old man said the same thing you did. That I look inward. If I tell you the end of the story, you'll find out how much I think your observation is worth. Wait here."

Felicia got up and went over to the bar. There she paid for a shot of scotch, which she downed instantly, and bought two beers, which she brought back to the table.

"I thought I was the one buying," he said.

"You were too slow." Felicia looked at him. She liked his face. He had coarse skin, and he needed a shave. A redeeming feature in a lawyer, she thought.

"What I realized was that he hadn't pointed to his chest, after all," she said.

"Where are we now?" he asked.

"Back in Alaska. With the grandfather. When he pointed at himself and said his grandson was inside. He wasn't pointing at his chest. He was pointing at his stomach."

"What are you saying?"

"My father went out there later that day and confiscated the cooking pot with the boiled meat. Tests showed that it was equal parts whale meat and human flesh."

"My God!"

"You were the one who wanted to hear the ending. That wise old man was totally psychotic. I had mistaken insanity for wisdom."

The lawyer sat there staring at her. Then he raised his glass.

"Here's to your excellent insight into yourself," he said.

They both laughed.

And that led to more toasts and more glasses of beer.

8

The day before it happened . . .

T*hat was how Felicia* had ended up in this apartment, drinking a cup of coffee and looking out at the unfamiliar street.

"I'm an alcoholic," she said laconically. She spoke the words aloud, facing the window, as if someone could hear her down there on the deserted street.

"I'm a two-timing alcoholic. Somebody who destroys things."

But what had she destroyed?

I love him. I was never really mad at him. That wasn't why I walked out. I just needed some distance. I think I was feeling like it was all too much—too much of us and him and his job.

She stopped herself there.

Why do I start all my sentences with the word I? she thought.

Then she drank the rest of her coffee and left the apartment.

Outside it was snowing, and the wind was so fierce that she decided to take a cab to Oslo Central Station. Besides, she might not be able to find her way there otherwise. For some strange reason, she took comfort in the fact that she had no idea where in the city she was. She didn't know the names of the various neighborhoods or the parks or the streets. It was almost as if none of this had happened, as if she'd dreamed the whole thing.

Even the express train to the airport had trouble staying on schedule. The weather was worse than the last time she'd gone out to the airport, and there was little hope that any flights would be leaving on time this morning.

Felicia considered turning her phone back on to call Odd. She knew he must be worried about her. But she decided to wait.

I need to see him. I actually need to see Odd again before I know what to say to him, and if I do decide to say something, I have to figure out how to say it.

She wouldn't know what had been destroyed and what was still whole until she looked into his eyes again.

"You're not going to get to Trondheim today. We have passengers still waiting here from yesterday's canceled flights. And they've already bought tickets, so they'll have priority if we get any planes off the ground today. It's even worse than before. A few planes departed yesterday, but I don't know about today."

She got the same answer from Norwegian Air as she'd heard from SAS.

The woman behind the service counter was already looking over Felicia's shoulder to the next person in the line of grumbling passengers. The airline agent hid her stress behind an annoying professional indifference. Felicia had an urge to scream at the woman that she needed to go home, that she couldn't wait. She was sweating and shaking. She felt like shit, in spite of the shower she'd taken that morning. But she realized there wasn't a special line for people who needed to find out ASAP if they were loved. If they could still *be* loved.

"You could try taking the train."

Felicia thanked the woman and took her suggestion.

There were no seats available until the night train, which left at

11:45 P.M., and she'd have to sit up all night because the sleeping cars were booked. She bought herself a ticket. Then she went over to the Radisson Blu Plaza Hotel and got a room.

It was still early in the day, and she knew she could sleep for hours. She asked for a wake-up call at eleven.

Then she went to the room and crawled into bed. But she couldn't sleep and decided to watch a movie instead on cable TV. *Casablanca*. She loved that film. But not today.

"It's sheer chaos. The worst day I can ever remember," said the Norwegian rail conductor as he walked along the platform to explain the situation to travelers.

An announcement over the loudspeakers had just informed everyone that the night train to Trondheim had been canceled due to weather conditions. For the same reason, there would be no bus to replace the train on that particular stretch of track.

"If I were you, I'd get a hotel room with a good selection of booze in the mini-bar. The forecast is for better weather in the morning, and sooner or later the traffic is bound to ease up. If you're really desperate, I think there are still rental cars available, but I can't promise decent driving conditions. If you want to wait for tomorrow's trains, the NSB railroad will cover a night's lodging, up to a certain limit. Please contact our information desk, which is in the airport arrivals hall."

The conductor took off his cap to wipe his brow, which was sweaty in spite of the cold temperature out on the platform. Then he moved on to the next group of frustrated and worn-out travelers.

Felicia stood there for a moment, staring after him. Then she made up her mind to rent a car.

An hour later, a little past one in the morning, she was sitting in a four-wheel-drive Subaru with studded tires, heading away from Gardermoen Airport. Whirling snow danced past her. It was like having thousands of scratches on the glass of the windshield, in a constantly flickering pattern. On the radio the main news topic was the bad weather and all the delays. Everyone was being advised to travel only if necessary, and otherwise remain patient and calm.

Nothing is more necessary than this trip, thought Felicia.

Otherwise there was little news. A boy was reported missing from a shop in Oslo, where a man had been found dead. The police considered both the disappearance and the death to be suspicious.

When she reached the E6, the light sculpture titled *Kepler's Star* illuminated the snowdrift like an enormous catalyst for the storm.

In fact, the road conditions weren't that bad.

Sure, a blizzard like this would be a disaster in Richmond, Virginia. Even a light snowfall paralyzed the whole city. There were hardly any snowplows, and no one even knew what studded tires were. Chaos would reign.

In Norway things were totally different. Here it was actually possible to drive in a snowstorm. The plows were all at work, and on the main highways there was enough traffic to pack down the snow into a hard crust that was safe for driving.

The biggest problem was really Felicia's lack of experience in driving on icy surfaces. She'd driven a little during that long winter she'd spent in Barrow. But there the roads were straight, with few curves, and the distances were never far. It was a community of only three thousand inhabitants, surrounded by a huge expanse of ice. In the winter, when eternal night descended and the sky shifted from black to a leaden gray, she'd mostly gotten around by riding on the back of her father's snowmobile. In Norway, on the other hand, driving in the winter was an everyday thing. That might be one of the most exotic things about this country—in Norway you had to take classes in how to drive on icy roads in order to get a driver's license. Right now she wished she'd taken that class herself.

She headed north on the E6. Overly cautious, she was probably driving a good fifteen miles an hour below the speed limit. She ended up with a long line of cars behind her, but she was patient, pulling over occasionally to let the other drivers pass.

At a rest stop south of Hamar she got out to study a map that showed various routes to Trondheim. She'd driven this way a few times before with Odd.

"I always drive through Østerdalen," he'd told her the first time they headed south from Trondheim. "Not much to see along the way, but it's a lot faster. The route through Gudbrandsdalen is for tourists."

"I'm a tourist," she'd told him.

That was after she'd been in Trondheim only a few weeks. They were going to the christening of Lars's child. Back then, she was still on vacation from the Richmond Police Department. She hadn't come up with the crazy idea of quitting and moving in with Odd in his run-down and drafty but charming apartment in this ice-cold land. She was just a tourist in love and nothing more.

"You can be a tourist when we get to Oslo," Odd had replied, which was unusually brusque for him.

She learned later that driving was one of the few things that could put him in a bad mood. The longer the trip, the grumpier he became, his ill temper escalating.

Felicia promised herself she'd go through Gudbrandsdalen when she made the trip alone. But she wasn't thinking of a day like today with this kind of weather, so late at night, and with such dark thoughts weighing on her mind.

A kilometer farther along, she turned off the E6 and onto Highway 3 toward Elverum. She tried to find an open café in Elverum, but it was almost two thirty in the morning, and everything was closed. Luckily she still had plenty of gas. She probably wouldn't need to fill up before she reached Trondheim. She headed out on the long, white stretch of road up through Østerdalen.

After Elverum, her car was the only one on the road. She was alone with the beam of her headlights, the frantic whirling of the snow, the humming of the heater, the lilt of the Norwegian language as people talked on the radio, and her thoughts about Odd, questions with no answers. The DJ, a woman with a sleepy voice, announced the last song of the night.

"Three minutes and twenty-six seconds with my favorite brooding song," she said. "Amazing, heavy, suggestive, depressing. That's it for me tonight. This is Joy Division, with 'Love Will Tear Us Apart.' Have a nice, dark night."

Ian Curtis's trembling, epileptic voice filled the car. Felicia imagined the snowflakes dancing in time to the music, whirling, flitting, stumbling, pieces of ash from a smoldering bonfire, scraps torn from the winter landscape. All of a sudden she began to cry. At first it was only one tear welling up in her eye, clinging like a drop of slush to her eyelashes for a moment. Then it rolled down her cheek.

More tears.

She gasped. Tried to take a deep breath and hold it in. But she couldn't. Gasped again and again. Thought she might run out of oxygen, faint, and drive off the road, putting an end to all her misery. The idea didn't scare her.

How selfish can I be? she thought. *How fucking selfish?*

Odd had been in the middle of a really big case. The kind that could leave permanent scars. The sort of case that no investigator wishes for.

The Music Box case was still in the news a week after it was resolved. A young girl had disappeared, and it took a long time to identify the perpetrator. Odd had taken the whole thing personally. He couldn't sleep at night. He was driven by everything that always drives a homicide detective: a sense of justice, a desire for confirmation and insight, fear, revulsion, and the hope of re-establishing some sense of order in a world that was falling apart. Odd was always fighting a battle against his own failing memory, a battle he might one day lose. All of this had consumed him completely. Felicia was fully aware of what was going on with him. She knew what she was getting into when she married a police detective. After all, she was one herself.

But what she hadn't realized was how much she had missed her own work. And that might be the reason she had wanted to run away. The thought gave her hope. If it was a problem that specific, they could work it out. Couldn't they? It was just a childish, primitive sense of envy.

It wasn't the fact that Odd hadn't told her about sleeping with Siri. That had happened before Felicia met him. It was a trivial matter, just casual sex. Right? No one could have known back then that she and Odd would become lovers, or that she would become good friends with Siri. They should have told her, but it wasn't important enough to have evoked such a strong reaction from her. Other things, other emotions had gotten mixed in.

Felicia realized that now.

She missed her job, she missed having meaningful work, being important to other people, the hunt for criminals, all of it. She saw Odd on the job and how he got caught up in his work, how it tormented him, but also how it made him feel alive in a way that few things other than police work could do. And that was what had made her jealous. Wasn't it? Yes. It definitely was not just that stupid affair with Siri Holm.

How egotistical could she be? Why had she made him suffer for something that really was all about herself?

She took out her phone.

She sat there holding it in her hand for a long time as she drove. She hadn't turned it back on since she phoned Odd at the hospital. Now she looked at her face reflected in the dead glass surface, casting a quick glance at the faint outline before she turned her gaze back to the road. It'll probably ding for at least ten minutes if I switch it on, she thought, with all the text messages and missed calls.

That phone had stories to tell. Stories about longing and confusion. Stories created by her, told by others.

How fucking selfish can I be?

It had been her decision to move to Norway. And now she was punishing Odd for it.

Do I love him? Maybe I don't.

She turned on her phone, wrote a text, keeping one eye on the road, and was just about to tap the SEND button.

But before she could do it, she hit a man.

He suddenly appeared around a curve in the road. Something that looked like a short rifle was pointing at her. She braked hard, making the car spin around on the road. The rear of the car struck the man, and he was thrown into the air, flailing like a gymnast who'd lost his grip on the horizontal bar. To Felicia, whose car skidded at breakneck speed, rotating away from him, he looked almost as light as a feather as his body sketched an arc in the air, hovered at the top, and then plummeted abruptly to the ground, landing on his back.

The car continued on, out of control, for several yards before it finally came to a stop, settling with a faint thud against the side of the snowbank, as if it were the finale of a carefully rehearsed stunt.

The headlights shone on the man as he lay on the ground, a lifeless shadow, a dead circus performer in the steady glow of the beams. Snowflakes fell on him like applause.

She tried to gather her thoughts, to think rationally, do the right things. First she took the key out of the ignition and put it in her pocket. Then she looked for her cell, which she found under the passenger seat. Her heart pounding, she got out of the car and rushed over to the man. She noticed a car half-buried in the snowbank nearby. The trunk of the car was open. A sawed-off shotgun lay next to the man. He was tall. Almost six foot six, she estimated. His eyes were closed, and his hair dark, close cropped, and well groomed. He looked as if he were smiling as he lay there on his back with his nose pointing up at the sky. The snow falling on his jacket looked like dust.

"My God!" she gasped. "Are you okay? Are you alive?"

She leaned down, pressed two fingers to his neck. No, no, no! She couldn't find a pulse.

All of a sudden he reached up and grabbed her by the ankle, his hand gripping hard, desperately. At first she was relieved. Then his eyes opened, and she saw his expression. Those blue-gray eyes were staring into the beam of the headlights.

Then her feeling of relief changed. A sudden gut reflex made her straighten up and kick.

He didn't loosen his grip on her ankle. Instead, he yanked it toward him so she lost her footing. She fell backward onto the hard crust of ice under the newly fallen snow. Her head struck the ground. A trembling, icy pain spread from the back of her head to her forehead. The cold from the ground found its way inside of her. But she didn't lose consciousness.

He let go of her ankle and got up.

Up to this point she had acted out of instinct, an innate suspicion, police reflexes. Now that she saw him standing over her, she was no longer in doubt. His gaze did not waver. His eyes hardly moved at all, assessing the situation, taking their bearings like sensors. They looked totally white, like chunks of ice covered with frost.

Her life hung in the balance.

Two quick strides took him over to the shotgun. He picked it up and turned toward her.

She rolled back onto her shoulders, did a back somersault, and landed on her feet.

By the time the gun fired, she had thrown herself sideways toward the car stuck in the snowbank. She jumped up on the lid of the trunk, closing it with the weight of her body. Buckshot from the gun sketched black patterns on the snow at the spot where she had been standing. They looked like markings from some rare and deadly disease.

He came toward her, racking the gun. He moved with confidence, his footsteps soundless. She could hardly even hear him breathing. He was aiming as he walked. She curled up. Automatically she conjured up images, instructions, movements practiced in the gym back at the police station in Richmond, punching and kicking, straight-arming her colleague Reynolds, the wall of the gym, gathering all those ingrained motor skills into a single smoldering point inside her.

Then she leaped.

Both boots struck him in the forehead before the gun went off. She landed behind him.

Now he lay on the ground again. But this time his eyes were open. A faint gust of icy vapor issued from his lips. His hands, white and unreal in the beam of the headlights. He fumbled for the gun lying next to him. She dashed forward to grab it first, but she was too late. Holding the shotgun raised, he swiftly rolled onto his side. Felicia again sprang up onto the trunk of the car. This time she pushed off and made it over the snowbank. On the other side she slid down the slope in the deep, powdery snow and into a tree. She got up and brushed the snow off her face, aware of the cold. She was even colder inside.

A shot rang out above the snowbank.

She headed into the woods, moving as fast as she could.

She wasn't dressed for this. Her boots had been a gift from Odd. They had high heels, something she wouldn't have bought for herself. The heels acted like awls in the snow, making her sink deeper than she would have otherwise. But she couldn't take them off. Her jacket was one she'd brought from Virginia. A leather jacket intended for chilly winter evenings, not the sort of cold that winter nights in Østerdalen offered. Luckily she'd put on a woolen sweater underneath. That sweater might be her salvation right now.

She waded through the snow as fast as she could. Every once in a while she paused to listen. She heard nothing but the wind rustling the trees. Yet she was sure he wasn't far behind.

Who was he? Why had he tried to kill her?

All her experience told her that such a desperate attempt to kill could only come from a desire to conceal something even worse. No one would attack a complete stranger like that unless he had everything to lose. But he'd been so calm. There was something terrifyingly methodical about the way he had acted. As if he'd been trained to kill.

She headed deeper into the woods. Tried to maintain a good pace, both to keep him at bay and to stay warm. But she knew he was better equipped than she was. He was stronger, faster, and had a sense of calm that she didn't possess. Then there were her footprints. All he needed to do was follow her tracks in the snow.

She turned around. Stopped, but didn't hear a sound. Then she saw it. The beam from a flashlight down the hill, not far away, maybe two hundred yards, four hundred, six hundred. It was hard to tell.

She came to a steep slope and followed the ridge, still climbing higher and deeper into the forest. A large birch tree had toppled halfway over in a winter storm. Its trunk hung over the slope, its roots partially pulled free. She continued past it for maybe fifty yards and then turned around once she was covered by a clump of spruce trees. From there she moved as fast she could back to the birch tree. She was careful to step in her own footprints so she wouldn't leave a new trail behind.

When she reached the leaning tree, she grabbed the roots sticking out of the ground and pulled herself up onto the trunk. She balanced along the trunk until she was standing at a place where the tree hovered in mid-air.

Again she looked for the flashlight beam. At first she didn't see it, but then spied it between the trees, flickering, searching. He was getting closer but still had a ways to go. Not hurrying, making steady progress, precise and cold.

The tree trunk dipped some under her weight, but the roots that were still in the ground refused to let go. She looked down and couldn't make out anything but darkness below. She couldn't hear him, yet soon he would be standing near the roots of the tree. So she took a deep breath and jumped.

One foot struck a big round rock. The other disappeared into the snow and got wedged into a hollow between two other rocks with sharper edges. She fell forward and had to twist and yank the foot that was stuck before it pulled free.

After that, she rolled down the slope.

Her body struck more rocks under the snow, and her back slammed against a fallen tree, bringing her to a halt. She was way down at the bottom of a ravine. She stifled a scream and couldn't help gasping for breath for several moments.

Then she lay very still, aware of the throbbing pain in her body. She'd suffered so many blows that she couldn't pinpoint all the cuts and bruises. But the worst was her foot, the one she had twisted between the rocks.

She looked up. A beam of light moved past in the night far above her.

Had he heard her over the wind and the rustling in the trees when she fell? Were all her efforts in vain? Or had she really managed to throw him off her trail?

The beam from his flashlight didn't stop. It never turned down toward her but continued to bob ominously along the edge of the ravine, and then it vanished from sight.

The snow had stopped falling temporarily. The moon suddenly appeared from between the drifting clouds, glittering faintly on the powdery snow. A slightly moldy odor came from the tree trunk she was lying on. Somewhere overhead she heard branches snapping. He was moving away from her.

Felicia Stone took several deep breaths and then stood up.

He'd fallen for her ruse. But soon he'd come searching for her again. Had she camouflaged her tracks well enough? Would he see instantly what she'd done, or would he end up wasting as much time as she hoped?

I need to call Odd, she thought. *I'm going to call him right now.* He'd be able to do things faster than if she called the emergency number. She was convinced of that. That was something he was good at; her husband could make things happen. Her husband. She savored the words. They didn't feel meaningless. There was at least some hope in them.

Please let there be cell phone coverage out here in the woods! She wasn't that far from the road. She pressed her thumb on the ice-cold button and waited for the familiar morning-blue glow, but the screen was cracked. Her phone was dead.

She felt a harsh, stabbing pain in her chest. Slowly, feeling resigned, her whole body aching, she stood up. She set her injured foot in the snow. Put as much weight on it as she could, testing it. Was it just badly bruised? Or was it sprained? Or even broken? It felt like an invisible knife was sticking into the flesh and jabbing at the bone. She considered pulling up her pants leg and icing her calf and ankle with snow. But that would be madness. She realized that. The cold was a worse threat than any physical injury.

She began climbing as fast as her footwear and injury allowed, out of the ravine and up the other side. Soon she reached level ground again. The snow was deeper here, reaching above her knees. The trees stood closer together, looking like an enormous flock of slumbering animals trying to keep warm in the night. The gray spaces between the tree trunks stretched on forever. A void filling up with snowflakes, a silent realm. Human beings very rarely set foot in a place like this, yet it was people she was seeking. After a few hundred yards she came to a ski trail. A snowmobile had traveled along it fairly recently, so there was a hard crust, and she was able to walk on it. In the meantime, powder snow had settled on top, acting almost like a blank sketch pad for her feet.

Felicia broke off a few branches from a fir tree next to the trail. She began walking backward as she swept away her footprints. Her track was far from invisible. But if she was lucky, the snowfall and wind would do the rest of the job so that by the time he got here, it would be impossible to tell which way she had gone.

And he will definitely find his way here, she told herself. *You can be sure of that.*

She headed in the direction of the highway, where she had come from. She hoped to get back to the car before he did. She still had the car key in her pocket.

When she came to a spot where the trail turned and headed back into the woods, she rolled out of it to leave the smallest possible track. Once among the trees, she stood up and headed in what she thought was the right direction. It was still the middle of the night, and she didn't hear any traffic. But she was able to move faster than she'd thought.

When she finally got down from the snowbank and out onto the road, she stopped to get her bearings. The road was straight in both directions. But off in the distance she was sure she could glimpse the beginning of the curve where she'd skidded into him.

Do I dare go over to the cars? she wondered. He might have come back.

That would be the natural thing to do after he lost track of her. Try to cut her off at the place where she was most likely to return.

I'll wait here. Sooner or later a car has to come along. Someone will stop for me. Someone will have a cell phone I can use.

So she decided to stay where she was, standing there and breathing heavily, feeling the pain in her leg, the numb feeling in her whole body, all the strangely contradictory emotions—nausea, resignation, defiance, anger, sorrow, regret—everything actually merging into one vast, nameless feeling, something that was all her, a bigger version of the person she had been in Trondheim, a more dangerous version, a smarter version, a more frightened version.

What if I go over to the cars? What if I sneak up on him and hit him from behind, take the shotgun, use his cell to call the police? She and Odd would have a lot to talk about afterward. In a strange way, she felt as if something like this might establish a sense of balance between them, fill an empty space in their relationship. Then she wouldn't be afraid of telling him what she'd done. And maybe she'd be able to ask for his forgiveness. Was she crazy to be thinking like this, when she needed to focus on saving herself, getting out of this situation in one piece? If she failed, then there wouldn't be anything to talk about anyway.

But maybe she was onto something. Overpowering him might actually be the best strategy for survival. She started heading for the curve in the distance.

That was when she became aware of the light shining from behind, and she turned around. At first it looked like the glow of a cold dawn, flickering beyond the snowbank. Then a headlight appeared, followed by another.

Felicia took up position in the opposite lane. Close enough to the center line that the driver would see her soon enough not to run into her, provided he was paying attention. Then she began jumping up and down and waving her arms. She needed the people in the car to realize this was important, that she needed help, and that she intended no harm.

The car gradually materialized behind the headlights, slowed down, and stopped only ten yards from where she was standing. She ran toward it. She was halfway there when the back door opened. A tall figure got out. Stood still over a few seconds. The man ran a hand through his hair and bent down to the car.

"That's her. Thanks a lot. No need to stop. We can manage on our own."

He slammed the back door. The tires spun a few times in the powdery snow before getting traction. Then the car drove off. Someone waved from inside, and they were gone. Felicia didn't bother to turn to look at the disappearing car. Instead, she looked at the man, who quickly opened his jacket and took out the sawed-off shotgun.

He didn't say a word. Just breathed calmly as he took aim.

Felicia threw herself full length onto the ground and felt the shot whiz past her head. Some buckshot grazed her back, but the only damage was to her jacket. In a flash she was on her feet while he reloaded. Then she rushed toward him at top speed. She leaped and hit him with both feet to the chest, which toppled him backward.

Yet he still managed to keep hold of the gun. He rolled onto his side, and got onto his knees, pointing the shotgun at Felicia, who was standing over him, furious and shaking. He pulled the trigger.

The gun clicked.

Felicia didn't know whether he'd failed to rack the gun properly, or whether he was out of ammunition. There was no time to think about that. She spun around and for the second time that night, she plunged over the side of the snowbank. Then she began wading through the snow, back into the woods.

He has more ammunition, she thought. *It's probably in his car. So I can't go back to the cars. But I've got a head start because he has to go back there before he can come after me.* She decided to make her way to the ski trail.

For a moment she paused to look ahead, in the opposite direction from which she'd come. On the other side of the valley was the house she'd seen with lights in the windows. Could she make it all the way there with her injured foot? She doubted it. As desperate as she felt, she had an urge to simply sit down. But she knew she couldn't give up. That was what he expected. That she would lose courage.

A guy like him can smell defeat, she thought. She had no idea who he was. All she knew was that this kind of situation seemed to excite him. It kept him going. She was sure her assessment was true. She'd seen it in his eyes.

She thought this must be her punishment.

I deserve this, she told herself. *I asked for this*. Most likely he was a convict on the run. A lone, desperate criminal. Someone whose life had taken a bad turn somewhere, someone she just happened to come across. That was the only explanation. Even so, she felt like it wasn't mere chance. This was happening for a reason, and he'd been waiting for her specifically. Of course that wasn't rational. But she couldn't get rid of the idea.

Felicia found her way back to the ski trail. Again she used tree boughs to erase her footprints. It had started snowing again, coming down harder than before. If he wasn't right behind her, if he had in fact been delayed because he needed more ammunition, it might be smart to do a better job of erasing her tracks this time.

After a while she caught sight of a dark cabin in the woods, and she veered over to the edge of the ski trail. There she wiped away the last of her footprints and moved in among the trees. Then she trudged through the snow to the cabin.

As she got closer, she saw with relief the electrical cord slung between the roof and a slender pole outside. Electricity meant the potential for heat. And heat meant she could sit still for a brief time to gather her thoughts, clear her head, and make a plan.

When she was almost up to the door, she discovered footprints in the snow. They crossed the yard in front of the cabin and disappeared behind it. She leaned down to study them as best she could in the dark. They seemed fresh. Judging by the snow that had fallen on them, she guessed they'd been made after the worst of the blizzard had subsided a short time ago.

Somebody was here in the woods. Were there others besides him?

The tracks seemed to have been made by at least two people. One had a significantly shorter stride than the other. A child? What were they doing out here in the middle of the night, and in such terrible weather? They couldn't have gone far, probably just over to another cabin close by.

Felicia decided to follow them. It seemed more sensible than just wandering about at random. From the cabin the footprints led deeper into the woods. Then they suddenly changed direction and continued up a hill to the top where only a single birch tree stood.

The storm was definitely beginning to let up. Again the moon emerged from the clouds, producing a sallow glow. Bare branches shone grayish-white, boughs stretched upward, thin and black like the fractures in an x-ray image of broken bones.

Felicia headed for the top of the hill and the birch tree, following the footprints. When she reached the crest, she saw the figure at the foot of the tree trunk. A slight shape that seemed suspended, something that had seeped out of the tree itself, pus, black sap, a nightmare that the forest had dreamed, a small, lifeless human body. She moved faster, feeling the pain in her foot, but she didn't stop until she reached the boy.

She leaned down to examine the motionless child.

His hands had been bound to the trunk. Maybe he'd originally been standing. But now he had slumped forward so he was sitting in the snow. His black pants were covered with a thin layer of snow, and there was frost in his hair.

She pressed two fingers under his chin. His skin was warmer than she'd feared. She felt for a pulse. Found it at last, beating slowly, very slowly, like that of a torpid reptile. Felicia pulled the key ring out of her pocket. Her fingers were frozen and felt like they'd break if she pressed too hard. She chose the key to her old apartment in Richmond, an extra key she'd kept after selling the place, a sentimental talisman. It had the sharpest teeth.

She used the key to saw at the thin plastic tie until it came off. A bloodred stripe was left on the white wrists of the boy.

Now he began to stir. Moving like a sleepwalker, he crossed his arms and doubled over. Felicia sat down and put her arms around him. Then she pressed her lips to his ear and whispered:

"We have to get out of here. We have to get you someplace warm."

When she raised his head, she saw the blood. His hair was stiff with it. A dark red trickle ran around his ear and down the back of his neck. A head wound. It didn't look life-threatening.

Then she stood up and saw the damage that had been done to the tree trunk. She recognized the dark patches. She'd seen the same thing a short time ago in the snow up on the road. Buckshot. This was his work. The man from the road had left these marks on the tree. For some reason he'd aimed above the boy's head before leaving the poor child to an icy and lonely death, tied to the tree trunk.

This was what he was hiding. This was the reason he'd tried to kill her. He didn't want to leave any witnesses. He didn't want to be seen on this stretch of road, not with the shotgun, not by anyone who would get suspicious and call the police. His plan was to get away unnoticed while the boy died here alone and the snow covered all the tracks. But why hadn't he simply shot the boy? The more she thought about it, the stranger it seemed. Cowardly and pitiful. A killer who didn't dare kill, but instead let the forest and the cold do the job for him. It was such a grotesque idea that she dismissed it, without any other explanation for why someone would do that. Instead she speculated how long the boy must have been out here in the cold. Not long, or he'd already be dead.

The perp left him here, she thought, *and went straight back to the road where I ran into him.*

How long ago was that? She wasn't sure. She'd lost all sense of time.

Now she took hold of the boy's arm. It felt like an icicle as she draped it around her neck and lifted him up. She held him in her arms and began wading back through the snow to the cabin. Pain shot through her foot with every other step, and the high heels of her boots didn't make walking any easier.

She set the boy down in front of the door. He groaned quietly, the first real sign of life. A gurgling sound, like from a newborn baby. That gave her strength. She forgot about the pain in her foot, how exhausted she felt, and her own fear.

She tried the door, but it was locked.

She went over to a window in back and broke the glass of one of the panes. By sticking her hand inside she was able to lift open the hasp and open the window. She jumped up on the ledge and climbed in.

She found herself in a tiny bedroom with bunk beds along one wall. Quickly she went into the main room and opened the front door. She picked up the boy and carried him into the bedroom. She'd noticed an electric heater on the wall under the window. She didn't want to risk lighting a fire in the woodstove in the living room. Smoke from the chimney would draw his attention and lead him here even faster.

He's going to find us soon enough, she thought.

There were quilts and pillows on the beds. Felicia lay the boy on the lower bunk and stuffed a pillow in the broken window. Then she closed the door to the bedroom and turned on the heater. Luckily the electricity was still working.

On the top bunk she found a rolled-up sleeping bag tucked under the quilt. She unzipped it, then got the boy out of his cold, wet clothes and helped him into the bag. He had started moving now, though lethargically.

Felicia whispered to him:

"Let's get you warm. You're going to be okay."

After getting him to lie down inside the sleeping bag, she went outside to take a look at the forest. She couldn't see anything moving in the dark. No sounds other than from an occasional car on the road far off. She broke off a tree bough and tried to sweep away their tracks around the cabin. But it didn't do much good. The snow had stopped, and he'd be able to see that they'd been here. There was little she could do about that.

Then she went back inside and locked the door.

Maybe he'll give up, she thought. *Maybe he doesn't have time for this. He's on the run from something. Maybe he's supposed to meet someone and has to get going.* She went into the bedroom and closed the door.

What I need to focus on right now is getting the boy warmed up, she thought.

For a moment she stood still, trying to recall the first-aid course she'd taken, and what she'd learned about hypothermia. She remembered something about gradually warming up someone with body heat. So she got into the sleeping bag with the boy. It was a tight fit, but the boy was thin, and she managed to zip the bag so it closed around them. Felicia put her hand on his forehead. There was still some warmth in his skin. If they didn't get interrupted, everything should be fine.

Considering the circumstances, the thought that now occurred to her seemed strange, even inappropriate.

Why haven't I ever thought about having a baby?

With Odd, of course, it would never come into the picture. He was approaching retirement. And besides, they were always careful with birth control. It was only their first night together that he hadn't used any protection, but nothing had happened. Now she realized that she'd never had the urge to have a baby. Naturally she'd thought about it. But she'd never had a desire to have Odd's child. Nor with anyone else before she'd met him. She'd never pictured herself as a mother, not even when she was younger. Why not? she now wondered.

She was suddenly struck by a thought that should have been worrisome, but it wasn't. They hadn't used a condom that night in Oslo. She'd had unprotected sex on that black, sweaty night with the lawyer from the bar. And it was right in the middle of her cycle. The likelihood that she was pregnant wasn't great, but it still existed.

What would that mean for her and Odd? And what should she do if she turned out to be pregnant? Felicia noticed she was holding more tightly to the boy's hair than she ought to, so she let go.

If that happened, she and Odd were finished. It wouldn't matter if he forgave her for running away, or for cheating on him. They wouldn't be able to live with something like that.

Felicia didn't remember much that her mother had told her when she was growing up. She wished she could recall more, but the memories had faded, like the wreath that she and her father had placed on her mother's grave every spring. But there was one thing she did remember. It was something her mother said while standing at the kitchen counter. The bread machine was kneading dough for a loaf of bread, or maybe rolls, white flour with lots of butter. One of her grandmother's recipes. Felicia had written it down somewhere but never tried it. Maybe it was still back home in the attic, the notebook bound in gray, with a few recipes from her maternal grandmother. Her mother had thought Felicia should have them, back when they still thought that someday they would understand each other. In spite of the noise from the bread machine, Felicia heard very clearly one of the few things she remembered her mother saying to her. Back then she hadn't understood what it meant. The words were abstract and strange, and she didn't recall the context, or what they talked about before or after. All she remembered were two peculiar sentences:

"Life is a series of missed chances," her mother said. "Replaced by rare moments that actually mean something."

What if what happened in that Oslo apartment was just such a moment that actually meant something? What did that say about her and Odd?

She brushed the thought aside. Of course she wasn't pregnant. *And I love him. Don't I?*

She lay there listening to the boy, his breathing irregular and slow. Every once in a while he seemed to be whispering something, but the words were too quiet. She couldn't make out what he was saying.

Then she noticed how exhausted she was. Her head ached, she had a faint churning sensation in her abdomen. She needed a cigarette. She wanted coffee, a beer. Her muscles ached, she felt sick to her stomach. She was still wearing her jacket, but there were no cigarettes in the pockets. She'd left the pack in her bag in the car. The cars. He must have gone back there long ago and reloaded the shotgun. Thoughts began whirling through her mind.

I've done this before, she thought. *Once before, a long time ago, I shared a sleeping bag with a boy about his size. But back then he wasn't smaller than me. And the boy wasn't shaking with the cold and fear.*

He wasn't afraid of anything. Brad Davis, the boy who lived next door to Felicia Stone. That was what he'd told her. He'd never been afraid of anything his whole life, not even that time when he was five and a strange dog came into their yard and attacked his family's dog.

Their dog, Rudolf, was a mutt, a mixture of pit bull and everything else, Brad had boasted. Not much pit bull and a lot of everything else. Felicia remembered him as a sleepy old dog with shabby fur. He was a terrible watchdog.

But back when she and Brad were both five, Rudolf was young and frisky. One night, a dog, a furious boxer that had gotten away from his owner, came rushing into the family's yard.

Felicia still vaguely recalled what happened. Maybe it was her first real memory, but it was just images, not sounds or smells. She saw it happen from her window. The two dogs barking at each other out on the lawn under the tree in the backyard, the spot where a few years later she and Brad would build a hut out of tree branches and she would have her first kiss. Brad came storming out and threw himself between the two snarling dogs. He landed on the ground, with them towering over him, their jaws wide, looking like the wolves who were their ancestors. The little boy was nothing but air to them. They barked, growled, and clawed at each other, paying no attention to the fact that Brad was trying to separate them. It went on for a long time. Every time they moved, Brad followed like a silly puppy, unthinking and unafraid. Time after time he landed in the middle of the furious dance of muscles and claws, blood-stained fur, staring, dark eyes, their bodies moving to a rhythm only they could follow. The whole time it seemed as if the small child didn't exist.

Suddenly Brad stood up, grabbed Rudolf's collar, and pulled him aside, managing to make eye contact with the agitated dog. And he calmed down. Gave a few halfhearted barks, as if snapping at the air, and then lay down in the grass.

Brad turned around and glared at the other dog, standing there motionless and staring back. Several seconds passed as the animal took the measure of this new adversary. Felicia was terrified that it might leap at him and tear him to bits. Instead, the intruder turned away and ran out of the yard.

Brad talked about that incident for years afterward. He claimed he wasn't scared.

He'd felt perfectly safe sitting between two dogs. It was like being inside a tent, with a storm raging outside. He had simply waited for the right opportunity to grab Rudolf's collar. He knew he could control the dog once he got hold of him.

Felicia listened to him tell the story every time without mentioning that she'd seen the whole thing. It took a long time before she got tired of the story. But that day finally came. The episode had almost faded from her memory that night when they shared a sleeping bag some years later. They must have been eight or nine. Nine. It was 1985. Felicia had never kissed a boy when that day began.

"I got it from Eddy." Brad held up a brown box with a couple of knobs on top.

"Eddy in the sixth grade?"

"Uh-huh."

"You mean you talk to people like him?"

"Sure. Look what he gave me."

"Is that something for a stereo?"

"It's a pirate decoder. Eddy says it works. His brother got it somewhere, and they've been watching HBO for free for months now, and their parents don't know about it. Cool, huh? I got it because they have a new one. This one is a little broken, but it works if you stick this card in the slot and wiggle it."

"Wiggle it?"

"Yeah. Back and forth like this, Eddy says. And it's true. It works. Want to try?"

"I'm not allowed to watch HBO. Mamma says it's nothing but bad movies, the kind kids shouldn't see."

"Your mamma? Come on. You've got a cable hookup in the wall, don't you?"

"Of course."

"Well, *A Nightmare on Elm Street* is just starting." Brad began attaching the cable. He'd done it before.

"Is it really scary?"

"Scary? I'd call it gory. And terrifying."

"Shouldn't we watch cartoons instead? Mamma and Pappa said we could watch cartoons until they come home."

"So what? They let us watch cartoons when they're here."

"Is there any blood in this movie?"

"Tons."

Brad had finished hooking up the box. He turned on the TV. A grainy picture appeared on the screen. Freddy Krueger's hoarse voice filled the room. Brad wiggled the card, and soon they could see Freddy's steel claws.

Felicia hid her face behind a big sofa pillow. That was where she stayed until the movie was over.

"Did you like it?"

She nodded.

"You weren't even watching."

She shook her head and laughed.

"Let's sneak outdoors tonight," said Brad. "After your parents come home and go to bed. Let's stay awake and then sneak outside."

"Isn't it good enough that you get to stay here overnight?"

"I know about somebody," said Brad.

"What are you talking about?"

"Marijuana growers."

"What about them?"

"They've got a place over by the river where my father and I sometimes fish. I've seen the house where they grow the stuff. One day when we were out fishing, I needed to pee, and I happened to look in the window. They'd forgotten to cover the glass, so I saw all the plants. I know what those kind of plants look like. There were lights and foil on the walls, and everything. I'll bet they go over there at night. We could report them and be heroes. Maybe even get our pictures in the newspaper."

"They're marijuana growers, Brad. Not bank robbers."

"So? They're bad guys. If we report them to the police, we'd get in the papers. KIDS UNCOVER MARIJUANA GANG."

"You're crazy!"

"I could only find one." Felicia came out of her bedroom closet carrying a sleeping bag. "The others are in my parents' room."

"We'll take turns sleeping," said Brad. "That's what they do on a stakeout. What about a flashlight?"

"In the drawer over there," she whispered.

Brad took the flashlight out of her desk drawer and stuck it in his belt. He also found an old package of Twinkies that Felicia had forgotten about.

Then they tiptoed out of the apartment, took their bicycles from the basement, and headed for the place on the James River that Brad knew about.

It was past midnight. It was October, and the air felt brisk. If the police or anyone else happened to catch sight of them, two nine-year-olds riding their bikes in the middle of the night, they would have been suspicious. So they stayed in the shadows as much as possible, only crossing the intersections when no cars were around. They were spirits in the night, small, dark figures. They weren't bicycling. They floated through the streets like disembodied phantoms. If anyone had asked Felicia in the daytime, she would never had said she'd agree to do anything like this. But now it was different. Now it was nighttime. Now she was here in this world of dark houses, empty streets, sweeping headlights, flickering streetlamps, loud voices coming from open windows, sirens somewhere beyond the corner, maybe her father's colleagues chasing down real criminals. While she was on an adventure, on her way to the river. It was on that night that she became familiar with the dark for the first time.

"There it is."

Brad was hunkered down behind a bush. He was holding the sleeping bag. They had left their bikes up near the road and clambered down the slope to the river. An old shed made of corrugated iron stood in the shrubbery between the slope and the riverbank. At first glance it looked empty, abandoned, dark. But then she saw it. It was like stardust that had fallen from the sky. Light shining on the leaves behind the shack, a silvery glow. A reflection of the light coming from inside, shining through the window.

"There's a light on," she whispered.

"They've covered all the windows except for the crack I saw. It's at the back."

Brad made his way through the bushes toward the shed. Felicia followed, mostly because she didn't want to be left there alone. The horror movie they had watched earlier was still vivid in her mind.

Brad went over to the window with the shimmering light. He stood on his toes and peeked in through the crack, standing like that for a long time. Then he turned around and whispered:

"Nothing but plants, just like last time. There's nobody here. They keep the lights on at night to make the plants grow."

"Let's go home," said Felicia.

"No, let's see if the door is open." Brad went around to the front.

The thought of Freddy Krueger was still more frightening to Felicia than any marijuana growers. So she followed close behind.

"Are you sure you saw the whole room?"

"Of course," said Brad.

He reached the door and tried the handle, but a huge padlock hung from it. Anyone could see that it was locked.

Felicia tried again.

"Let's go home now!"

"No, we're on a stakeout. I'll take the first watch. You can sleep."

They found a good spot in the bushes where the grass was soft. It was a mild night.

"Are you going to be warm enough?" Felicia got into the sleeping bag.

"What are you, my mother?" Brad was sitting on a fallen tree trunk. Then he turned to look at the shed, which was visible behind them. "I'll wake you up when it's your turn."

In the middle of the night she woke up. The sky was dark and filled with clouds that looked like leftover scraps of food.

The sleeping bag was too hot and stifling. Groggily she turned over, sitting up halfway, and saw that he was lying next to her inside the bag.

He was snoring, but not loud enough to be annoying. More like the purring of a contented cat. She lay back down beside him, studying his face in the faint light.

"You're so handsome," she whispered.

Then she fell asleep again without really understanding what she'd been feeling.

It was the beams from the headlights up on the road that woke them, and the sound of the engine before the car stopped in the parking place. Doors slammed.

"It's them," whispered Brad.

They quickly got out of the sleeping bag and crept over behind a tree trunk to peer through the bushes at the shack. Two figures came toward them. In the gray light of dawn, they looked blurry, like a photograph out of focus, as if partially conjured by the sunrise. They were carrying sacks. Neither of them spoke. Soon they disappeared behind the building. From where they were sitting, the children heard them unlock the door and go in. They heard them moving around inside.

"What do we do now?" Felicia hardly dared even whisper.

"I don't know," said Brad. "We should have brought your father's police radio along." He stood up. "I want to get a look at them at least. Then we can give the police a description."

"Have you thought about the fact that we should have told my father about this last night? He would have sent somebody out here."

"What's the fun in that?"

Brad laughed quietly, sounding a little uncertain, she thought. Trying to make himself seem tough.

Then he moved toward the shack, creeping through the underbrush. She followed. He stood on his toes and looked inside.

"I can only see the back of one of them," he whispered. "The other one . . . Shit!" He stepped back and fell to the ground.

Then Felicia heard the door slam. They came running around the side of the house toward her and Brad. Brad got up and turned to face her.

"Run!" he yelled.

But she couldn't move. He gave her a shove.

"Run!"

She stepped back and was about to head for the bushes, but by then it was too late.

One of the men grabbed Brad by the arm, spun him around, and pushed him to the ground. Felicia backed up some more but didn't want to leave her friend behind. She saw Brad fumbling for something on his belt. He pulled out the flashlight and switched it on. The beam landed squarely on the man's face. The difference between the gray dawn light and the beam was so great that it blinded him, and he had to turn away. But Felicia had recognized the man. She looked at Brad sitting on the ground. He lowered the flashlight. Felicia went over to him so she could look into his eyes. His gaze shifted, filled with disbelief and disappointment.

The man stood over them, not saying a word, not moving either. The other man had withdrawn and was on his way down to the river.

"Dad!" Brad cried after a moment. "What are you doing here?"

His father's hand slapped him hard in the face.

Riding back home in the family pickup, Brad's father tried to downplay the matter.

"It's legal if you grow it for personal use," he explained. "And I don't use much. It's mostly for the other guys."

He stopped the car in front of the building where Felicia lived. The curtains were still closed in her parents' bedroom.

"I won't say anything if you don't," said Mr. Davis.

Felicia looked at Brad. He was sitting next to her, looking like he'd fallen asleep with his eyes open.

She nodded and got out of the truck. She would never forget the look on Brad's face. There was nothing there. Absolutely nothing. Everything was hidden somewhere deep inside of him.

Two days later everything had returned to normal. Brad was just as cocky as ever. They were sitting inside the tree house they'd built in his yard. Felicia wanted to try to wrangle something out of him.

"Are you disappointed by him?"

"Who?"

"You know who."

"I don't give a shit."

"It didn't exactly go the way we'd planned."

"I said, I don't give a shit. So shut up! Your father is a cop. Mine smokes grass. So what? Fuck it. I'm not going to be like him. Let's talk about something else."

They sat in silence for a while. She looked at him. The glint was back in his eyes. Then she leaned forward and kissed him. Just like that. Right on the lips. It was one of the bravest things she'd ever done.

"What was that?"

"Something else to talk about," she said.

He laughed.

"You're the one who's crazy, not me," he said.

Felicia was sure about two things. She liked him. A lot. And she would never kiss him again. It hadn't tasted very good.

Now she laughed. More than twenty-five years later, worn out, scared, with an injured foot, bruised and feeling the effects of alcohol withdrawal creeping through her body like maggots in acid, lying in a sleeping bag with a half-dead, ice-cold boy, she all of a sudden laughed out loud. Something had let go inside of her. Her stomach muscles rippled. She couldn't hold back. She laughed like a weeping child who has forgotten why she started crying in the first place. *I can die now,* she thought. *Now I can die.*

But then she thought of something.

The boy couldn't die. *If there's no other reason for me to be here, it's to save him. I'm here for him.* The thought calmed her down. She focused on her breathing. She lay there and touched his forehead. He seemed warmer, didn't he? She noticed how this gradually steadied her. The pain and the nausea didn't go away, but the exhaustion after all her efforts and the lack of sleep slowly took over, and at last she fell asleep.

9

Very early, before dawn, on the day it happened . . .

You're a free agent," said Odd. "It's totally your decision." He lay in the water below her. Around him floated slushy ice. "I won't force you to jump."

She looked at him, her husband, her beloved, this eager "ice bather." She'd never before gone in the middle of winter to swim in the sea with him. To her it seemed insane. She looked down at his wet gray hair plastered to his head, his arm moving in the ice-cold water. She had no idea what she was doing here. She was standing naked on the pier, with snow under her feet. She wasn't cold. She was just staring at him.

"You're a free agent!" he shouted.

Should she jump? Did she dare? Did she want to?

He ducked under the water.

Then she heard a strange knocking sound, as if someone was trying to punch through the pier beneath her.

Felicia Stone woke from her dream. The first thing she thought was this: *I have to talk to him. I have to talk to Odd.* That was one more reason she needed to survive.

Then she heard the knocking again. It wasn't merely part of her dream. It was real. A hammering from out in the living room. It was the door, she realized. *He's found us. The man from the road is pounding on the front door.*

Felicia got out of the sleeping bag. The boy moaned softly, but she didn't wake him. She went into the living room. That was when she heard his voice:

"I know you're in there."

It was the first time she'd heard him speak. His voice was strangely clear and sharp, loud but deep, and very calm.

"You can't escape."

But he doesn't know the boy is here too, thought Felicia. She looked around. She caught sight of a trapdoor high up on the wall above the doorway to the bedroom. A crawl space.

She ran back to the boy.

"Come with me!" She pulled him out of the sleeping bag and off the bunk as carefully as she could. He was able to stand on his own now. Felicia put her arm around him and led him into the living room. There she got a chair from the table, set it under the trapdoor, and climbed up. She opened the hatch, then got down.

More pounding on the door, louder, steadier. He was using something hard. Maybe the butt of the shotgun?

"Come out right now, or I'll break down the door!"

So what are you waiting for, you fucking coward? she thought.

The boy had regained his mobility. He had returned to life. And for the first time he spoke.

"That's him. The man who killed my father."

"He killed your father?" she asked, unable to stop herself. She knew there was no time to talk, and they had to be as quiet as possible. If he heard them, he'd know the boy was here with her. She pressed her finger to her lips and pointed to the trapdoor. He nodded.

"You'll be safe up there," she whispered.

Again he nodded.

Then she helped him up onto the chair and lifted him up, pushing on his feet until he was inside the crawl space. She handed him the sleeping bag, which he took, staring at her with an expression that wasn't fearful, but there was a lonely look in his eyes, as well as a wish to survive. She closed the trapdoor, got down from the chair, and put it back in place.

Then she closed the door to the bedroom and stood in the middle of the living room to think. The man was still pounding on the door. Felicia realized what she needed to do.

He has to see me, she thought. *He has to see me as I run away. That's the only way to keep him from searching the cabin.*

She stood still, taking several deep breaths as she considered various escape routes.

Suddenly two shots were fired, one after the other. The first time the door merely shook. The second time, however, the lock flew into the room, fell to the floor at her feet, and then skidded over to the woodstove. Buckshot sped past her like lethal horseflies.

The door burst open.

A swift movement off to the side. After that she saw only darkness through the doorway. He was standing to the side of the opening, waiting to hear a sound from inside. He wanted to get his bearings and not take any unnecessary chances. Even though he knew she was unarmed, he didn't want to give her an opportunity to surprise him. He'd already fought with her once. And apparently she'd shown him enough of what she was capable of doing under pressure.

She turned and ran. There was only one option: the bedroom. She could close the door behind her and get out through the window.

The next instant she heard him in the living room. Heavy footsteps crossing the floor, a pause, several metallic sounds. Was he loading the shotgun?

She fumbled with the top latch on the broken window. Nothing was going as fast as she'd hoped. Finally, she was able to push open the window. She put one foot on the sill and was about to jump when the door opened behind her. She looked over her shoulder and caught a glimpse of him in the doorway. He was holding the gun in one hand, like some maniac cowboy. He had to duck his head to enter the room. His all-weather jacket was open and fluttered around him. His eyes were just as calm as before.

She threw herself into the snow as the window slammed shut behind her and a shot whizzed over her head. The glass shattered, and several shards landed on the back of her head.

She got up and ran full speed along the side of the cabin.

The next shot came after she had rounded the corner. She dropped to the ground, gasping for breath. She was shaking all over now and almost couldn't get up. But she had no choice. She had to keep going and get as far away as possible, away from this cabin and the boy hiding inside, as quiet as death, up in the crawl space right above his father's killer.

So that was the secret the man was so desperately trying to conceal.

Using the cabin for cover, Felicia ran toward the woods, going in the opposite direction from the birch tree on the hill and the footprints in the snow that would reveal that she'd been up that hill and found the boy. When she paused briefly, she was relieved to find the man following her. Maybe the boy was saved. Not her, but him. She heard the man coming closer through the trees. He was now hunting at a different pace. Time was no longer on his side. It would soon be daylight.

Felicia continued on, limping because of her injured foot. It was clear that she wouldn't be able to evade him much longer. All she could do was postpone the inevitable. Desperately she looked around. Saw a tree with branches close to the ground. She tried to climb up, but slipped down because of the ice and frost on the first branch she grabbed. She fell again when she tried to grab another. She stayed on the ground until she felt the muzzle pressed against her forehead. The gunmetal was almost warm compared to the ice-cold void inside the metal barrel. He was standing over her. A shadow blocking out the sky.

"The question you ought to ask yourself is this," he said quietly, whispering as if didn't want to disturb the forest. "You've heard two shots since I loaded the gun inside the cabin. This is a Browning pump-action shotgun, a classic 1893 model. It belonged to my father. A gun like this takes five shells in the magazine. But in Norway the magazine on a pump-action shotgun has to be plugged so it can fire only two shots before reloading. So what you need to ask yourself is this: What sort of man was my father?"

Felicia was breathing hard. Assessing the situation. She had no good cards left. She could try to shove the gun away and attack the man. Roll off to the side and kick his legs out from under him. Maybe grab the gun and render him harmless that way. But he was on high alert. After tapping her forehead with the muzzle, he'd taken a step back. Very professional and deliberate. She'd need to make at least two different moves to reach him. He'd have more than enough time to pull the trigger before she was able to do anything to him.

"What do you think? Was my father the kind of man to follow the letter of the law? Was he someone who wouldn't dream of making any changes to a gun like this? So ask yourself now: Are there any more shells in the magazine?"

"Someone did alter the gun," said Felicia, mostly just to buy time.

"What do you mean?"

"The barrel."

"Ah. That was me. And I regret it. But it's easier to handle like this. Do you know what a sawed-off shotgun is called in Italy?"

"It's called a *lupara*," said Felicia. "But that's not a *lupara*." She'd switched to English. "A *lupara* is made from a traditional shotgun, the kind you have to break open, not a pump-action shotgun."

"I'm impressed," he said.

"The *lupara* was the preferred weapon of the Italian Mafia. Armed with that type of gun, they won the war against Mussolini."

Felicia kept on talking, trying to drown out her own fear and dread. Her voice quavered.

"It's rare to meet a woman who knows so much about guns. But maybe that's an American thing? Even though this is all very interesting, I don't think it's moving us in the right direction. What do you think? Do you want to risk me pulling the trigger? If I don't have any more shells, you have a chance of overpowering me or taking off again. Or would you like another option?"

He took the bag off his shoulder and dropped it in front of her.

"Look in the bag!" He raised the gun to his shoulder. Took a step back and aimed it at her.

She did as he said. What else could she do?

Inside the bag she found a fanny pack.

"Not that. The other one. The toiletry kit."

Felicia found it at the very bottom and pulled it out.

"Open it!"

Inside was the type of paraphernalia she'd seen many times before on the job, lying on filthy tables between empty beer cans, on beds with mattresses stinking of urine and blood, between used diapers tossed on the floor, underneath cribs in which sweaty babies with their hair plastered to their heads screamed like crazy hour after hour without being heard until they fell down, exhausted, malnourished, feverish, and alone. Felicia had started in the narcotics division before she became a homicide detective. She'd seen just about everything that happens in the void left behind by addiction.

She'd only ever used this sort of paraphernalia once herself. One time in the basement of her childhood home. That awful summer after high school, during those months after the rape, when she still believed that the rapist had taken everything from her. She'd gotten the overdose of heroin from her friend, the dope dealer Brad Davis, the boy who said he'd never be like his father.

She dumped everything out into the snow: the syringe, rubber tubing, spoon, lighter, and the little plastic bottle containing what she assumed was a mixture of lemon juice to make the drug dissolve more easily.

The man reached under his sweater and pulled out a little container hanging from a cord.

"You seem to know an awful lot. So do you know how to use this?" he said, dropping the container next to her.

She nodded and opened it. She was freezing now, shaking hard. *Soon I won't feel the cold anymore*, she thought.

She stuck her finger inside and tasted the powder.

"Heroin," she said.

"Here's your choice. You can take the risk that my father was a conscientious man who plugged the magazine on this gun, or you can shoot up the heroin. I decide the dose."

He leaned down to pick up the spoon and container. He was quick, but he still left himself open. Felicia could have seized the opportunity and punched him as hard as she could in the temple, then grabbed him by the back of his neck and shaken him. But she no longer had the energy to fight anymore. It was over.

He filled the spoon with heroin. Felicia saw at once that it was an overdose, no matter what the quality of the dope.

He handed it to her.

"That's enough to kill me," she said.

"Most likely," he replied.

"Why do you want to kill me?"

"You saw me with the shotgun," he told her. "It's that simple. If I'd managed to put away the gun before you ran into me, you wouldn't have been suspicious, and I could have let you live. But you saw me very clearly. Holding the gun."

"There's something you're trying to hide," she said, looking directly at him, holding his attention. At the same time she used her thumb to brush some of the heroin out of the spoon.

He didn't notice.

"Of course I have something to hide. So, what's it going to be?"

Felicia picked up the lighter and began preparing the heroin.

When she was done, she filled the syringe.

She kept on talking to him as she spilled some of the drug from the spoon onto the snow every time she caught his eye.

"I want you to know that at least I don't have any children," she said. "So you won't be killing anyone's mother."

"Shut up!" Something had crept into his voice that wasn't there before.

"Do you have kids?"

"One more word out of you, and the drug option goes away."

By now the syringe was filled, with much less than the original dose. She pulled up her sleeve and tied the rubber tubing around her arm, but the cold made it nearly impossible to find a good vein.

Finally, she found one and pressed the needle to her skin. She managed to spill a few more drops before the needle went in. She also left a little in the syringe. She'd reduced the dose by more than half, right in front of his eyes. If it was average-quality heroin, she was saved. If the dope was pure, she wasn't sure how things would go.

Felicia closed her eyes and felt the rush almost immediately.

She saw Odd. He was laughing. His torso was bare as he sat there eating herring. Odd again. First in her dream, now with the heroin. That had to mean something. Did she love him? Was she capable of love? Questions like that would have to remain unanswered.

The night turned as white as snow, a white night that ran straight through her.

10

Before it happened . . .

S*he was lying* inside a well. It must have once been a well, but it had dried up. She was lying in a circular space with walls of granite. Above her stretched gray stones, extending upward to a sky fading to dusk. The distance was too great for her to climb up the stones and get out.

She had only a vague memory of how she'd ended up here.

She remembered lying in the car that belonged to the man in the woods—that was the only way she could think of him, even though she'd talked to him. She was placed on the backseat, her hands and feet bound with plastic zip ties, a gag stuffed in her mouth, drugged to the edge of consciousness, adrift in reality, strangely still possessed of hope, although she had no idea whether that promise would be kept.

Then she recalled how the zip tie began to cut into her wrists. The pain and nausea returned.

Why didn't he kill me out there in the forest? Felicia wondered. *He could have just shot me. He fired at me up on the road.* But that was when he was filled with panic. He hadn't been able to bring himself to shoot the boy, or Felicia when he had her right in front of him, easy prey. Maybe there was still some scrap of mercy in him, despite everything. Or was it merely cowardice? Maybe it was due to something even simpler. Maybe they were no longer important to him, after he took control. It seemed like the only thing he cared about was not being stopped, not letting anyone get in his way. But what was he up to? Felicia thought the only reason he wouldn't care whether she lived or died must be because he was planning to disappear for good, to take off somewhere. He was on the run and doing whatever he had to do in order to get to his destination. That was why he killed only if absolutely necessary. That was why he'd taken her along.

She hadn't been able to see out the window, so she had no idea where they were headed. At last the car stopped. He got out. A few minutes later she heard an enormous crash, worse than thunder in Virginia in the fall. Then he pulled her out of the car and removed the restraints and gag.

Then there was a boat speeding out to sea, away from her. She thought she was free. That was when she heard something behind her, turned to look, and saw the baseball bat come whizzing through the air. And everything went black.

She must have sustained multiple blows. More than a person could normally stand.

Much later she awoke, lying on an old mattress with blood all over her clothes.

Someone must have used the well as a garbage dump, because there were pieces of old furniture and empty paint cans scattered about. Surrounding the mattress were discarded electronic equipment, the guts from several radios, a smashed TV, a few old-fashioned dial phones—Felicia couldn't remember the last time she'd seen that kind in use—batteries, and other things she couldn't identify. Everything was old and rusty. All the laughter, sorrow, and joy that these pieces of equipment had once generated were long gone. The whole mattress was covered with blood. She was spitting up blood. It ran down her throat, which she found strangely soothing. Her teeth were loose. Some of them had fallen out. Her head pounded and ached, as if fractured.

Felicia didn't know how long she lay there, looking at everything, as if she were merely an anonymous passerby.

She slipped in and out of consciousness. The cold wasn't as bad down here as it had been in the forest. It was a different kind of weather, a marine climate, and the storm had subsided. And what was left of the wind couldn't reach her. She quickly realized that she badly needed help. And soon.

She didn't know how long she'd been inside the well when she heard someone up above. She tried shouting, but only a gurgle came out of her mouth. Something was tossed down to her. It looked like charred fragments of some sort of technical equipment. Something that had shattered into a thousand pieces. She brushed them off the mattress into the trash lying all around. It was probably the person with the bat who'd come back to get rid of something. Another object was tossed down from above. This one was bigger. Gray plastic, cables, a circuit board, microchips, intricate mechanisms. Felicia had no idea what it was. Only that it had been severely damaged. It was covered with dark patches, and it looked partially melted. She stared upward to see if there was more coming, but whoever had been up there left quickly, and once again there was only silence.

In a lucid moment she discovered a cell phone. She remembered that she'd broken hers in the woods. But this one was intact and still working. How had it ended up next to her on this mattress? Was she dreaming? Had she slipped into that final slumber in which hope displaced reality and remained as the only possible form of awareness?

No, Felicia could feel pain in her whole body, so she knew she wasn't dreaming. Her fingers numb with cold, exhaustion, and blood loss, she tapped in the number she knew by heart. The display got smeared with blood. Someone had to pick up. Someone had to answer. If not, then it was all over. She knew that if she passed out again, she was finished. She would never wake up.

II

Sometime, no one knows exactly when . . .

Look at the boy.

Can you see him there in the dark? The dawn light shines through the floorboards, making a pale line on his face. His dark eyes blink rapidly, as if releasing his thoughts from imprisonment. Slowly he begins to move, sliding out of the sleeping bag that has kept him warm and given him his life back. Finally, he kicks it away. It lies there like a dark lump at the very back of the crawl space.

Then he listens, lying very still. The boy has tasted death. It may have left some remnant inside of him, a shadowy feeling, a phantom in his mind, his stiff joints and aching muscles, in his heart, fumbling between beats. Maybe he's no longer sure whether the world is real.

Finally, he crawls over to the trapdoor in the wall, feetfirst, and tries to push it open. It's latched from the outside, so he kicks and kicks until at last it gives way.

Bright morning streams in from the room below.

He slips out of his hiding place, hanging by his arms until he lets go and lands on the floor. Then he searches the cabin, moving quietly and cautiously. He finds some food, a few stale crackers, a can of pears that he opens with an ax.

He eats them so fast the juice runs down his chin, slurping and swallowing, even licking up the pear juice that dripped onto the floor.

His clothes are lying at the foot of the bunk in the bedroom. They're still wet, but there are clothes in the wardrobe, cold garments intended for grownups, things that had been left hanging there, things that only had value out here in the forest. He puts on a jacket that is much too big and is covered with grease spots.

Then he leaves the cabin.

Look at the boy as he walks:

The jacket like a coat that reaches below his knees. He doesn't follow any of the footprints leading away from the cabin. He puts behind him the tracks left by the drama in which he's been embroiled all night. The boy is making his own path through the snow, heading for the road. No one can possibly know what he's thinking. He trudges onward, making his way toward something new.

Page 10 of 48

Melhus: February 21, in the morning. Twenty-four hours since you reported Felicia missing. The Trondheim police discovered that she had rented a car at Gardermoen Airport, close to midnight the previous day.

Singsaker: As I understand it, this was the result of a combination of coincidence and good police work.

Melhus: Excellent police work, considering it was a relatively low priority matter. Wouldn't you agree?

Singsaker: The information came to light in connection with what was then considered a far more serious matter.

Melhus: The boy from the forest?

Singsaker: As you know, early that morning a boy was found, cold and weak, near Highway 3 in Østerdalen. He said that he'd been taken into the forest at night and tied to a tree by a man who had apparently killed the boy's father. It took a while for the police to make the connection with the disappearance and death in Oslo the day before. The interesting thing was that the boy said he'd been rescued by a woman, but he didn't know where she went. He also said that the man who had tied him up was still at large. It was during the investigation of this case that a description of the car and a license plate number came in. A tow truck driver reported what he'd observed in the night. He'd become suspicious of an individual who acted strangely when he arrived to tow his car. He'd also seen blood on the sleeve of the man's jacket. It turned out that the towed car was registered to a police officer. A narcotics detective from Oslo named Rolf Fagerhus. But the tow truck driver had also taken note of the model and license number of another car. A vehicle that Fagerhus claimed to have rented. This turned out to be false. The car was traced to the Hertz office at Gardermoen airport. It had been rented to Felicia around midnight the day before.

Melhus: And all of this information, along with an APB on the car, was sent to the Trondheim police?

Singsaker: That was the logical next thing to do,

given these observations and considering the most likely route Fagerhus would take.

Melhus: And at that point your wife's disappearance was upgraded to something more than just the result of a domestic squabble.

Singsaker: That's right.

Melhus: And it was then that word came from Hitra?

Singsaker: Yes.

Melhus: Where were you at that moment?

Singsaker: I was at work . . . I mean, at the police station. Jensen had asked me to come in so he could tell me about the rental car and the possibility that Felicia might be caught up in something serious. He wanted to tell me face-to-face.

Melhus: So you were with him when he found out. Who contacted him?

Singsaker: Gro Brattberg. Head of the violent and sexual crimes team. The request for assistance was officially sent from the sheriff's office on Hitra.

Melhus: What specifically did the inquiry involve?

Singsaker: First and foremost, interviewing and taking statements from the survivors out at sea. The crime techs were supposed to make inspecting the wreckage their highest priority. The site of the explosion on land was not yet considered safe enough for the police to examine. For a long time the explosion itself was thought to be an accident, since the owner of the cabin had reported that she had stored old dynamite on the premises and she wanted to turn it in to the authorities.

Melhus: And the dynamite was still on the property?

Singsaker: Apparently.

Melhus: At any time did the police see a connection between the two events--the explosion and the accident at sea?

Singsaker: No. As I said, the explosion was considered an accident.

Melhus: What did you think about it?

Singsaker: I didn't give the matter much thought at first. My focus was on Felicia and the rental car that had been seen in Østerdalen. But with two such dramatic events happening in such a small area, the thought did cross my mind.

Melhus: So Jensen was assigned to the case. Why did you go with him?

Singsaker: He asked me to come with him. We hadn't finished talking about the other matter, the one that Felicia was involved in. He wanted to discuss it on the drive there. Maybe he also thought it would help me to think about something else.

Melhus: Think about something else? A bombed-out cabin? A boat sinking at sea? Didn't he know you were still on sick leave?

Singsaker: Yes, he did.

Melhus: When did the two of you leave the station?

Singsaker: Around three.

Melhus: The vehicle was logged out at 3:15 p.m. Does that sound right?

Singsaker: Sure.

Melhus: According to the log book, that's exactly one hour and five minutes after Gro Brattberg heard from Hitra for the first time.

Singsaker: Okay.

Melhus: What do you know about the information that was received during those first conversations between Hitra and Trondheim?

Singsaker: Only what I've already told you. It was a request for assistance.

Melhus: According to Sheriff Birger Anthonsen on Hitra, a car that was parked in the yard of the bombed-out cabin quickly became part of the investigation. He says that he mentioned the car and its license number in his first conversation with Brattberg. He also claims that he said it was a rental car.

Attorney Gregersen: As I understand it, he added that he's not positive about that. He may have mentioned it in a later conversation. What does Brattberg have to say about this?

Melhus: She also says that she's not sure. She thinks the information about the rental car came later on. But let's not get too hung up on who remembers what. This much we know: A rental car was parked outside in the yard at the site of the explosion when the police arrived at 12:05 p.m. It was determined that the car had been rented from Hertz. The license number was quickly checked and linked to Hertz at Gardermoen and to Felicia Stone. Do you understand that I think it's possible that the Trondheim police may have connected the event in Østerdalen with the explosion before 3:15 p.m., when you and Jensen left the police station and headed for Hitra?

Singsaker: I follow what you're saying.

Melhus: So I'm going to ask you point-blank: When you drove to Hitra with Jensen, did you know that a car, rented in your wife's name, had been found at the explosion site? Was that why you went there with Jensen?

Attorney Gregersen: You don't have to answer that question.

Singsaker: I went to Hitra because I wanted to talk to Jensen some more. That's all.

Melhus: Did you know that Felicia had been linked to one of the sites being investigated by the police?

Singsaker: The situation was still unclear. No one knew yet what exactly had happened.

Melhus: I'm going to ask you one last time: Did you know about the rental car that was parked in the yard?

Singsaker: I got in the car with Jensen because I wanted to talk to him. I was on sick leave and went along as a civilian. There were no plans for me to participate in any active police work out there.

Melhus: And yet that's precisely what happened.

Attorney Gregersen: The prosecution knows full well our view of the matter. Everything that Singsaker did during those dramatic hours on Hitra, he did in his capacity as an off-duty officer, but he had not been suspended or put on leave from his job on the police force. He was merely on sick leave, and did nothing that would not be permitted for any citizen of this country to do. Much of what he did was purely in self-defense.

Melhus: We will come back to the motive for his actions at a later time.

12

Two weeks after it happened . . .

S*ingsaker looked at his* watch. It was almost eleven thirty. He put the documents in his bag and got up.

Then he went over to the counter and did what he had vowed not to do: He ordered a shot of Red Aalborg, which he downed in one gulp. Finally, he left the restaurant and headed off to work.

On his way there, he was lost in thought. He hardly noticed Trondheim in the sunshine or the almost springlike air, the snow glittering as it slid down the slanted rooftops and hung perilously from the eaves, or the bare pathways in the snow on the sidewalks, the light footsteps of the old women, or the dog shit that had spent the winter hidden in the snowbanks and was now emerging.

Odd Singsaker was thinking about Kurt Melhus. He was thinking about Horten. That time so many years ago. The Philosopher was not the only nickname that Melhus had been given. After an incident out on Bastøy in Oslo Fjord, he'd also been called Mr. Gray Matter.

As comical as it sounded, there was something frightening about that name. Singsaker knew that he couldn't fool Melhus. He needed to stick to the truth as long as he could, but no longer.

As he walked along Kjøpmannsgata, he thought about the Bastøy affair. It occurred to him that old memories were often more vivid to him than recent ones. Except for the events on Hitra. Those hours were frozen solid in his mind, but otherwise much of what had happened in recent weeks was a blur, as if those events were somehow less important than what had happened in the distant past. He could still recall sounds and smells from long ago, as if his senses had just registered them. Memories of things that happened thirty or forty years ago seemed strangely fresh. That was true of the Bastøy affair and the dinner right before. He remembered that dinner so well. He and Melhus were supposed to be getting to know each other better.

"We should have planned something fancier."

"What do you mean?"

"When we had dinner with Kurt and Anne last weekend, I noticed their china was from Porsgrunn."

"What does it matter where the china is from as long as the plates aren't cracked? They're just meant to hold the food, not entertain us with a song and dance."

"And their forks and knives were Georg Jensen."

"Georg Jensen? Who's that? Some sportscaster I've never heard of?"

"You're kidding me. Don't you remember our trip to Copenhagen?"

Singsaker remembered it well. One of the best things about living in Horten was that it was easy to go abroad. The boat to Denmark went right past. But that was no reason not to take the job in Trondheim. They were moving there soon, but the trip to Copenhagen had been an amazing experience. They'd had a cabin on board. And Anikken practically had to carry him to the hotel after their antics in that cabin, all the Danish beer and aquavit, the herring—and an evening when he couldn't get enough Red Aalborg.

"Georg Jensen was that silversmith shop we went into on Strøget."

Now he remembered.

"You went in," he said. "I sat near the fountain on Højbro Plads and drank a beer, if I recall correctly."

"I came out to get you."

"Oh, that's right. But we agreed it was way too expensive."

"I'm just saying that we ate with silverware from Georg Jensen when we had dinner with Kurt and Anne. That's all."

"Let them be the snobs. We'll concentrate on happiness instead," he teased, giving her a smile.

"Eternal happiness?"

"What good would happiness be if it wasn't eternal?" he said.

Anikken gave him a quick kiss. Then she put the last stainless steel fork in the silverware drawer. A perfectly fine set of cutlery that his mother had given them.

The doorbell rang. Singsaker was struggling to get the cork out of a bottle of red wine, so Anikken went to open the door for their guests. When they came into the dining room, he was hacking at the broken cork with one of the knives that Anikken found so embarrassing. Wine squirted onto the linen tablecloth when the cork was finally pushed inside the bottle. He smiled at Kurt Melhus.

"Yet another good reason to stick with beer, if you ask me."

Melhus politely smiled back.

"I don't think we'll ask you," said Anikken. She took the bottle from him and wiped if off with a napkin. Then she poured a little salt on the stained tablecloth. "We're having rib eye steak."

"Sounds lovely."

Melhus's wife, Anne, was an attractive woman. But her beauty was only superficial. The opposite was true of Kurt. He wasn't much to look at. But his head was screwed on right. He was both intelligent and a good person.

"Nice china," said Anne. "Porcelain?"

"Yes."

"Egersund?"

Anikken nodded and smiled. The game had begun.

After dinner Singsaker got out the aquavit.

"I bought cognac," Anikken whispered. "VS. It's in the cupboard above the sink."

Singsaker was about to object. He didn't want cognac. But he felt a sense of solidarity with her.

Then the phone rang. Singsaker went out to the hallway to take the call.

"Singsaker here."

"This is Ambjørnsen. I'm trying to get hold of both you and Melhus, but he's not home."

"Melhus is here."

"We need backup."

"What happened?"

"There was an assault. A crazy man with a knife, and he's on the run. Possible attempted homicide."

"Homicide? Where?"

"Out at Vernehjemmet."

"The prison out on Bastøy?"

"About time you learned some geography down here."

Singsaker didn't think it was the right time to joke around, considering the situation.

"Should we come into the station?"

"Yes, then all of you can go to the ferry dock together. We've requisitioned a boat. We need a lot of manpower to secure the area. We don't know whether he's still out there on the island."

How strange, thought Singsaker. *That's what I remember best.* The dinner, the awkward mood, the passive-aggressive comments from Melhus's wife, and the fact that Melhus spoke only when absolutely necessary. But when he did say something, it often turned the whole conversation in a different direction. His comments were so clever it was almost frightening.

Not until they got out to Bastøy did he actually become talkative.

Two other detectives went with them. Lier and Horst, if he remembered correctly. Both of them outranked Melhus. But it was Officer Melhus who found a solution for what had happened out there. He was able to turn the whole case on its head.

Bastøy used to be a notorious home for boys. Plenty of kids had suffered a miserable fate there. Back then, in 1972, it was used as a home for people who were unfit to work, recovering alcoholics, and other homeless people. It reminded Singsaker of a prison.

The stabbing victim was a man who'd been on guard duty that night. The suspect, an alcoholic inmate, had taken off in a boat. That was the presumed state of things when they arrived, and Lier and Horst decided to proceed accordingly. But Melhus quickly observed that someone had recently been digging in the potato field. He also noted a wet guard's uniform, a good deal of blood on the floor of the crime scene, and an ax missing from the tool collection. After putting all these facts together with some background information about the suspect that he'd had the presence of mind to look up at police headquarters before leaving, Melhus convinced everyone that the suspect was the real victim, while the victim in the case was the perpetrator.

And of course Melhus had been right, Singsaker thought as he walked across the canal bridge to Brattøra.

All the technical evidence on the island supported his theory. The boat was quickly found, with the body of the suspect inside. He turned out to be a former police officer from Oslo by the name of Teodor Olsen. Presumably he'd never touched the knife at all before he was struck down by the guard wielding an ax. The motive behind the murder came to light during the investigation. A rumor had long circulated that Olsen had stashed a large sum of money, taken from some investigation he'd been involved with.

And it was discovered that he'd buried the money in the potato field on Bastøy.

When the guard eventually confessed, he also revealed that Olsen had told him where the money was hidden. The guard had planned to kill the man and make off with the loot.

This story, which was Singsaker's very first murder case, had always fascinated him. It taught him something that he'd later had confirmed many times. Brutal crimes are often the result of stupid and sloppy actions. It was almost like the perpetrator is dumber when he kills than at any other time in his life. That was true of crimes that were solved, at any rate. A minimum of thought, planning, and precision was necessary to carry out a successful crime, if such a thing even existed. But a surprising number of crimes were based on erroneous ideas.

The case had also shown Singsaker that such erroneous ideas were not part of the thought processes of Kurt Melhus. And he was the man who almost forty years later would question Singsaker about possible breach of duty committed on Hitra. The man who, after his performance on Bastøy, was nicknamed Mr. Gray Matter, a name he retained for the rest of his time in Horten. He worked there longer than Singsaker, who got a job in Trondheim a few months later and never looked back. But after a while a man like Melhus was bound to end up in Oslo. There he spent a long time working for Kripo, the Criminal Police, before finally transferring to Internal Affairs and moving to central Norway.

"You smell," said Jensen.

Singsaker stared at him in surprise. On his way to the interview, he'd dropped by his colleague's office to say hello. He thought it would be a sensible thing to do. Jensen might have something to tell him that was important.

"Booze," said Jensen. "Aquavit. Don't pretend you haven't had a snort."

"You can smell it?"

"Yeah."

Singsaker was confused. Jensen had never before said anything about his habit of starting the day with a shot of booze. Even if he'd noticed, it hadn't bothered him. Singsaker had been convinced the same held for the rest of his colleagues at the station.

"Have you . . ." Singsaker didn't know how to ask the question.

"Sure," said Jensen. "I've noticed once in a while. I know you never come to work drunk. But did you really need to have a drink today? It's one thing for me to smell it on you. It's another story if he does."

"Melhus?"

"Who else?"

"True enough. That wouldn't be good."

"Have a cough drop."

"Fisherman's Friend? I'm all out."

"So go buy some. We're talking about your job here. And mine."

Singsaker looked at his colleague, who was probably also his best friend. He had rarely—no, never—seen him look so tense.

"I'm not trying to stress you out." Jensen gave a strained laugh. "But we need to do things right."

"Have you seen him today?"

"Only from a distance, but you know how he is. He never wastes time on small talk. And he's already talked to me."

Singsaker had to run over to the train station across the street to get some cough drops. When he got back to police headquarters, he was out of breath and two minutes late for the appointment. He had also begun to sweat. Not a good start for another lengthy session.

Melhus was already sitting in the interrogation room. Singsaker's lawyer, Evald Gregersen, a well-dressed and precise man who was an expert on such matters, was waiting for him in the hall. He straightened his tie and gave Singsaker a reassuring look, as if to calm him down.

"I hope your tardiness is because you've been preparing yourself," the lawyer said with a smile.

"Just some last-minute things I needed to take care of," replied Singsaker.

"Those last-minute details are always the most important," said Gregersen. "Let's stay on the same track as yesterday, meaning tell the truth, but only say what is absolutely necessary. Try to steer away from your feelings about what happened to your wife. Facts. Just facts. And as the facts now stand, they've got very little on you. Focus on that. It's only when you reveal your emotions, which they don't need to see, that things may appear different from what they were. They want to try and show that you acted out of passion. We want to show that everything you did was done out of sheer necessity."

Singsaker nodded. He had no intention of lying to Melhus. That man could trace the curvature of the gravitational field around any lies, no matter how well concealed they might be. But at the same time, he had no intention of giving Melhus what he was after. Singsaker knew that it was as much a matter of point of view as it was of the truth. This was going to be a battle between different versions of what happened.

PART III

BLOOD

The human being is warmest during the first days of his life, coldest at the end.

—HIPPOCRATES

13

Approximately a week before it happened . . .

"*You've always seemed* to have more blood in you than other people, Knut," his mother once said as she was changing the bandage on his knee. He had fallen and skinned his knee on the rocks again, one day during his childhood out at the cabin, during a summer like so many other summers. "But there's also more life in you."

The laugh he uttered was for his mother. He had a different laugh for each family member. This one was for his mother, something he'd created just for the two of them, for times when they were alone, like now, when his siblings were off roaming over the rocks. The blood seeping out of the cut was their only worry in the world, at least for a brief time, until everyone started talking about the twin towers on the radio. There was no electricity out there. His father preferred it that way. "We inherited the place like this, and it's going to stay just the way it is," he'd said about the cabin on the island of Tjøme in southeastern Norway. His father had inherited almost everything they owned. Very few changes were ever made at home. Maybe it was his way of showing gratitude. The cabin had no computer or TV, but it did have a gas stove, water in the well, an outdoor toilet, reeds that rustled in the wind at night, grasshoppers, apple trees, phosphorescence in the surf, tar that was tough and silent, a horizon in which the seagulls could disappear, the smell of his father's cigarettes coming from beyond the silvery islet where he occasionally went to smoke in secret. And in the midst of all that silence: a radio. Knut was twelve years old. His mother had gone back inside the cabin with the box of Band-Aids. A clear voice was speaking to him about destruction. He turned off the radio, and that was the last thing he remembered about that day. The summer days didn't change. He kept on growing up.

Now there wasn't much life left in Knut as he hung from his feet. But there was plenty of blood. It gushed from his face and into his hair. From there it dripped onto the floor beneath him. He squirmed, making a creaking sound come from the lamp hook from which he was hanging. The hook wasn't intended to hold the weight of a grown man, especially not his weight. Soon he would fall to the ground, like an overripe apple. When that happened, he was hoping to swing himself over toward the table in the room. That would break his fall.

Coming to Trondheim to study hadn't taken the direction Knut had imagined. How had he ended up here? A boy like him, a merry boy from the Briskeby district of Oslo?

14

Approximately three weeks before it happened . . .

E*veryone else's life moved* slower than his. They spent their lives in still photos, while he was living in a motion picture. At least that's how he felt.

But sometimes he'd meet someone and recognize that they were alive too. He could see they were experiencing things the same way he was. There was a sense of momentum in their lives, they had things to look forward to, things to laugh at. But it was rare, very rare.

Yet now Knut wasn't sure. Maybe it was just her red hair. She'd been staring at him. That much he knew. Then she'd held up the book she had in her hand, as if she wanted him to notice the title: *A Clockwork Orange* by F. Alexander. Strange. He thought somebody else wrote that book. Wasn't it Stanley Kubrick? No, he directed the film. The book made her seem more exciting. She smiled at him. Then she swiped her card and punched in the PIN code. She looked at him again as she put the bottle of wine in the bag. Knut smiled back. Then she turned and left the liquor store. He had an urge to follow her, to put down what he was buying and run after her. They hadn't exchanged a single word. But there was chemistry between them. He'd felt it in his fingertips. He'd felt it in his toes.

He paid for his items, put them in the bag, and dashed into the street outside the Byhaven shopping center on Karl Johans Gate in Trondheim. He looked in both directions but couldn't see her. She was gone. Maybe this was both the first and the last time he'd ever see her.

Just a little flirting, Knut thought. It didn't mean anything. But why had he felt that she was someone special, that she was different from all the others? Was it just her hair? Red hair, green eyes. He knew he wasn't going to forget her anytime soon. And wasn't there something special about her figure too?

The bag of liquor was awfully heavy, as usual. He stood still, laughing at himself, chuckling out loud.

Someday I'll meet her again. Someday.

His cell rang. It was Jonas.

"Hey," Knut said.

"Hi," said Jonas. "Feel like some coke tonight?"

"Shit, Jonas. Where'd you get it?"

"I have my sources."

"Sure. Why not? It's supposed to snow," he said.

Cocaine. That was a new twist. He was actually careful about things like that. But what harm could it do?

"What happened?"

Jonas had inhaled it through his nostril, then sat still for a long time, breathing slowly. Suddenly he shook his head hard, before relaxing again. A white patch under the tip of his nose. Now he was stroking his pet rat.

"Hell if I know. But it's cool. I don't want it to stop."

Erling had gotten higher than anyone else. He shouted wildly: "Fucking awesome!"

Jonas looked around.

"Hey, Knut. We're not talking about you. You know that?"

"Shut up!"

"This is cooler than you." He bellowed with laughter.

Knut Andersen Stang got up, unbuckled his belt a notch, and tucked his shirt back in his pants, acting insulted, but he wasn't. He was used to those sorts of remarks. They didn't bother him. He knew the other guys actually liked him.

"Where are you going?"

"I need to fuck."

"Hell, you're 265 pounds, but you're always the one who ends up with the girl. How do you do it? It goes against all the laws of gravity, or something like that."

"I don't fixate on appearances."

"You've got a point there."

"I've got a sense of humor. Unlike you guys, I can laugh at myself. Not just at other people."

"That's how it is when you're always the funniest person in the room."

"Kiss my fat ass! Go ahead and snort the rest of that shit and die."

Knut laughed so hard he was shaking. He didn't care if they drowned in shit. He left them sitting there in that IKEA hell that was Jonas's place and went into town, still laughing. With one of his thousand different kinds of laughter burbling inside. He was a happy devil.

He drank beer on top of the rush from the cocaine. Then a woman bought him a tequila. He bought her one in return.

"*Crimes and Punishments*," he said. "That was the book that made me go into law."

He was lying. He was in pickup mode now. Everything he said was pure bullshit. He got into law because that was the department he could get into. Not medicine, not business school, and not any other law school except here in Trondheim. And it was only a pre-law program. Eventually he'd have to get into the university in Oslo. That was the only route for a man like him.

"Have you read the damn thing?"

She nodded. She could lie too. Things were looking good for the rest of the night.

He laughed slyly and went on. All this stuff he was spouting about Dostoyevsky was something he'd once heard from a woman at the Waterfront. He was good at remembering shit like that. He had the memory of an elephant. That made it a lot easier for him to talk about things, even if he really didn't have a clue about the topic. He was going to make a good lawyer.

"Raskolnikov. I've always thought he knew the whole time. He knew before he bashes in the old woman's head. He's going to get caught. He knows that, and it's what he wants. The crime is really just a means to the punishment. He needs to be punished. Otherwise he's finished. Raskolnikov's greatest wish is not to be something great but to be something small."

He laughed, feeling wise and cunning. He'd never read the book.

She nodded.

"How about another one, Shakespeare?"

"Not Shakespeare. Dustoflesky, if you don't mind," he said.

Now it was her turn to laugh. She had nice dimples. She was thinner than him, but no sylph.

The better to plow into, he thought.

An earth spirit, not an air spirit.

When Knut woke up the next morning, her head was resting on his shoulder. Under his buttocks he felt his cell phone vibrating. He dug it out to take the call.

"I'd rather be in hell!" he said.

"It's a cruel world," said Jonas.

"So you've come down too?"

"I know where we can get more," he replied. "I'm going to a party tonight. Want to come?"

"Of course. What do you take me for?" He chuckled hoarsely.

"That's my Knutie boy. Hey, listen, sorry about last night. Too much shit talking, I guess. You know how cool we think you are. You can handle it, right?"

"Forget it. I just filter out stuff like that. Want to grab a coffee?"

"In an hour? Dromedar on Nordre?"

"Sure. I just need to get rid of something that's snoring first."

He ended the call and lay in bed relaxing.

When am I ever going to find a girl that I don't want to get rid of? he asked himself. But there was no rush.

"Paulaner? What kind of shit is that?" Jonas made a face.

"German wheat beer. Thought I'd give it a try," said Knut.

"Well, keep it away from me. I'm allergic to wheat."

"Seriously? Wheat? Don't you eat bread?"

"You can make bread without wheat."

"What about pasta, for fuck's sake? Are you telling me you can live without pasta?"

"Have you ever seen me eat any?"

"No, now that you mention it. And you're right about one thing, anyway. This beer tastes like dishwater."

Knut had taken a swig and was now giving the bottle in his hand a skeptical look.

"Good luck with the next three!"

"Give me some of your wine, okay?"

"What's mine is yours," said Jonas. "At least until I get me a woman."

Knut went to get another glass from the kitchen. He put the bottles of beer in the fridge. *I'm sure somebody'll drink them before the party gets going,* he thought. They were expecting a lot of people that night.

Good thing Jonas had bought enough wine. The bottles were dancing like crazy. All the IKEA furniture and IKEA pots and pans were dancing too. All of Rosenborg Park was shaking and rocking under their feet.

When they left, his thigh muscles were still jiggling, tight little cramps that made him feel alive, as if he had laughter in his bones. He was sweating like a pig. There would be no ladies tonight. Being fat was one thing, but sweaty was another story. Talking wasn't going to distract any chick from noticing the sweat. But what did it matter?

They left the others behind and went to the party Jonas knew about.

Jonas had promised him more dope, and he came through. He and the guy who owned the apartment, a smiling smooth-operator type, went into another room where Jonas bought more than enough for the two of them. Now they were sitting on the floor of the living room, feeling like they were floating. They were shrieking like seagulls at each other.

"What the fuck!"

"I know!"

"This is fucking awesome, dude!"

"I know!"

They laughed so hard they cried.

Somebody had put on the wrong kind of music. The party was somewhere in the Lademoen district. How'd Jonas ever find people like this?

"I saw where he had the stuff stashed. What if we just walked out with it?"

"Rip it off from Mr. Smiley Face? Have you seen the muscle he's got for bodyguards? You don't fuck with people like him."

"But it's such good shit. Don't you think?"

"Fuck, yeah. But Jesus H. Christ."

"Okay, have another snort."

He did. He took some more. And some more after that.

"Shit, you're bad!" Jonas's shout seemed to fill the whole empty park near the Lademoen church. "You're a bad motherfucker!"

"Still don't know how cool it was for a big guy like me to sneak into that bedroom. I'm not exactly hard to miss."

"Screw it. Those junkies in there aren't going to notice anything until morning. There must have been a hundred people in that apartment. If anybody saw you, they just thought you were going in the bathroom to jack off."

"Jack off at this!"

He pulled a bulging plastic package out of his waistband. Half a kilo, at least. He didn't even dare think about what the street value might be, but it had to be insane. He dangled the package over Jonas's head, making him jump for it. Jonas finally tackled him to the ground. They rolled around in the snow, bellowing.

Then they went back to Jonas's place, their nostrils quivering.

For several days they were careful about how much they snorted.

Then they got greedier, but also more generous, sharing the dope with anyone and everyone. They sold some of it and then spent the money on expensive restaurants and passable drinks. Focusing on anything but their law books, making only quick visits to the library reading room, attending only a couple of hazy lectures, the words flying toward them and then disappearing. Exhausted days, busy nights, a few girls, but nothing promising. Knut laughed a lot, sang a good deal, danced off a few pounds in weight, and made plenty of pithy and carefully considered remarks that were quickly forgotten.

Then came the fatal day when that rabid bitch dumped the dope down the toilet. How could Jonas have ended up in such a fight with a girl he'd met at the Student Association the day before? Something went wrong. Jonas tried to get rid of her the next morning, but he didn't do it in a nice way, and all of a sudden she just seemed to snap. At some point in their argument the whole snowstorm landed in the toilet.

They could have lived with losing the coke if they hadn't gotten caught. If somebody hadn't started retracing their steps and finally caught up with them—two detectives, one fat and one thin, Laurel and Hardy on cocaine.

15

Approximately a week before it happened . . .

"*Just think of this* as the beginning of a tragedy."

He'd introduced himself as Sving before he barged in. Just Sving. No last name.

They'd broken open the door, hitting Knut in the face so he'd ended up flat on the floor. Then they hit him with something heavy. He didn't see what it was. It knocked him out for a while. Long enough for them to hang him from a hook by his feet, which was the position he found himself in now. But by the time he came to, Sving was the only one left in the room. Now he was sitting at the rickety table, looking up at Knut as he hung there with his head pointing down.

"It's meant to be a positive statement. According to Aristotle, tragedy always leads to catharsis."

"Catharsis?"

Knut felt the pressure building inside his head as he talked. It was like all the blood in his body had collected inside his skull. How long could somebody hang upside down before passing out and eventually dying? Was it true that Roman prisoners asked to be crucified upside down so they'd lose consciousness and die faster?

Sving was still talking:

"To be honest, I don't really give a shit about all that catharsis crap. Personally, I'm here for practical reasons. We're missing half a kilo, and we want it back. Either in powder form or in cash. My employer is a reasonable man, and he'll settle for a quarter of a million kroner. He even told me I didn't need to kill anyone if the money was forthcoming. 'We'll just think of it as a business deal,' he said." Sving laughed, shrugged, and gave Knut a look that almost seemed to convey some shred of empathy.

Your employer should have thought things through before he decided to have an open house with a quarter of a million worth of cocaine under the bed, thought Knut.

But what he said was this:

"Why do you think I took the stuff?"

Sving laughed. His laughter seemed genuine, as if he really couldn't contain his mirth.

"My second favorite thing is when people I work with give me some reason to slug them. My favorite thing is when they give me a reason to laugh. And you've given me both."

The guy punched Knut in the stomach. It hurt, but no more than intended.

Sving was still laughing.

"We could keep this up for a while. I like you. I like hitting you. You're like a high-quality punching bag. But the thing is, I'm running out of time. I'm working under contract here."

He punched Knut again. Harder. In the chest this time, though making sure not to break any ribs.

"So why don't we quit talking shit and move on? I know as well as you do that you were the one who took the goods. So I don't think it's necessary for me to waste half the morning telling you how I found out. I'm sure you'd believe me."

"I'll pay the money. Give me two weeks. That's all I need."

"See? That's more constructive. I don't doubt that you'll pay up. But a week should suffice. And just to give you a little more incentive . . ."

Sving bent down and picked up something from the floor. His fists were no longer enough. Knut hadn't noticed the baseball bat when they broke in, but now he realized that must have been what they'd used to knock him out.

"Say hello to Mr. Louisville Slugger, my most loyal friend," said Sving, tapping the bat against the forehead of young Knut.

He gave Knut a slight push, making him swing backward a few inches. He felt dizzy. He was trying hard to focus as Sving launched into a brief lecture about the legendary baseball bat that had been produced from American white ash and maple trees since 1884. Did Knut know that the world's biggest bat was outside the factory in Kentucky? Or that the baseball legend Babe Ruth had never used any bat except a forty-two-ounce Louisville Slugger?

No, Knut didn't know that.

Did he know that even a skinny little girl could bash in the skull of a grown man with a well-aimed blow from this bat?

Knut got the picture.

"The thing is, either you put an end to this tragedy, or Mr. Slugger here will do it for you," said Sving after finishing his lecture. "A spiritual or physical catharsis. You decide."

He lowered the bat and leaned down so Knut could feel him breathing in his face. He smelled of badly digested food.

"You've got a week," he said and straightened up. "And by the way, I brought in your newspaper for you."

Knut wanted to protest, say that he didn't get the paper, that he must have taken the landlord's paper.

But Sving was gone.

So now he was still hanging here. For a little while longer, hanging here like a big, heavy bundle of fun. The rope tightened, making his ankles ache. Slowly he started swinging back and forth. He had to get down before he lost too much blood. His goal was to loosen the rope as he swung over to the table and be able to drop onto it. He realized the table legs would give way under his weight. His landlord hadn't exactly filled the room with the sturdiest of furniture. It was mostly teak crap from the '60s. But the table might still break his fall if only he could reach it.

But the exact opposite happened.

When Knut was farthest away from the table, the ceiling plaster let go of the hook with a resigned croak. Luckily the weight of his body was tilted forward, so he fell onto his stomach. He managed to use his hands to break the fall slightly and didn't suffer any more injuries than those he already had.

Only now did he register the fact that he was naked. He had gone to open the door wearing his bathrobe, so they must have stripped it off him before hanging him upside down from the hook. He looked for his underwear from yesterday but didn't find it before someone knocked on the front door. Everybody who came to visit him had to pass through the small outside entryway that led to his rented room. That was also how Sving had entered. There was only one person who ever knocked on his door from the main hallway in the house. That was where his bathroom was located and where another door led into the house itself. There was only one person who would even consider visiting him this early in the morning. The door opened a second later. Guttorm Gjessing's shiny bald head appeared in the doorway.

"Sorry. I guess this isn't a good time for me to drop by," he said, though he didn't budge from the doorway. "Rough night?"

Evidently the deaf old guy hadn't heard all the commotion in his room.

Knut wiped the blood from his nose.

"You should stuff some cotton up your nose," said the old geezer. "That helps."

"What was it you wanted to see me about?" Knut said as politely as the situation allowed. He picked up a towel from the floor and wrapped it around his waist.

"It's that time of month, you know. Rent is due," said the landlord.

Panic seized hold of Knut at the thought of more due dates. The only one he could focus on right now was the one in a week's time.

"Oh. Right. I'll bring it right over."

Knut stood where he was, feeling dazed and dizzy, as if his blood was having trouble flowing back down from his head into his body after dangling from the ceiling. He was also bruised and hungover, and he could use something other than cotton up his nose.

His eyes suddenly fell on the copy of *Adresseavisen* from February 15, 2011. It was the newspaper that Sving had brought in. He blinked twice, realizing now that it was over. His days as a dumb and happy student stopped right now. Everything stopped. At this instant.

He was looking at the headline: STUDENT DIES IN MYSTERIOUS FALL NEAR ROSENBORG PARK.

Underneath it said:

A young law student died last night after falling from the balcony of his apartment by Rosenborg Park. The police are treating his death as suspicious, but as yet they have no hard evidence of foul play.

The photograph showed the apartment complex in Rosenborg. No one needed to tell Knut who that law student was. He knew without reading the rest of the article.

His knees buckled. His heavy body was suddenly too much for them to bear. He collapsed onto the floor and lay there on his stomach. A moment later he got onto his knees and vomited, then kept on heaving. It was like having cramps from laughing too hard, except it hurt. Finally, it stopped and he lay back down, his mouth wide open.

After a while he finally stood up, got dressed, and went out.

He grabbed his bike from where he'd parked it in Gjessing's garage. Then he headed down the steep streets of the Singsaker residential district toward Rosenborg Park. When he got there, he didn't dare ring the bell. Instead, he rolled his bike in between the buildings to a small hill behind with a cluster of trees, some benches, and a flagpole on top. From here he had a view of the Kristiansten Fortress. But more importantly, from here he could see right into Jonas's apartment.

Knut could see it even before he parked his bike. Police tape had been strung up between two lampposts that lined the path under Jonas's apartment. From the lampposts, the tape was stretched over to the wall, blocking off the area directly under his friend's balcony. In the middle Knut could see some red patches on the ground. They were small, but big enough for him to tell they were blood. Inside on the wood floor of the apartment, where he had danced so often over the past few months, two white-clad men wearing rubber gloves were moving about. He couldn't see their feet, but he knew they were wearing blue plastic booties. These guys had to be the police crime scene techs. He let go of his bike without using the kickstand, and it toppled over onto the slope as he sank onto a bench. He pulled his knees up and wrapped his arms around them as he rocked back and forth. That sick fucker had killed Jonas. There was no longer any doubt. That bastard had thrown his friend off the balcony. Why else would he bring a copy of the newspaper with him? Obviously he wanted Knut to see the news. The article hadn't mentioned Jonas by name. It was too soon for that. He'd died yesterday, yet early enough for the newspaper to print the news in the morning edition. While Knut was still out partying, blissfully ignorant of what had happened, not knowing that Jonas was gone. *Suspicious death.* He thought about that phrase. There was nothing suspicious about it. Jonas had been killed by the man who called himself Sving, the man who was now after Knut. What he really wanted to do was scream at the top of his lungs. But he couldn't. He didn't want to attract attention from the police inside the building. In fact, he needed to get out of there before they noticed him.

So how much money did he actually have? None? To be honest, he really had no idea. There had been so little reason to worry about trivial matters like that. He'd had a bunch of cash on him yesterday when he was at . . . where was it now? That place where he'd gone dancing with that lame chick who didn't come home with him? He couldn't remember. Didn't really matter.

He checked his bank account online. Eleven thousand Norwegian kroner. He got ten thousand from his father every month. His next rent payment was due. He'd squandered most of his student loan long ago. When he got back to his place, he went through his jackets and found seven thousand kroner in the inside pocket of his down jacket. Probably payment for a sale that he'd forgotten about. He collected another three thousand from the pockets of other jackets and a couple of hundred in various pants. Altogether he had a total of twenty-one thousand. His rent was six thousand a month. Gjessing insisted on cash, always cash. Knut decided that six thousand kroner was so far from a quarter million that he might as well pay the rent. It made little difference if he had twenty-one or fifteen banknotes with Edvard Munch's picture on them when he owed two hundred and fifty of them to a psychopath with friends like Sving. Small change wouldn't do him any good. He needed a fucking miracle.

He clutched the money in his hand and, strangely enough, felt a surge of hope. Hope was his thing, blind and reckless hope, pale and paralyzing.

He went into the bathroom and took a shower. Tried to rub off the thought of Jonas and an image that had settled in his mind of the lifeless body underneath the balcony where he'd seen the police tape. He pictured it in various crumpled positions, lying on patches of blood. He wished he could wipe the image away by rinsing his throat. But he couldn't. He was never going to be rid of it.

"Come in!" Gjessing shouted shrilly through the keyhole.

A double oak door led into his living room.

He was sitting in the dim light with the curtains drawn. They were old and dusty, looking as if they hadn't been touched since Gjessing's wife had died. The folds were stiff with age, with thin strips of sun in between. Dust motes whirled in the sunlight, trembling like heart murmurs.

"I've brought the money," said Knut.

What am I doing here? he asked himself.

"Good. You look better. Did you find some cotton?"

"Cotton? Oh, sure, right. The bleeding stopped by itself."

"Do you often have nosebleeds?"

"Uh-huh."

"I have a nephew whose nose would bleed if you just looked at him. Back when he was a kid, I mean."

Knut laughed without knowing why. How could he be laughing after what had just happened?

"He doesn't bleed as much anymore. He's a lot more serious nowadays."

Knut was taken aback.

"Is there a connection between nosebleeds and seriousness that I'm not getting?"

"Of course."

Again Knut couldn't help laughing at what the old man had said. It wasn't rude laughter. Nor would he call it amiable laughter. Just casual. Disarming. Giving no indication of what he'd just been through.

"You're a sanguine fellow," said Gjessing.

"Me? Hardly. You should hear me sing. I only sing at parties, and then only drinking songs." That was true. It was a custom he'd acquired back home.

"I didn't say you were a singing fellow. I said you're sanguine."

"Oh, sanguine. Not a word I hear very often. I've heard it before, but what exactly does it mean?"

"Come over here and sit down." Gjessing pointed to an armchair with velour upholstery.

Knut was afraid that his landlord's wife might have been the last person to sit in that chair. She had died more than ten years ago. Or was it twenty? Nevertheless, he sat down, relieved to see that the chair would hold his weight. Actually, it was quite comfortable. It hardly creaked at all. The velour tickled the back of his neck.

"A sanguine person is an eternal optimist."

"That's me in a nutshell," replied Knut, even though he was feeling the opposite right now. How could he ever be optimistic again with Jonas lying in the morgue, or wherever it was the police stored bodies in this town?

"Have you heard of the four bodily fluids?"

He was familiar with bodily fluids. Of course he was. A man like him. But it was news to him that there were four.

"Would you like something to drink? There's tea in the pot." Gjessing pointed to a flower-patterned pot on the coffee table. "You'll find cups in the sideboard." Again the old man pointed. His finger was pale, with thin blue veins. His nails were gray like hardened chewing gum.

"There's port wine too. If it's not too early in the day for you."

Knut got up and went over to the sideboard to get out the port wine.

"We could do with a glass, don't you think?" he said.

Gjessing smiled.

"Don't see why not."

Knut held the bottle in his hand as he surveyed the volumes in the bookcase next to the sideboard. It was a low bookcase made of dark, polished wood. Three rows of leather-bound books. For some strange reason he was in the mood for a chat. It wouldn't take his mind off Jonas entirely, but he also had his own problems to solve. He needed to come up with some ideas, plain and simple. And he had no clue where to find them.

"Lots of old books here," he said.

He saw titles and author names that he'd never seen before. All the books were in English, arranged alphabetically by author. He ran his fingers over the spines. Paused to read some of them. He'd always enjoyed looking at the book spines on other people's bookshelves. Sometimes he thought he'd read more outsides than the insides of books. But he'd always been more interested in what was possible than what was real. What he *could* experience meant more to him than what he'd actually experienced. It was the same with reading. He liked the titles of Gjessing's books.

The Worm of Midnight by Edgar Allan Poe. *Songs of the Long Land* by Lallafa. *History of a Land Called Uqbar* by Silas Haslam. *A Princess Among Slaves* by Sir Elmer Bole. *In a Network of Lines That Intersect* by Ermes Marana. *One Human Minute* by J. Johnson and S. Johnson. And *Necronomicon* by Abdul al-Hazred.

What he liked best was the fact that he'd never heard of any of these books before. For him, they could just as well be the working titles of books that he hadn't yet written.

"Lots of interesting books here."

"Very interesting, if I do say so myself." Gjessing was looking at Knut with those colorless old man's eyes of his.

Knut pulled a book from the shelf, turned to the title page, and read aloud:

"*The Anatomy of Melancholy, What It Is: With All the Kinds, Causes, Symptomes, Prognostickes, and Several Cures of It. In Three Maine Partitions with Their Several Sections, Members, and Subsections. Philosophically, Medicinally, Historically, Opened and Cut Up.*"

"It has a certain flair to it! They really knew how to come up with titles in the old days. Today we simply call that book *The Anatomy of Melancholy,*" said Gjessing. "Written by Robert Burton. Odd that you should select that particular book. It's about one of the four bodily fluids: black bile, *melas choli*, as it's called in Greek. Bring it over here and sit down."

Knut carried the book in one hand, the wine bottle and two glasses in the other.

He wondered again what he was doing here. He'd come over to pay the rent and then was going to go back to his room. To think.

To come up with a solution. But how was he going to find it? A quarter million kroner? His father would die if he asked for that kind of money. Not that the old man didn't have it. But he couldn't ask him. That was impossible. How would he explain the situation? Nothing like this would ever happen in his father's world. Never. He wouldn't give Knut even one øre.

"Phlegm, black bile, blood, and yellow bile. Those are the four bodily fluids, called *humors*. In antiquity it was believed they influenced a person's state of mind. If there was an imbalance in the bodily fluids, it could also lead to various illnesses."

"You mentioned your nephew who used to get nosebleeds. Does that have something to do with the four bodily fluids?"

"Yes. He had an excess of blood, *sanguis*, as the Romans called it."

"In other words, he was sanguine?"

"Yes. Like you."

"What do you know about me?"

"Not much. But a person's temperament is the first thing that becomes apparent. It's rare that anybody can hide it for long, even if they try. Someone who is sanguine wouldn't bother. A sanguine person is extroverted, full of blood and easily moved, cheerful, easygoing, and fun. It's a compliment to be called sanguine."

Knut thought about this as he sat in silence. He liked Gjessing. The old man was a dreamer. You could almost see his thoughts whirling in his head when you looked into his eyes. There was a glint in his eyes, the remnants of a youth that should have faded long ago.

"In modern times we dismiss the wisdom of the bodily fluids, but many people, also within the field of psychiatry, think that each human being is born with a fundamental temperament, which is constant and independent of more situation-based shifts in mood. That temperament can be changed only by decisive events, illnesses, or injuries. What's interesting is that temperament is still regarded as something inherited and relatively static; something that is still influenced to a certain degree by fluids in the body. Today we call these fluids hormones. Here's to progress!"

The old man picked up his glass of port, which he'd filled as they talked. Knut poured himself a glass, and together they drank a toast.

"You can borrow the book. Even though you're a lighthearted kind of person, it would do you good to read about the dark side."

Knut looked at the spine of the old book. It was the same color as the trunk of a spruce tree. The gilded letters looked like they were about to sink into the bark and disappear.

Lighthearted? he thought. *If you only knew.* He studied the old man sitting across from him. He resembled a squirrel, hunched over his glass of port wine as if it were a pinecone.

"*Skål* to melancholy!" said Knut.

He downed the rest of his wine and then refilled his glass.

Gjessing set down his glass and lit his pipe. The tobacco had a sweet fragrance. With a tinge of plums, nuts, and old man. The topic of conversation then shifted to deep-sea fishing. It was one of Gjessing's great passions.

"Some people think it's sheer madness to fish at a depth of a thousand feet," said Gjessing, suddenly transformed. A deep-sea fisherman near the end of his life, but with fire in his voice.

"But it's at those depths that something incredible can happen. I once pulled in a ling weighing 110 pounds. Imagine that! That's more than an average ten-year-old child weighs, even today when all the kids are overweight. It took me five hours to haul in the beast. I was all alone in the boat and enjoyed every second of it. Never any question of giving up. Finally, I got it over the gunwale. You should have seen the eyes on that thing. It was one of those blue lings with bulging eyes. It stared at me as if it had seen the very core of the earth and knew more about the world's secrets than any man of science. I had to let it go. But you should have seen it! Almost five feet long! There's nothing to compare with a blue ling from the deep like that."

"*The Old Man and the Sea*," murmured Knut.

He hadn't read the book of that title. The phrase just slipped out of him. He didn't mean for the old man to hear, and he realized that the remark could be taken as snide. But Gjessing wasn't offended.

"Ah, Hemingway. So you're a literary man?"

"You know I'm studying law," replied Knut. "But I like reading other things too," he added untruthfully.

"Reading and fishing," muttered Gjessing ambiguously, wetting his parched lips with more wine.

"Do you have any family, Mr. Gjessing?" asked Knut. "Brothers? Sisters? Cousins?"

"I have several cousins. The nephew I mentioned comes to visit now and then. But Else and I never had any children. It took too much time from what we thought was life."

Knut poured more port wine into Gjessing's glass. He emptied the rest of the bottle into his own and took a big swig.

Suddenly a thought occurred to him. A liberating thought.

"Why don't you ever want me to deposit the rent in your bank account?" He took out the six thousand-krone bills from his pants pocket.

"I don't trust banks. I only keep enough in my account to pay the bills, and an old man doesn't have many bills to worry about."

He spoke as if that were a sad state of affairs. And maybe it was. *Someone who doesn't pay for things never receives anything either,* thought Knut.

"Is there anything safer than a bank?" he asked innocently.

"Maybe I shouldn't be telling you this, but I trust you. I don't know why. I just do. I'm one of those old guys who hides my money under the mattress. Don't know why. The money will probably still be there when I die. But I like the thought of whoever cleans up after me finding the money."

Knut leaned forward and placed the rent money on the table in front of Gjessing.

"Well, here's a little more you can tuck away."

Then he stood up and emptied his glass. The last drop was sweeter than the first. He inhaled the smell of tobacco from

Gjessing's pipe and saw how the smoke was hovering near the ceiling above him. White clouds indoors.

"Thanks for the wine. I'll buy you another bottle the next time I go to the liquor store."

"Don't bother. I'm going out traveling, and I always pick up some duty-free booze."

"Traveling? Where to?"

Gjessing never stopped surprising him.

"I to go London every year. To see QPR play. Are you familiar with British football teams?"

"Sort of."

"Sort of? Young people today have no passion, but then you didn't grow up playing the pools. For you, British football is all about brand names, like colas or Santa Claus."

"Do you really go all the way to England by yourself?"

"I'll keep doing that as long as I can stand on my own two feet. After my wife passed away, I was left with three things in my life: fishing, books, and QPR. And I'm not going to be doing much fishing anymore. Arthritis in my fingers. Soon I'll only have my tall tales left from my life as a fisherman. When was the last time I was out in a boat? When could it have been? At least a year ago. I'm always thinking that I should go out one last time. But I've still got books and football. That may not sound like much. But it's enough to fill my life for a few more years."

"When are you leaving?"

"Tomorrow."

"What about the house?"

"What about it?"

"Who's going to take care of the place?"

"This house takes care of itself. Besides, you're here. But it'd be nice if you'd take in the newspaper. I'll be back on Saturday, February 19."

"Okay, I'll do that."

Knut Andersen Stang gave the old man a casual, reassuring smile.

But inside, he was in an uproar.

He lay in bed, staring up at the slanted ceiling where the lamp hook had been. A long crack in the ceiling tiles pointed to the spot where he was lying.

He spent a lot of time in bed. It was the only piece of furniture in the place that was his own. He and his father had driven it over in a trailer from Oslo. He'd lasted a week on Gjessing's creaking plank bed. What was that mattress filled with anyway? Hay? Gravel? The very first weekend after he'd moved away from home, he was back in Oslo. He couldn't live without a decent mattress. He and his father had enjoyed the drive north. Stopping to swim in Sjoa. His father wore the same swimming trunks he'd had since Knut was a boy. Brown and orange, but by now the flower pattern was completely faded.

Knut made the most of his bed, sleeping in it, eating in it—honey puffed wheat for breakfast and bacon for supper—dreaming, and going on Facebook, although not often. He spent less time on the Internet than most people. His father's opinion had stuck with him. "The Web makes you restless," he'd said. "And you're restless enough as it is." That's why Knut didn't even have a smartphone. He knew that not having one made him a freak, but he didn't care. People liked him the way he was. But right now he was in trouble. He stared at the hole left by the hook on the ceiling. Some of the loose plaster drifted down from the hole. White powder filled the air.

Of course he was out of coke. He'd gone into town and tried to get some, but no luck there either. He hadn't dared contact anyone he knew because he didn't want to talk about Jonas. Naturally people had been calling him, but he'd given only terse replies, saying that he was fine and he had no idea what had happened to his friend.

What was he supposed to say? He could have tried telling them the truth, explaining that he wasn't able to think clearly anymore. No. He couldn't do that. He wasn't like that. This state of shock had turned him into someone he didn't recognize. Something Gjessing had said rang true: only really decisive events could alter a person's innate temperament. Could that be what had happened? Had Jonas's death fundamentally changed him? Was he a different person now?

Instead of getting high, Knut had gotten drunk at a bar where he felt sure he wouldn't be recognized. He'd gone home with a girl but couldn't stand the sight of her in the glaring light of her kitchen. So he'd left before they made it to the bedroom. Back home, he threw up in the sink in the little bathroom down the hall.

Now he was lying in bed, feeling sick to his stomach. He wasn't thinking about anything specific. He was simply waiting, and listening.

Early in the morning the sounds started up. The oak door slowly opened, then shuffling footsteps, a suitcase set down on the floor for a short time as Gjessing paused in the entryway to put on his beige coat, hat, and wool scarf. Gjessing's clothes had a certain flair—Knut had to give him that. He tried to picture the old man standing there, knotting his scarf, but ended up envisioning those small gray eyes of his, hovering all alone and weightless in the dimly lit hall.

A few minutes later Gjessing picked up the suitcase and went out the door.

Knut Andersen Stang—a dork and a coke addict, a drunk, seducer, and sanguine guy in a shitload of trouble—lay in bed listening to Gjessing close the front door and make his way down the stone stairs outside, moving cautiously on the wide slate steps, holding his cane in one hand and clutching the wrought-iron railing with the other. Old Gjessing probably wasn't wearing cleats on his shoes, and no doubt he was worried about slipping on the thin layer of ice that covered the stairs in the morning. Frozen dew, shiny and nearly invisible, treacherous. Even Knut had slipped once in the winter on his own steps, which were narrower, but they were also made of slate.

Gjessing stood outside for a long time. Silence descended. Maybe he was studying the view of the town. Knut wondered whether he should get up to see if the old man was still out there. Could he really have disappeared without another sound? Drifted away into the air? But Knut decided not to budge. He didn't want to be seen in the window, peering out, as if he were up to something.

Then he heard a car pull into the gravel driveway. Probably a taxi. So Gjessing was still there. He spoke to the cabdriver, then got in, the doors slammed, and the cab drove off.

The last sound Knut heard was the creaking of the gravel as the taxi headed into Overlege Kindts Gate in the Upper Singsaker district of Trondheim. Gjessing, apparently a long-retired physician, had left. Setting off for a trip to England. A man well over eighty, maybe even ninety, was on his way to a football match in London.

And Knut was alone in the house.

Moving slowly, as always, he got out of bed. His stomach felt heavy, the same sensation he got when he ate a steak without chewing it properly. He exchanged his Hugo Boss underwear for Armani and got dressed. It felt like more work than usual.

He went out to the hall and looked around. Hanging on Gjessing's coat rack was a plaid smoking jacket. On the floor underneath were his slippers. Knut turned on the light and inspected the oak door leading to his landlord's rooms. Suddenly he coughed, then strode over to the door and grabbed the brass handle. He gave it a tug, but the door was locked. That was no surprise. He tried to recall if he'd heard Gjessing turn a key in the lock, but he wasn't sure. Probably Gjessing had locked the door as it closed. A soundless maneuver, with one hand on the door handle, the other turning the key. Then he'd slipped the key into his pocket. Automatic movements that even stiff, old fingers remembered.

Knut felt a pang of guilt about what he was going to do, though he didn't know why. Gjessing had said it himself. He had no plans for the money other than to surprise distant relatives that he seldom saw. If he found more than two hundred and fifty thousand-krone bills under the mattress, he planned to leave them there. Right now, it was a matter of survival. Going back to the life he'd been living. Maybe even giving up the dope. Who knew? That was an idea. A thought occurred to him. What about Jonas? Jonas was part of the life he'd been living. So that meant Knut really couldn't go back. Not to his former life. That was gone for good. But no matter what, he had to get himself out of this situation, one way or another, and he had to do it alone. The thing was, he needed that money lying in there under the old mattress. He needed it more than anybody else did. That money could do more for him than it ever could do for Gjessing.

He went back to his room. Put on the down jacket, a pair of mittens his mother had knitted for him, and a Busnel knit cap. Then he went out into the freezing cold, exiting through his own door.

The air was colder than a mug of whiskey. It hadn't snowed. The storm everybody had been talking about in the media had passed south of Trondheim. It had also subsided a bit but was expected to return with even greater force over the weekend, and to this part of Norway as well. A few rays of sunlight penetrated the clouds like unexpected guests.

He trudged across the icy gravel toward the garage. He moved aside the shovel leaning against the garage door. The neighbor boy used the shovel to clear the driveway once a week. Otherwise it stood propped against the old door, holding it shut. Inside was the old, burgundy Mercedes that belonged to Guttorm Gjessing. Knut walked around the car to where the tools were kept at the back of the garage. He knew where to look. He had borrowed tools from Gjessing before. From the biggest drawer he took out a crowbar.

"No, no. Not in there!"

A fat dog with shaggy fur and floppy ears came running into the yard. Knut was going back to the house and stopped midway, holding the crowbar in his hand, as if it were the metal tool that had brought him to an abrupt halt.

The voice was coming from out on the street, beyond the winter-white hedge.

"Aphrodite! Come here, Afro! Come to Mamma!"

Then he caught sight of her.

Her red hair hung over one shoulder, almost like a scarf. She wore a knitted cap with multicolored stripes, like a psychedelic snail with her hair sticking out. And she had freckles. Snowflakes fell from her gray coat with blue embroidery across the front. She had brushed against the snow-laden hedge on her way in. It was her. The girl he'd seen at the liquor store a couple of weeks ago. Before everything went to hell.

"Oh, you'll have to excuse my dog. She has no manners at all."

She laughed as if she really wasn't the least bit sorry. Both of them looked at the dog, who was peeing near the corner of the garage.

Knut laughed. It was one of those laughs he couldn't control, a spontaneous sort of laughter. She laughed too, as if imitating him.

"She doesn't get her bad manners from me," she said.

"Let's hope not."

He caught sight of the leash in her hand. She was also holding a book. Didn't she have a book the last time he saw her?

"Let me have that," he said, pointing.

He set the crowbar on the ground, feeling guilty. Did it look weird for him to be walking around with a crowbar on a cold day like this?

As she raised her hand to give him the leash, he read what it said on the cover of her book: *Campi clysteriorum* by Symphorien Champier.

"You read Latin?" he asked.

"Only when I'm bored." She gave him a teasing smile.

Was she flirting with him?

"Just kidding. It's an English translation. They just kept the Latin title. Mostly I read detective novels, but sometimes I try something really old. This is a treatise from the Middle Ages. Pretty dry. Stuff for work. The original is archived in the library where I work. I brought it along so I could read it while I'm walking my dog."

"You read while you're walking?"

"I like to live dangerously."

"I read old books too," he said. "Dostoyevsky, for example. *Crimes and Punishments* is my favorite book."

"You've never read even one sentence by Dostoyevsky in your whole life." She laughed.

He loved her laugh.

"What makes you say that?"

She'd seen right through him. Nobody had ever done that before. He liked it. He found it exciting.

"I just know it's true," she said.

"How can you know that?"

"I could tell you, but then I'd just scare you off. I have a tendency to scare people. It's a bad habit of mine."

"I'm not easily scared."

"If it really was your favorite book, you'd know that the title is *Crime and Punishment*, not *crimes*, plural. Are you going to help me catch my dog or not?"

He held up the leash, staring at it foolishly.

"Sure. Right," he stammered.

When he got close to the dog, it ran past him and straight over to the red-haired girl. She grabbed the dog's collar, holding it carefully, lovingly.

"Better bring the leash over here," she said, laughing.

He handed it to her.

"So you named your dog Aphrodite?"

"Mostly I just call her Afro."

"Both names suit her," he said, grinning.

He watched her fasten the leash to the dog's collar. Then she said good-bye and went on her way.

As she disappeared from sight, he noticed her stomach. She was thin, but under her coat he could see a slight bulge. Was she pregnant? He didn't know why, but the thought made him even more excited. He leaned down and cautiously picked up the crowbar. It was so cold he could feel it through his mittens.

Back in his room Knut placed the crowbar on top of the electric heater. He knew it was irrational and crazy, but he wanted it to be warm to the touch. After eating a portion of honey puffed wheat with milk he put his hand on the crowbar and decided it was the proper temperature.

Then he carried it into the hall, where he stood and stared at the oak door.

No, he thought. *This is wrong. A burglar wouldn't come in this way.*

There was no reason for any suspicion to fall on him. Gjessing was out of town, and burglaries occurred frequently on Overlege Kindts Gate. And the old geezer hadn't installed a security alarm in his house. He'd asked his young lodger, who was often out, to keep an eye on things. With newspapers piling up on the front steps—Knut would forget about taking them inside, and that was merely an oversight, not a crime—and with all the lights off inside Gjessing's house 24-7, it wouldn't be at all strange for someone to try and break in. Nobody would suspect Knut, as long as he went about it the right way.

He went back to his room and wiped off the crowbar with a T-shirt he found lying on the floor. Then he set it on the bed and lay down next to it. He tossed and turned for a long time. He could have used some stuff up his nose.

Then he started thinking about her. At first it seemed coincidental that she would appear in his thoughts. He happened to think of what she'd said. That she scared people. But as soon as he began thinking about her, he couldn't stop. She wasn't especially pretty. And he found that annoying. But not ugly either. Definitely not ugly.

She was slim, except for her stomach, and she had red hair and freckles. Not his type at all. So what was it about her?

Aphrodite? Who would give a name like that to their dog? Was it really possible? But Afro was cool.

He laughed out loud.

It struck him how wrong this all was. He shouldn't be thinking about such things right now. He had just lost his best friend. And he was in danger of losing his own life, or at least getting the shit beat out of him if his plan didn't succeed. That was what he needed to focus on. But what was it about her? He was attracted to her, wasn't he? Wanted to sleep with her? He wasn't sure. Maybe it would be good. Maybe it would be better with her than with anyone else. Could she be the one? The one he didn't want to get rid of the instant he woke up?

But she was pregnant. She was with someone else. Maybe she was even married. What was he thinking about now? Those freckles of hers. He couldn't get them out of his mind. They were red like Mars, seen with the naked eye from earth on a clear night when he walked home, semi-drunk, from a failed attempt to get laid. She was otherworldly.

Finally, he fell asleep.

He woke up in a sweat several hours later, and she was still in his thoughts. He'd been dreaming about the snow that had settled on her coat, and pictured himself brushing it off. Brushing and brushing until her whole coat crumbled away. Underneath she had on bright red panties and nothing else.

It was not yet dark. He searched all his pockets but then realized he'd already done that several times earlier. No more white powder anywhere.

Instead he went down to the basement, which could be reached from a door in the hallway. It wasn't locked. There he had a storage space with a fridge inside. He found some beer—six bottles of Sol,

Mexican piss—and a salami that his mother had brought him from Italy.

He went back to his room to eat while he waited for darkness to fall. And finally it did. Just as it always does.

He'd also brought upstairs from the basement some coveralls his father had left behind after helping him move in. That was so typical. His father had clothes for every occasion. Knut pulled on the coveralls over his jeans and shirt and buttoned them all the way up. He put on his Busnel cap, tugging it down over his forehead like a crook might do. Then he put on his gloves and grabbed the crowbar, which was lying on the bed.

He went out through his own private entrance and hurried around the corner of the house, away from the street. On that side no one would be able to see him except for the neighbors who lived in the property at the back, but only if for some reason they should decide to shine a flashlight out their window. But there weren't even any lights on in their house. They probably weren't home. Knut was feeling confident.

He paused to survey the old man's house. There were four big windows on this side, and at least two of them led to Gjessing's living room, while one was the kitchen window. But all of them were too high up for him to climb through from the ground. There were also a lot of basement windows, but he didn't even consider using any of them. They would just give him access to the basement stairs and up to the oak door in the hall. And he'd already ruled that out as a possible entrance into Gjessing's part of the house. So he decided to go back to the garage and get the stepladder. As he crossed the yard, he kept an eye on the road, but it remained deserted.

He placed the ladder under the kitchen window.

Then he climbed up, pausing at the top to catch his breath and collect himself. He took a look around, but the neighbors' house was still dark. No sounds, no movement outdoors, just him, a dark kitchen window, and a cloudy night sky. Cold gusts of wind blew into his face.

He shattered one of the six windows with the crowbar, then cast another glance around but saw no lights anywhere. Everything was quiet. The wind instantly found its way inside the house along with some drifting snowflakes that blew in from the windowsill.

Knut stuck his hand inside and unlatched the window. He had to reach in with his whole arm to find the latch at the top. A shard of glass left in the frame made a big rip in the coveralls he was wearing. He realized he could have gone about this more efficiently, but finally the latch released.

With the window now open, he was able to climb inside. Two hundred sixty-five pounds was actually about a hundred thirty pounds too much for a burglar, but fortunately a big, fancy house like Gjessing's had windows as wide as doors. Knut managed to get inside, dropping onto the pine floor of the kitchen. Then he closed the window behind him.

From the kitchen he headed for the oak door of the living room, the one that led out to the hall and his own room. He stood looking at the door, butterflies in his stomach. So, he was inside now. There was no way back to his room except via the thief's route: out the window and through the snow.

Shit, he thought. *I've got to get rid of these boots. I've left footprints in the yard.* Peak Performance boots? Not exactly cheap. What burglar would wear heavy boots like that?

Then he told himself: *Stay focused or this whole thing could go to hell.* That was always a danger. Just remain focused, keep your mind on the task at hand, like a ski jumper. So what was the task? Oh, right. The mattress. And didn't Gjessing talk about it as if there was only one mattress? Knut wasn't sure. There had been something ambiguous about Gjessing's tone of voice that he hadn't fully understood.

There were more rooms upstairs. A guest room with a sofa bed from the '70s. It had a mattress on slats, open underneath. He looked but found nothing. He glanced inside an office and a room lined with bookshelves. There he saw newer books than in the living room—book club editions from decades ago, piles of newspapers, and lithographs hanging on one wall that had no bookcases. Prints by artists that might be well known, though he had no clue who they were.

Gjessing's bedroom had the only bed with a separate mattress. The room smelled of licorice, pipe tobacco, and time gone by. Two photos of his wife were on the nightstand. Clearly at least fifty years had passed between the two pictures. In the black-and-white photo, she was young, wearing a hat tilted flirtatiously, with a glint in her eye, at the beginning of a long life. In the other photo, she was sitting in a chair, smiling. It was the same smile as in the first picture, except that her lips were now on the verge of disappearing. Above the bed hung their wedding photo. Gjessing was shockingly young, without a single wrinkle. He looked so proud, as if he'd achieved something no one else had ever done before. He was a pioneer, an explorer of new territory, a man who had invented love.

The bed was neatly made up with a colorful patchwork quilt on top. Knut tore off the quilt and threw it on the floor along with the duvet and pillow. Then he ran his hands over the mattress. A thin mattress with coiled springs that were undoubtedly a bear to sleep on. Maybe a little softer than the mattress Gjessing had given Knut in his room, but not much. From the outside he couldn't feel anything except the coiled springs.

There's got to be an opening somewhere, thought Knut, turning the mattress over. The bottom surface was just as smooth and even as the top. No rips or slits anywhere. The only seams were along the edges, and they seemed solid and machine-stitched. The mattress had never been opened. He was positive about that. He picked it up to shake it. No indication that any money was hidden inside.

Then he lifted up the bed frame, but found nothing under there either. He pulled the cover off the duvet, which had only down inside.

He also carefully examined the pillow and quilt with the same result. Finally, he remade Gjessing's bed and left the bedroom.

A steep stairway led up to the attic. The steps creaked under his feet. The light didn't work in the attic. He took out his cell and switched on the flashlight. At first glance there didn't seem to be anything but newspapers. Gjessing was apparently a newspaper collector, or used to be. Stacks and stacks of old issues of *Adresseavisen* reached up to the ceiling beams all the way to the very back of the space. Knut was about to leave when he saw it. Under five or six piles of papers, not far from the stairs, was an old mattress. Excitedly he tossed the newspapers aside, pulled out the mattress, and discovered the rip running across the top of it.

Knut Andersen Stang—unorganized, cynical, and romantic, stressed and fearing for his life, with an exhausting grief over the death of his friend hovering over everything he did—felt his heart lurch, pressing against his chest.

Had he found the money? Was he saved?

All of a sudden he began thinking about the red-haired girl. Why? He couldn't get the sight of her freckles out of his mind. Then he realized that this wasn't just about the money. It wasn't just about escaping Sving's clutches. It was a question of getting free, of being able to start over, do things differently than he had in a very long time. This could give him the opportunity to get to know her better. Maybe it was a path to his salvation. It might somehow give meaning to the circumstances that were threatening to consume him, the sorrow and guilt he felt at being alive while Jonas was dead. Maybe it was for her sake that he'd survived Sving's assault. But she was pregnant, and he had no idea who she was. He didn't even know her name. Maybe he would find out.

He felt a prickling sensation down his back as he looked at the mattress. Breathing fast, he leaned down and stuffed both hands inside the gap in the mattress, spreading open the edges. He shone the light inside, but didn't see anything. He lifted up the mattress and shook it. Then he tore off the whole cover. He cut his fingers on the sharp threads of the material, but he didn't stop until one side of the mattress was completely bare. Then he inspected the springs inside. They trembled like peals of laughter. Finally, he caught sight of it. A blue slip of paper was attached to one of the springs. He took it off and held it up to the light from his phone. He saw the picture of a man he remembered from his schoolbooks. Wasn't it Fridtjof Nansen? He'd heard that the explorer's portrait used to be on Norwegian banknotes, but he'd never seen it before. This piece of paper claimed to be worth ten kroner. But he doubted that. Not anymore.

Gjessing once kept money inside here, Knut thought. *But it must have been long ago. There must be another mattress somewhere.*

He spent the rest of that evening and a large part of the night searching the house for the mattress. But he couldn't find it anywhere. He cleaned up after himself, then crawled back out through the kitchen window, twisting his ankle as he went down the ladder. He took the ladder back to the garage. Afterward, he used a broom to erase his footprints in the snow, hoping that there would be more snow over the next few days. He searched the basement and found the mattress that Gjessing had loaned him. But it too was empty.

Back in his room, Knut lay in bed brooding. Which was not something he normally did.

He had a sudden urge to cut up his own mattress.

That wily bastard. Maybe he doesn't have any money. Maybe that banknote I found up in the attic is all he's got left. Maybe he spent all his savings on these trips to London. In that case, I'm back to square one.

Knut rolled onto his side. He was still wearing the coveralls. And the boots.

He got up, changed his clothes, and went into town. In the third bar, he finally scored. But it wasn't coke.

Outside he paused on the sidewalk, in the midst of the wind and the snowdrifts, and looked at the pills in his hand. Jon Blund had it all wrong, he thought. If you want to fall asleep, you don't need sand or coke or snow. Sleep comes in solid form. He went home and took the pills. At last they worked like they were supposed to.

Fortunately, he had no dreams.

He slept like a rock. And woke up with a jolt. The garbage cans were being emptied in the driveway outside. It was eight o'clock. No sun. Daylight outside, but just barely. He felt like shit. It occurred to him that he hadn't eaten anything since yesterday morning. He got up to look in the fridge. No milk. He remembered emptying the big fridge down in the basement the day before. So he wouldn't find anything there either. He sat down on his bed with the box of honey puffed wheat and ate it by the handful. The cereal clung to his lips and the inside of his cheeks. Some landed on the sheet. The air in the room was as stifling as his thoughts.

He got up and went over to the window. The garbage truck was moving on to the next house with a huffing and puffing garbageman hanging on to the back. A brisk wind was blowing through the hedge and whirling the snow into the air. The big trees across the street were swaying. Knut could remember a time when he enjoyed staying indoors on a day like this. He would have made hot chocolate. Worn his slippers all day long. But now he didn't care where he was.

Suddenly he caught sight of her. She was passing Gjessing's driveway, with her fat dog plodding along behind her. Again she had a book under her arm. Her coat flapped around her legs. The cap she wore was different, made of gray felt with a rose of the same material. Was she humming as she walked along? Was this her usual route? She'd walked past two days in a row now. Did she do that every day? He'd never seen her here before. But he rarely got up this early. Maybe she came this way because she wanted to talk to him again. See if he might be in the yard. Run into him.

Knut was naked. That was how he'd slept. The dog had stopped to pee. She waited for it, a bit too impatiently, in his opinion. Did he have time to get dressed and run outside? He doubted it. That would be too obvious. Wouldn't it?

Then his phone rang. He'd forgotten to turn it off before he fell asleep. Automatically he turned away from the window and searched his bed. It was under the pillow. He didn't recognize the number. He went back to look out the window as he took the call. The dog had left what looked like a yellow question mark in the snow. She was gone.

"Am I speaking to Knut Andersen Stang?"

"That's me."

"My name is Thorvald Jensen. I'm with the Trondheim police. The team that handles violent and sexual crimes. I'm investigating the death of Jonas Fredly Holm."

Knut sat down on the edge of the bed. Hunched forward.

"Yes?" he said.

"First, let me offer my condolences. As I understand it, the two of you were close friends."

"We were college classmates. I didn't meet him until I moved here to Trondheim last fall."

"So you've known him only six months or so?"

"Something like that."

"Yet witnesses have described you as being very close."

"Jonas," he said and suddenly felt overcome. A lump settled in his throat, making it hard for him to talk. What he said sounded stiff and formal compared to what he was feeling. "Jonas and I liked each other. So yes, we were good friends. Or rather, we would have been if there'd been more time."

"How did you happen to hear about his death?"

"I read about it in the newspaper."

"I see. You may be able to give us some help with the investigation. We'd like you to come over for an interview, if that's possible."

"Oh, er, sure. When?"

"What about tomorrow morning? Nine o'clock?"

Knut thought about the girl with the dog. She'd walked past early on both days.

"Could we make it twelve?" he replied.

Jensen was silent for a moment. It sounded as if he were leafing through some papers.

"Twelve. That's fine. Check in on the ground floor, and I'll come and get you. One more thing. We've started working on mapping out the movements of everyone in Jonas's circle of friends. That means we don't yet have a suspect. This is just something we have to do. I'm sure you understand. Can you tell me where you were on the night of February 15?"

Shit! Knut tried to remember. That was the night he'd gone dancing and didn't score. Why hadn't he brought that girl home with him? Then he'd at least have an alibi. What now? Did they think he had something to do with Jonas's death?

"I was in town. First with some guys, but Jonas didn't come along that night. He wanted to chill out at home. I got a little drunk. Don't remember everything. But I went home early. My landlord might be able to confirm that. Guttorm Gjessing."

He said that part about Gjessing just to win some time. He doubted the old man had heard him come home that night. But now the police would have to talk to him, and Gjessing didn't live in 2011 like everybody else. He didn't have a computer or a cell phone. So he could be Knut's alibi at least until he returned home. If he was lucky, the police would track down that crook Sving before then.

It occurred to him that maybe he should put all his cards on the table. He'd thought about doing that before, but each time he'd dismissed the idea. If he went to the police, he'd have to admit to his own role in the matter. There was no way he could avoid mentioning the theft of the cocaine. And what about the break-in at Gjessing's place? He could have lived with making a confession. It might have even given him some form of relief. He could have done it for Jonas. Yet he was positive that people like that slimebag they'd stolen the coke from had many more friends than just Sving. He wouldn't feel any safer if he squealed to the police. From what he'd heard, it was no picnic to be a snitch in prison, and once he got out, he'd still be easy prey. Talking to the police wasn't going to erase his debt to the drug dealers. That much he knew. So there was only one way out. He had to get the money. He needed to buy himself more time. If the police found their way to Sving on their own, that would be fine, but he couldn't help them.

"Guttorm Gjessing? Was that his name?" said the detective on the phone.

"Yes, but he's in London for a few days."

"Do you have his cell number?"

"I don't think he has one."

"No cell phone?"

"He's old. Over ninety, I think. He should never have gone to London by himself." Knut had to hold back a laugh. It wouldn't be appropriate.

"We'll talk more about this tomorrow, Stang. Twelve o'clock?"

"Sure. Twelve o'clock."

He put the phone down on his desk. There he caught sight of the book he'd borrowed from Gjessing. He looked at the dark brown color of the spine and the faint, shadowy pattern on the leather. He picked up the book and leafed through it. Then he had an idea.

If she shows up again, I'll do it, he thought.

Then he went into town. This time he found some cocaine. Enough to get him through the clouds of the rest of the day and far into the night. Luckily he didn't run into any of his classmates from the law school. At one point he thought he saw Sving, standing at a bar with a pint of beer between him and a tall woman with big, intense eyes. But it could have been somebody else.

He left and stayed out of trouble the rest of the evening.

His cell phone rang, playing the French national anthem. He didn't remember programming that for the ringtone. Must have been drunk. He also didn't remember setting the alarm to ring at seven.

The clothes he'd worn yesterday were draped over the end of his bed. He gave them a careful inspection but then took clean clothes out of the wardrobe. It was clear that he'd need to do laundry very soon.

Taking the clean clothes along, he went out in the hall to the bathroom. He showered and then got dressed. It was seven thirty. Way too early. He still hadn't bought any groceries. He hoped he'd managed to eat something the night before, but he couldn't remember. He was famished. He drank two glasses of water from the sink in his room. Then he went over to look out the window. He stared down at the hedge where he could get a glimpse of the street before it vanished behind the neighbor's fence. *I wonder if she's a creature of habit*, he thought. *Maybe this is part of her regular route. Maybe I haven't seen her before because I'm almost never out of bed by eight. She probably has a job. Takes her dog for a walk before work, always the same route.* Knut considered this possibility, but he couldn't be sure. She didn't look like a creature of habit, but he wouldn't mind if she was.

His back was stiff. And he was feeling excited too. He knew what he was doing wouldn't help him in the least. Yet he couldn't stop staring out the window. And there she was. Fluttering past the gap between the hedge and the fence, like an unsteady image from a handheld camera. What was she wearing today? A green coat?

Knut put on his down jacket, grabbed the book, and went out.

He ran into her as she turned onto the street.

"Hey. It's you." Why was he out of breath?

"Were you just sitting there, waiting for me?" she asked.

"Why do you say that?"

"You started talking a split second before you looked up. So you must have already seen me."

"That's creepy. I'm starting to see why you scare people."

"I don't really mind. I'd kind of like it if you were waiting for me."

"Really?"

"I've never had a stalker before."

They laughed.

"I saw you through the hedge. But I was actually on my way out. I'm not trying to stalk you."

"You're carrying a book. Is that a coincidence too? On your way to the library?"

She showed him the book she was holding. A detective novel with a yellow cover.

"Okay. You got me. I was waiting for you. I wanted to talk to you again."

"Shall we go to your place?"

"You want to?"

"No, I just said that because I'm so naïve. All of us redheads are."

He stood there staring at her. Green eyes. Red hair. Green coat.

"You're about as naïve as Dr. House," he said.

"Who's that?"

"He's from a TV show."

"I don't watch TV," she said.

She stayed with him a couple of hours. They drank tea. That's all. It felt right. Then she said she needed to get to work. She'd make excuses, saying that she had an unexpected dentist appointment, but she couldn't stay away all day. She didn't want to make any promises about meeting him again. Just said that sometimes she walked past his place in the morning. Sometimes she didn't.

"But you've walked past three days in a row," he couldn't help saying.

"So maybe it'll be a while before I'm back here again."

He tried to think of something to say. Felt like he was about to lose her. Just when everything was going so well.

"Would you like to borrow my book?" he asked, pointing at the volume lying on the desk. "I finished reading it, and I think you'd like it."

She looked at the book.

"*The Anatomy of Melancholy* by Robert Burton. That sounds like my kind of book, but . . ."

"You can keep it."

"You can't just give it away."

"Sure I can."

"But you don't know if—"

"Do you want it or not?"

She gave him a long look.

"Okay, but I'm just borrowing it," she said, picking up the book. "I take walks in the evening too," she said as she put on her green coat.

He looked at her stomach, wanting to ask if the baby's father was still in the picture, but he couldn't think of the right way to say it.

Then she left.

He sat in his room gasping for air. He'd screwed up everything. He'd acted just like the stalker they'd joked about. "But you've walked past three days in a row," he'd said. Shit. As if he was keeping track. And Gjessing's book. Why had he given it to her? So stupid. So desperate. He really wasn't himself. But he consoled himself with the fact that the book was old and worthless, though clearly it had value for Gjessing. He shouldn't have given it away. Luckily she'd said it was only a loan. And the fact that she planned to return it also meant that he'd have a chance to see her again.

Detective Inspector Thorvald Jensen, a slightly pudgy and serious officer, had pushed him pretty hard about the alibi. But Knut had acquitted himself well. Jonas was killed around 11:00 P.M., and at that time Knut had still been in town. And he'd even come up with the name of the place where he was. If he was lucky, there would be witnesses who remembered seeing him there.

On his way home from the police station he was feeling all right. He had a line of cocaine left from the day before. It was in a plastic bag in his pocket. So he snorted it on his way through the park by the fortress, after stopping for a beer.

When he got home he found a dead rat on the stairs. The bloodstains on the top step indicated it had been brought there alive and then killed. It looked like the pet rat that Jonas used to carry inside his shirt. On top of the lifeless, bloody animal someone had placed a Louisville Slugger bat. A note was stuck in the doorframe. He pulled it out and read: *Hope the cash collecting is going well.*

The handwriting looked like it had been done by a child.

Knut crumpled up the note and stuck it in his pocket. Then he leaned his forehead against the door and felt his stomach clench. He wanted to scream at the top of his lungs and kick at the door, but he managed to go inside before doing anything that would attract the neighbors' attention.

Once inside, he kicked at the teak table so hard that the empty cereal bowl flew over the bed and struck the wall on the other side of the room, where it split in half and fell to the floor. Then he leaned forward, grabbed hold of the bed frame, and gasped for air.

A short time later he went back outside with a plastic bag from the supermarket. He picked up the rat and put it in the garbage. For a moment he considered saving it as evidence if he did decide to tell the police about everything. But no.

He picked up the baseball bat from the steps and took it into his room. There he swung it in the air a few times before deciding on a target. Then he aimed several blows at the table he'd just kicked, smashing it to pieces. He swung the bat so hard the tiles on the tabletop shattered, and he didn't stop until he'd made two big dents in the pine floor under the table. Fortunately, he managed to stop before he attacked the desk too. At that point he started to cry, sobbing loudly. Then he tossed aside the bat before he stumbled over to the bed and collapsed.

The next day Gjessing came back from London.

"If the kitchen window weren't broken, I might not even have noticed they'd been here."

Gjessing didn't look sad. His cheeks were just a little more flushed than usual.

Knut had asked him about his trip to London. It had almost been ruined by the snowstorms raging over all of northern Europe the past week, with lots of air traffic delays and canceled football matches. But Gjessing had been lucky, and he got to see his beloved QPR team play. He'd had a good trip and seemed really pleased until he abruptly changed the subject back to the break-in. Wasn't it strange that he should be talking about that with his lodger? Knut wasn't sure.

"Nothing was stolen. Hardly anything was even touched. It's just a little tidier than I remember. That's all. Who breaks in to somebody's house to tidy it up?"

Knut had to smile. He was glad that Gjessing could at least see some humor in the situation.

"So nothing was stolen? That's odd," he said, taking a big swig of the whiskey that Gjessing had bought at Heathrow, as if he knew he'd need something stronger than port when he got home.

"Well, my TV isn't exactly the latest model."

Knut looked at the old TV set. It was brown. That said a lot about it.

Gjessing went on:

"I don't have all those newfangled devices that burglars are looking for. And I sold all the silver after my wife died. But they should have . . ." Gjessing raised his wineglass, which now held whiskey, and took a sip. Then he cleared his throat and stared at Knut.

"They should have what?"

"I've got valuables here. They may be hidden, but they're here."

"The money in the mattress?"

Knut thought asking such direct questions would make him seem less guilty, like a man who wasn't trying to hide anything.

Gjessing nodded, but Knut wasn't sure whether the old man was answering his question or thinking about something else entirely. He couldn't rid himself of the feeling that his landlord harbored suspicions about him, in spite of the good act he was putting on. Maybe because of the simple fact that he was here, that he'd knocked on Gjessing's door to ask him about his trip to London. A week ago he would never have done that. Not without some ulterior motive. Gjessing was old, but he wasn't stupid. He must have sensed that something was going on.

"Have you talked to the police?" asked Knut.

"The police?"

"Shouldn't you report the break-in?"

"What good would that do?"

"It's customary to report a burglary. Don't you want to get the thieves off the street?"

"Yes, if that would be the end result. But I don't have much faith in the police. They'd hardly pay any attention to something like this."

"Aren't you afraid the thieves will come back? What about your money?"

"The thieves—or thief—didn't find anything valuable here in my house. Why would they come back?"

I'm not going to get anything more out of him here, Knut thought. *He's never going to tell me where that mattress is, at least not directly. But maybe he'll let it slip out if I make him think about something else. Maybe we need a change of scene.*

"Why don't you go fishing anymore?" he asked then.

Gjessing's eyes lit up at the question.

"It's my body. I don't dare go out in a boat alone. My balance isn't what it used to be. My knees give me trouble. And then there's the arthritis in my fingers. I can't even put bait on the hook anymore."

"But you still know how to do it, don't you?"

"Of course I do. It's all up here." Gjessing drummed his index finger against his forehead.

"You could tell me what to do. I could be your hands for you."

"What do you mean?"

The old man's expression told Knut that he knew very well what he meant.

"I could go fishing with you. You tell me what to do, and I'll do all the work. All you have to do is sit in the boat, nice and easy. What do you say?"

Gjessing considered the offer for a long time before speaking.

"When?" he finally asked.

Knut didn't need long to consider. The deadline that Sving had set was approaching way too fast.

"Tomorrow," he said.

"Bad weather," said Gjessing. "But it's supposed to blow over in a couple of days. Shall we say Monday?"

"Monday, February 21? Sure, why not."

That's the day before I have to pay Sving the money, Knut thought. *This fishing trip better loosen up the old guy's vocal cords, and fast.*

The following day he stayed in bed. Slept, sweated, took large quantities of painkillers, experiencing emotions he didn't even know he had.

What fucking bad luck he'd had. Goddamn it.

Why did they have to have cocaine at that party? What good was it? Why had he stolen it? And so much of it!

A few weeks ago he wasn't even interested in drugs. He drank. He was a happy guy. He didn't need that kind of shit. There was something about this whole mess that he couldn't explain. He hadn't really had a good reason to try it. And then he'd had a crazy idea—or rather, they'd had a crazy idea. He and Jonas. And now Jonas was dead, and he was almost dead too. How did that guy with the big smile find out they were the ones who took the stuff? He probably just guessed. There were lots of people at that party, coming and going. No way to know for sure. He'd guessed. And then they'd beaten up Jonas, beaten him up too hard. So now he was the only one left for them to go after. People like Smiley Face and Sving were first and foremost businessmen. They'd rather have the money than kill someone. Jonas's death must have been an accident. That was his only hope. The money could set him free. Give him a second chance.

Why was all this happening at the same time he'd fallen in love? How could he even be thinking about love in the middle of everything going on? There must be something wrong with him. There was no doubt about that. But he really was in love. That didn't happen to him often, not like this, that he could sit over a cup of tea with a woman for several hours and afterward feel like they'd made love. Had he ever felt this way before?

Knut knew that he had to find a solution. Get the money and get out of here. And he needed to do something for Jonas. He had no idea what that might be, but he had to do it. Then something good might still come out of all this. *It's a test*, he thought. *It's a fucking test.*

Then he spent a long time thinking about Guttorm Gjessing. What did he need to do to get the old guy to reveal his secret? He seemed clearheaded enough. But when it came to that mattress, he became secretive and slightly confused. Did it even exist? Yes, it had to. The money had to be somewhere. It wasn't like Knut to have such doubts. That wasn't like him at all. Some of his old self had to be left inside. His former optimism and hope. That insane feeling of hope.

The old Mercedes coughed weakly a few times before the engine finally got going. By the time they'd left the city limits behind and accelerated up the road south of Trondheim, the car was purring contentedly.

Knut drove, with Gjessing dozing next to him in the passenger seat. It was just past seven in the morning. They'd started early, at his request. At first Gjessing had wanted to wait and see how the weather was going to be, but luckily the wind had subsided by morning.

They didn't talk much until they'd passed Orkdal. It was going to take them almost two hours to get to Hitra.

"They hide out in the scree," said Gjessing. "In the big, stony slopes down in the deep. Where we're headed, you won't fall into the water. If you drown there, your body will slowly sink into utter darkness, to be eaten up by pollack and ling."

"Not a good way to go," Knut remarked.

"I don't know," said Gjessing. "You'd be dead long before the fish started gnawing at you. Personally, I wouldn't mind going back to nature that way. It might be the only way that this old carcass of mine could be of any use. There's a lot of nutrition in an old man's heart." He laughed as if he meant what he said.

"What does it feel like to be old?" asked Knut, genuinely interested in what Gjessing would say.

"It's fine. I don't have any other choice. You can't go back. Life is only a one-way street, you know."

"What you said about the four bodily fluids. Do you believe that?"

"Hmm. I guess it's just one of many ways to talk about human beings. When it comes right down to it, we're really just stories."

"Stories?"

"Stories, memories . . ."

"I don't think I'm following you."

Gjessing looked at Knut and laughed.

"I just told you that in life you can't go back, but actually you can. I do it every day. Everything's inside here. Old stories. There's nothing else left of me." Gjessing tapped his forehead like he'd done before, back home in his living room. "We're stories, not bodily fluids or hormones. Keep that in mind! And stories are more sinister, less reliable. In a story everything can always be turned upside down. Things shift and change."

When they reached the Hitra tunnel, the traffic was backed up. The tunnel had been closed because a semi carrying farmed salmon had overturned at the lowest point inside. They had to wait almost an hour before they could drive through. It was approaching ten by the time they reached Gjessing's boat. It was moored in a small marina near Kvenvær, a place that swarmed with Germans, who arrived in the summertime in RVs with big freezers. But right now, in the winter, all was quiet.

Knut had grown up spending his summer vacations in boats, so he'd have no problem maneuvering Gjessing's fifteen-foot wooden fishing boat.

They'd found everything they'd need in the garage, so they were well equipped. Good knives, a long rope, a sturdy grapnel and chain, excellent fishing rods, a sea chart, heavy nylon cords, and an echo sounder. Gjessing's nephew had once given it to him as a Christmas present, but the old sea wolf insisted it wasn't necessary.

"I've got the seafloor imprinted up here," he claimed, tapping his forehead.

Gjessing leaned against a bollard at the end of the pier to watch Knut carry all the gear from the car to the boat. When that was done, he went on board.

There he took up position at the tiller, insisting on steering since he was the one, after all, who knew the best fishing spots. So seaman Knut Andersen Stang took his place on the bench along the side of the boat. He sat there studying the old man, whose eyes were the same color as the variegated gray of the sky overhead. Gjessing headed the boat out of the archipelago toward the open sea.

That was when Knut suddenly felt his stomach turn over. He'd never been seasick before, but he had an urge to lean over the side to throw up.

"My favorite spot isn't very far out!" shouted Gjessing over the thudding of the motor and the rushing of the wind. He was sucking his pipe, which had probably gone out a few minutes ago.

"That's where I pulled in that huge ling. It's on the outer edge of an underwater crevasse where a big cliff drops off at least thirteen hundred feet."

No sooner had he said those words than they heard a tremendous boom behind them. It sounded like a big explosion coming from shore. Knut turned around. At first he didn't see anything beyond the rocks. But a moment later black smoke began rising up in the sky from the area of the marina. *What could that be?* he wondered. He thought about Gjessing's Mercedes. No, that was parked a good distance away. No matter what it was, it had nothing to do with them. No doubt some sort of exercise. Maybe the Home Guard.

Knut turned back to look at Gjessing, who was still gazing out toward sea. No indication that the partly deaf old man had noticed what had happened behind them. Reassured by Gjessing's calm expression, Knut stayed where he was, watching the dark smoke fill the sky behind them like a highly localized storm.

They continued on for a ways, the waves getting bigger. Eventually they could see the foam from the underwater rocks, which at low tide lay just below the surface. Gjessing elegantly maneuvered past and stopped alongside the rocks, about a hundred yards away. Then he stood up abruptly, standing there on his wobbly legs, with his feet wide apart and the tiller in his hand, pointing at the anchor, which was lying in the bottom of the boat.

"When I say the word, drop it over the side," he said.

Knut lifted the heavy anchor, which had to weigh at least forty pounds, and set it on the gunwale. He pretended to be checking to make sure the chain was properly attached and fastened to the winch screwed onto the boat.

He looked at Gjessing, who was still surveying the rocks, presumably trying to find just the right position. His internal echo sounder was on the alert.

Then, just as Gjessing turned to look at the skerries one more time, Knut got out his fishing knife and sliced through the rope just below the chain.

Then he threw the grapnel overboard.

Gjessing heard the splash and looked at him in horror.

"Did I tell you to drop anchor?" he asked, narrowing his eyes. His pipe fell out of his mouth, and something that looked like sea spray appeared on his lips.

"The rope broke," said Knut, holding up the end.

"Broke?!" Gjessing practically shouted. "Broke?!"

Then he seemed to reconsider. As if he'd realized something. A strange calm came over his face. The decrepit old man leaned forward and turned off the motor. Then he stood there at the stern, and it was as if he knew what was about to happen. He was waiting for it. When Knut leaped toward him and gave him a shove in the chest so that he toppled over against the gunwale, he was almost sure he saw Gjessing smile.

"The money in the mattress," Knut said. "You have to tell me where it is."

"So it was you," said the old man. He sat with his back to the gunwale, his arm stretched out along the edge. "You were the one who broke in? I thought as much."

"Yes, it was me."

"What sort of trouble are you in?"

"Just tell me where you put the mattress with the money that you've been talking about."

"Sorry," said the old man. But he didn't seem sorry at all. Again a smile slid across his face.

"Are you laughing at me?"

"No. I'm laughing, but not at you. There's nothing laughable about you, my boy."

"Maybe you don't think I'm serious."

"Oh, I know you are."

"So tell me. Tell me where the money is, and I'll let you go back with me."

He grabbed hold of the old man's jacket and lifted him up so he was sitting on the gunwale, swaying.

"And if I don't?" asked Gjessing calmly.

"If you don't, there won't be any more trips to London for you."

"I've started to lose faith that QPR will make it back on top," said Gjessing.

This time he was definitely laughing.

"You think this is a game? Huh? Do you?"

He flung the old man around so he landed on his back in the bottom of the boat. Then he launched himself forward so he was sitting on top of him.

"You old bastard! That money would save me!"

Save me from what? Knut thought to himself. What was he talking about? Was this how he would be saved?

He had an urge to punch the old guy, but then he saw it.

Gjessing was lying very still, his face as white as in a black-and-white movie. *What the fuck? What have I done?* shouted a voice inside of Knut. The old man had hit his head on the bottom of the boat when Knut tackled him with his full weight. Knut put his hand under Gjessing's neck and felt the blood. Then he opened his hand and slapped Gjessing in the face several times. But there was no life left in him. Guttorm Gjessing was dead. All those ninety years of his were now gone.

Knut howled. He tipped his head back and screamed at the clouds up above. Then he got up in a daze. The nausea had subsided, to be replaced by numbness, or maybe it was a bizarre form of relief, dark and paralyzing. It was all over now. Everything ended here.

He put his arms around the old man and lifted him up. His body weighed almost nothing, as if only his soul had kept him here on this earth the past few years. Then Knut threw him over the side.

"That was the kind of death you wanted," he said aloud. "Wasn't it?"

The thought was intoxicating. Was this what Gjessing had wanted? Was this his personal wish? One last trip out to sea, a burial on the seafloor? What did it matter? Knut stood there, watching the bubbles rise to the surface at the spot where Gjessing had disappeared. Were they trying to tell him something?

That was when he noticed the sound. A furiously roaring motor and the slapping of a big hull against the water. He realized that he'd been hearing it for a while. It was getting louder. He turned around and saw what the sound was coming from. It was a speedboat, at least twenty-five feet long.

It was heading straight toward him at full speed. Knut stood up to his full height, waving at whoever was steering the other boat, but he couldn't see anyone on board, and it didn't change course. It couldn't be more than a hundred yards off now, and it was definitely going to collide with him. He stumbled over to the dashboard but couldn't find the key to start the engine. Gjessing must have stuck it in his pocket. So it was now several hundred fathoms deep. He spun around and grabbed the biggest life vest, which was on top of the blue mattress on the bench along the gunwale. A wild thought occurred to him as he put it on.

No, that couldn't be possible, he thought.

Then he jumped into the sea.

A second later the big boat struck the smaller one. The speedboat rose up from the water in an arc. It turned 180 degrees in the air, like a breaching whale, and crashed back down about fifty yards farther on. Gjessing's boat, where he had stood only seconds before, was split in half by the impact, and soon both parts were on their way down to join Gjessing. A crazy thought occurred to Knut.

If I hadn't killed the old man, he'd be dead anyway right now. I stole five minutes from him. Five minutes. That's all.

Knut Andersen Stang floated there in the life vest, feeling the icy cold of the water. He wouldn't survive here for long.

Who the hell had run him down?

16

Two weeks after it happened . . .

O*dd Singsaker always* sat with his back to the door whenever he conducted an interview in this room. It gave him the upper hand, psychologically.

Now he was sitting on the other side of the room with his back to the wall.

The room was still white. The size was the same. But it felt smaller, more claustrophobic. Only the ventilation system seemed unchanged. The air was just as bad as always.

Next to Singsaker sat Attorney Gregersen, moving his papers into neat stacks and lining up three pens parallel to his notepad. Singsaker studied the man's hands. Long, thin fingers, perfectly manicured nails, the wedding ring that was a tad too big so that it was loose on his finger. It looked as if it might slide off if he wasn't careful.

Kurt Melhus sat across from them. His hair had grown grayer with age than Singsaker's. Whiter.

The white hair of a philosopher, thought Singsaker.

The Philosopher. Mr. Gray Matter. There was something so innocent about the nickname. That's what made it so deceptive.

The two policemen, contemporaries, looked at each other and smiled.

"What do you make of the term *quintessence*?" asked Melhus, fidgeting with the tape recorder that sat on the table between them.

"Has the interview started?" asked Singsaker.

Melhus paused to consider.

"Yes, I suppose it has," he said. He pressed a button and cleared his throat. Then he read off the day's date and who was present in the room.

"Quintessence. You've heard the term, haven't you?"

"Of course. It means the core of the matter, or something like that."

"Today, yes. But the word comes from alchemy, the prescientific chemistry of the Middle Ages. It's the fifth element."

"What are you getting at?"

"I like to warm up. Don't you?"

Now Gregersen intervened.

"If this isn't relevant to the case, then I suggest we move on to more factual issues."

"This is a complicated case," said Melhus calmly. "I don't yet have a full picture of what is relevant and what isn't. Do you, Singsaker?"

"I agree that it's complicated."

"The factual circumstances are starting to become quite clear. It's the meaning behind the various events that we're looking for. Right? The motives, causes, and connections."

Melhus paused, but no one spoke, so he went on.

"The strange thing about this case is the way in which completely unrelated events become strangely intertwined. On the surface, it seems to be random. And there are undoubtedly a number of sheer coincidences, but still. What we're looking for are the connections. As you know, Singsaker, I have a weakness for Aristotle. In his teachings about physics, he says that all things are composed of four elements. Do you know about this?"

"Sure. I took a philosophy class back in my day."

"The four elements are earth, fire, air, and water. All real things, but since there was no such thing as an empty void, Aristotle maintained that outer space had to be filled with something. He called this ether. And this is what the alchemists termed quintessence, the fifth element."

"I understand," said Singsaker, who was amused at the long introduction that Melhus was making. He dreaded the moment when he would get to the point.

"In many ways, our case can be viewed as multiple cases. Multiple different stories that coincide and lead to one hell of a mess. Do you agree?"

"Mess?"

"Maybe that's a rather insensitive term to use. A tragedy. Shall we call it that?"

Singsaker merely looked at Melhus and nodded. Melhus was good with words, yet he'd never be able to get anywhere close to describing what Singsaker felt about this matter.

"But what interests me is all the things that bring these different stories of ours together, the space in between them, the 'fifth element' of the case, the flow of events, the coincidences that cause things to evade us. No matter how much we wish to understand a crime and human nature, we aren't always successful because frequently they can only be understood in a hazy context marked by coincidences. The job of the investigator is to move around in this space between the various events, in the lost time, the unknown rooms, in the silence between incidents. And that's where you and Jensen come in."

"Are you saying we're the quintessence?"

"No, but it's what you're looking for. So, to get back to the case: When did the two of you realize how complicated and intertwined the case on Hitra actually was?"

"The first connection that we—or rather, Jensen—discovered was between the boat wreck and a case the police were already working on. The homicide in Rosenborg Park."

"The law student who was beaten and thrown off a balcony?"

"That's right."

"Please explain."

"Jensen recognized him."

"Let's go back to the beginning. I'd like you to describe in your own words exactly what happened when you and Jensen arrived on Hitra."

"We got to the island around 5:30 P.M. There we were told that there were two survivors of the boat wreck out in open waters, and that they were under the care of the chief physician at the Hitra clinic. Subsequently, we drove over there. At that time the site of the explosion had already been secured by the Hitra fire department.

"At the clinic we found out that both survivors had escaped the accident with only minor injuries. Both were going to be kept under observation for a few hours, but it wasn't necessary to move either of them to Orkdal or St. Olav Hospital. Both would be discharged from the clinic during the course of the evening and would be able to leave on their own."

"At that point did you know anything about the nature of the accident?"

"Yes, an officer from the sheriff's department met us at the clinic. He told us there were witnesses to the accident."

"And who were they?"

"Two fishermen on their way to an island farther out had seen a big motorboat moving at high speed collide with a smaller fishing boat. That's all they saw because they were far away from the actual collision site, but they could tell it was serious, and they went right over to help. They pulled the two survivors into their boat and notified the police and the coast guard."

"Did they mention any other people?"

"They were too far away to determine whether anyone else was in the boats. But one of the survivors, the young student, told them an elderly man had been with him. They made an initial search for the man. The coast guard continued the search when they later arrived on the scene. But by the time we got to the clinic, everyone assumed that he was gone."

"And this was the man named Guttorm Gjessing?"

"That's right. A retired physician from Trondheim, ninety years old. When Jensen heard the name, he decided that the first survivor he wanted to talk to was the young student."

"Knut Andersen Stang?"

"Yes. He had been taken to one of the rooms in the clinic. It wasn't until we entered his room that I realized Jensen knew who he was. I remember what he said to the student: 'Who would have thought we'd meet again so soon, and under such circumstances?' Stang was a quite a large young man. He looked pale, and his expression was glum, but he still managed to crack a smile. He didn't seem surprised by Jensen's words. He'd probably been told who was coming to see him. Then Jensen said something about how accidents seemed to follow him. First his friend fell from the balcony of an apartment building. Then he almost drowned on a fishing trip. Stang didn't offer any comment, and Jensen then asked him if the man in the boat with him was his landlord. When Stang nodded, Jensen asked him what he thought about the fact that the very man who was his alibi in the Rosenborg Park case had now disappeared into the sea. It was clear that Stang was no longer happy about Jensen's questions. I sat on a chair and listened without interrupting." At this point Singsaker took a brief pause.

"Because you weren't on duty, right?" said Melhus.

"I was not on duty."

"And maybe you were more interested in news about Felicia Stone?"

"Of course I was."

"So you would have preferred to go over to the site of the explosion?"

"To be honest, I really didn't know where I wanted to be. If your wife is missing and you fear that something serious might have happened to her, there's really only one place you want to be."

"And where's that?"

"Back home. Back home with her."

Melhus sighed heavily. Was it sympathy that Singsaker saw in his eyes? A vague memory of the camaraderie they'd had during that year in Horten?

"Let's go back to the clinic on Hitra. That's where you were, since you had no choice but to accompany Jensen. But at that point the two of you must have heard that Felicia's rental car had been found at the scene of the explosion."

Singsaker thought for a moment, decided he was on safe ground.

"Yes, by then we'd been told. I'm very sure about that. But the fire department and the rescue team had also told us that Felicia had not been found out there. So that wasn't where we should be searching for her. For my part, it seemed most sensible to go with Jensen as he carried out his job."

"All right. Let's continue there."

"Sure. Let me see now . . ."

Singsaker suddenly felt disoriented. That often happened to him if the conversation jumped around. That was a consequence of his brain injury, part of his illness that at some point might do him in. He closed his eyes for a moment and in his mind went back to the clinic on Hitra.

"Jensen questioned Stang about the accident. There wasn't much he could tell us. Only that he and Gjessing were getting ready to do some fishing when the other boat was suddenly coming toward them. Gjessing wasn't wearing a life vest, and he disappeared in the waves. I think that was when Jensen tried to catch Stang off guard. He knew things that I didn't. He asked Stang if he knew that someone had broken into Gjessing's house while he was in London. Stang asked Jensen how he knew about that. He seemed surprised and said something about Gjessing not wanting to report the break-in. Jensen said that Gjessing must have changed his mind, because he'd reported it to the police the day before. Jensen also said that the police were a bit surprised the old man had waited so long. But that happens now and then. Gjessing had apparently explained that he didn't consider it a serious matter, and nothing had been stolen. Then Jensen asked Stang who he thought Gjessing suspected of breaking in. Stang said he had no idea, and I could see these questions were making him uncomfortable."

Singsaker stopped to catch his breath before going on.

"Then Jensen told him straight out: 'It was you. Gjessing suspected you.' Stang tried to laugh it off. He said that Gjessing was an old fool, ninety years old and with little grip on reality. But Jensen was having none of it. He said that Gjessing had seemed quite lucid when he'd talked to him."

"From what I understand," said Melhus, "Stang didn't deny having been inside Gjessing's house."

"That's right. He said that he used to help Gjessing with things, and he assumed the police would find his fingerprints in the house."

"Can you tell me what happened after Jensen finished putting Stang through the wringer?"

"It was at that point that the officer from Hitra came in and asked to speak to Jensen outside the room.

"Both of us went with him.

"The office told us that the coast guard had found some interesting pieces of wreckage. More specifically, a blue mattress covered with sailcloth was found floating on the surface of the water. They figured it had come from the fishing boat. Upon closer examination, they found a large number of banknotes inside the mattress. Soaking wet and stuck together, but a considerable sum. Maybe close to half a million kroner." Singsaker picked up the pitcher of water on the table and filled his coffee cup.

"What did Jensen do with this information?" asked Melhus.

"We went back into the room and confronted Stang with the news. After some hesitation he admitted that Gjessing had talked about keeping money inside a mattress, but he hadn't realized the old man meant the mattress on the boat. He thought it was a mattress in his house in Trondheim. At that point Stang was no longer looking so confident. He was sweating. And it was clear he knew more than he was saying. But even though things were becoming obvious, and even though he had to realize what we were thinking, he didn't confess to the break-in. I almost felt sorry for him when we left the room again."

"Both of you are experienced police officers," said Melhus.

Singsaker didn't reply.

"Would it be correct to say that you should have known—no, maybe *known* is too strong of a word. Shouldn't both of you have sensed that the witness you'd just spoken to was suicidal?"

"In hindsight it's always easy to see things like that. I'd never met the individual in question before. Jensen ran a background check on him when he was working on the Jonas Fredly Holm case. But in that connection witnesses had described Stang as a cheerful young man. He was well liked, a bit irresponsible, but a nice guy, someone who would never hurt anyone. Personally, I thought there was something in his expression as he sat in the clinic bed. We were almost sure that he was the one who'd broken into Gjessing's house. He seemed desperate. And then he heard the news about the money that he'd missed. He'd probably been sitting on that blue mattress in Gjessing's boat on their way out to the fishing spot. It was like the old man had made a fool of him. With hindsight, I realized it was wrong for us to leave him there, all alone with his thoughts."

"When you say 'wrong' you don't mean in a legal sense, do you, Singsaker?" said Gregersen, who had been sitting in silence for a long time, just listening.

"Of course not. And besides, the police don't have the professional training to fully evaluate the psychological state of a witness. At that point Stang was a witness and nothing else. From a legal standpoint, and maybe even a moral one, there was nothing wrong with leaving him there."

"What did the two of you do after that?"

"We went to have a cup of coffee in the waiting room. Jensen filled me in on the Rosenborg Park case. I hadn't known much about it before listening to him question Stang. Then we discussed the interview we were going to do with the next witness."

"The man in the motorboat? Who was in the other room in the clinic?"

"That's right. But we never got that far. While we were sitting there, a nurse came running to find us. She said she'd heard a crash in Stang's room, and when she went in to see to him, she found him lying there with his wrists slashed. Jensen and I jumped up and ran to his room. And there we found him, just like the nurse had said. Blood was still gushing out over the sheet on the bed. He had knocked a pitcher of water off the nightstand, and it fell to the floor, presumably at the moment of death. That was the noise the nurse had heard. And the worst part was . . ." Singsaker took a cough drop out of the package he'd bought at the railway station a short time earlier.

"The worst part was?"

"The worst part was that he was smiling as he lay there. Of course, that was just a result of the death throes. But he was grinning from ear to ear. He almost looked happy."

"Death is often very strange," said Melhus. "Sometimes it reveals the truth about a person."

"At any rate, the nurse had tried to revive him, but it was too late, and he'd already lost too much blood. When the doctor arrived, there was nothing for him to do but call the time of death. I'll never forget what the doctor did. First he reached out and closed Stang's eyes. Then he pressed the palm of each hand on the boy's cheeks and pulled his lips down. Then he wasn't smiling anymore."

Singsaker thought back to that scene. Afterward it almost seemed as if what the doctor did had finally killed the young man.

"We found a note on his chest. It said:

"It was Gjessing's plan all along. He wanted this to happen. He even reported me to the police before we left on the fishing trip, so I would be arrested for his murder when I got back."

"Do you consider that a confession of murder, Singsaker?" asked Melhus.

"Hard to say. Maybe he was just feeling guilty. Gjessing is a thousand feet down in the sea. We may never know for sure. But I think Stang was right about Gjessing playing a deadly game with him."

"What happened after you and Jensen found the note?"

"We searched the room. Under the bed we found a scalpel. The doctor acknowledged that it must have been taken from his office. He'd stepped out for a short time to have a smoke while all of this was going on. I put the scalpel in an evidence bag, labeled it, and then put it in my pocket."

"Why didn't Jensen do that? He was the one on duty."

"I don't remember. I suppose we were just following old habits."

"Then what happened?"

"We went back to the waiting room. Jensen and I. Drank our coffee in silence, as far as I recall. You've been a policeman for a long time yourself, Melhus. You know how something like that affects you. It's your job, but still. You've been there before. It doesn't feel good. You feel like it's your fault."

"And you weren't even on duty," said Melhus with no trace of sarcasm in his voice.

Singsaker nodded. How often was Melhus going to repeat that fact?

"Was it a long time before you and Jensen got moving again?"

"No, not long. In fact, no more than fifteen minutes before the same nurse came back to tell us something else. This time she said that the second witness, the man in the other clinic room, was gone. She'd actually seen him jump out the window, run over to the doctor's car that was parked outside, and take off in it."

"So this is when things really took a dramatic turn, am I right?"

"Yes, I suppose that's an accurate description." Singsaker sighed.

"The fifth element. Things start to happen that neither of you could have foreseen, things that result from an inexplicable connection between events, things that you can't control."

"Up until then we didn't know much about the man in the other clinic room. The doctor was able to tell us that his injuries were not consistent with a boating accident, but otherwise there was little to indicate that he was behind any of the other events that had occurred before then."

"But that would eventually become clear."

"Yes. Very clear."

"I think this would be a good place to take a break," said Melhus, looking from Singsaker to Gregersen. "Why don't we meet again in half an hour? At one thirty?"

Singsaker nodded with relief.

PART IV

YELLOW BILE

Most types of fever arise because of yellow bile.

—Hippocrates

17

Three weeks before it happened . . .

They lay on the floor around a low table, half-asleep, like neglected farm animals, stinking of urine and vomit, wearing down jackets because of the ice-cold air indoors. There were food stains and blood on their clothes, dark blotches with colors of the life they lived.

Beer bottles covered the table along with cigarette butts and syringes.

A child was crying in a crib in the corner. The toddler's head had gotten stuck in the gap left when one of the bars had broken.

He stepped over the people scattered over the floor. They didn't notice him at all. Then he went over to help the child get free. He picked up the toddler, who stopped crying but refused to look at him. The child's eyes flickered from lack of mother's milk and heroin. Impossible to tell whether it was a boy or girl. The child stank. A brown streak ran down the inside of the nightie all the way to the footies. He carried the child out of the room. At the bottom of the stairwell he found a baby buggy and inside was a pacifier, which he stuck in the toddler's mouth before heading back to the apartment.

The child sat quietly in the buggy, staring after him, like a tiny sprout someone had stepped on.

"Which of you zombies goes by the name of Tjoms?" he said in the voice he'd developed during his time as a sergeant in Poland.

One of the people on the floor roused himself enough to sit up halfway. Didn't look at him, but reached for a joint on the table. His hands were shaking as he tried to flick the lighter, but it wasn't working.

He leaned down over the guy, sticking a baseball bat under his chin. Then he got out his own lighter and lit the joint for the poor schmuck, who took a toke. They were garbage, these people. Nothing but garbage, but he felt sorry for them. Occasionally, that is, when he allowed himself to think about it. He could have been one of them. It took so little. He'd once held a syringe in his hand too, when he was staying with his uncle in Gdańsk. But he'd made a different choice.

The guy with the joint showed a glimmer of light in his eyes after the first toke.

"Are you Tjoms?"

"Tjoms?"

He seemed to be thinking about it. The guy was only a kid, not even twenty. And that didn't fit the description he'd been given.

"Shit, no. Is Tjoms even here? Oh yeah. He's over there."

The kid pointed at a guy with long, greasy hair who was lying under two gray woolen blankets. He was the only one who seemed to be sleeping with his eyes closed. Next to him lay a woman with blond curls. She was awake but didn't say a word, just stared up at him with a surprised expression, as if she thought she had dreamed him.

"Over there? That's Tjoms?"

The kid nodded. Took another toke on his joint.

"Are you sure?"

Again he nodded.

"Shit, why wouldn't I be sure?"

He straightened up, switched the bat to his right hand, and went over to Tjoms.

"Please move over," he said to the blonde.

She merely stared at him.

"Didn't you hear me?"

He leaned down and grabbed her arm, squeezing it hard. He was starting to get tired of these people. He hated these sorts of assignments. And the pay was lousy.

The woman moved away. He took up position over Tjoms, his legs astride. Then he began poking him in the stomach with the bat.

Slowly the man woke up and threw off the woolen blankets.

"Tjoms?"

"What do you want?"

"What do you think I want?"

"Is this about the money?"

"I don't know. What do you think, Mr. Louisville Slugger?" he asked, speaking to his baseball bat. "Could it be about the money?"

He raised it up and struck. First in the man's stomach a couple of times. Not hard. But enough to knock some air out of the guy. Then he moved down his body, increasing the force of each blow. The first one that really hurt struck him in the hip. Then he started pounding on the man's knees, trying to crush them.

"I'm so fucking sick of people like you!" he bellowed, the way a sergeant yells at recruits on the first day of boot camp. It was the voice used to weed out the weaklings.

"I hate you! You're all scum! Nothing but shit! Human waste!" He raised the bat and walloped the guy one last time. In the jaw. He heard it snap.

Tjoms spat out blood and teeth.

Then he took out a handkerchief from his jacket, wiped the blood off the bat with it, and put it back in his pocket. He stood there staring down at the poor wreck wriggling on the floor like a worm.

"Tomorrow. Karlstad wants the money tomorrow. So get the money."

Not a sound in the room as he left. But they were all awake now.

The toddler was howling as he came out into the hall. The pacifier had fallen on the floor under the buggy. He wiped it off with a clean handkerchief—luckily he had more—and gave it back to the child. Then he rocked the buggy for a few minutes until the child had calmed down. After that he left the building.

Near Lademoen Park he found a public telephone. There weren't many left, but for someone like him it was sometimes necessary to make an anonymous call. He dropped in a few coins and phoned child protective services to tell them about the little tyke in the stairwell of the apartment building. When they asked for his name, he said Jonas Berg. That was a lie.

In reality, his name was Jerzy Malek, and he worked as a blaster in a mine. An important job that required security clearance from the police.

People called him Sving.

His cell rang just as he was stepping out of the phone booth. It was Karlstad.

"Did you deliver the message?"

"Loud and clear."

"Good. Are you coming in soon? There's a woman here who wants to meet you."

"A woman?"

"Does that surprise you?"

"Not really. But I don't usually meet girls that way."

"She's an old acquaintance of mine. I told her a little about you. She said she'd like to meet you."

"Really?"

"I guess she likes bad boys."

18

Six weeks before it happened . . .

W*hen are we going* to see Pappa again?"

The mother looked up from the book she was reading. *Love Can Be Murder* by Raymond Chandler. It wasn't his best. She gave her daughter a somber look.

"Soon," she lied. "We'll see him again soon."

"Pappa was going to take me to the park tomorrow."

"I don't think that's going to happen. Some other time."

"Are we almost there?"

"We'll be in Hamar soon. So about four more hours after that."

The girl didn't know how long four hours was. Only that it was a really long time.

"Will Aunt Liss be waiting for us?"

"Yes. She's going to meet us at the station. Then we'll drive straight to her house."

"I'll be happy to see her."

"Me too."

She sat there looking at her daughter. *I'm doing this for her,* she thought. *He's pretty much knocked the life out of me. But there's still hope for her. I'm doing this for her. He's never going to be allowed to see her again.*

Then she picked up her book and went back to reading. It was hours ago that they'd left the apartment in Homansbyen. He was at work. She hadn't told anyone where she was going. The plan was for him to find her in the end, but not until everything was ready. Not until she'd made all the arrangements up there. She had decided who she would talk to. There was really only one person who could help her with this.

19

Three weeks before it happened . . .

K*arlstad was leaning* against a pile of tires, smoking a cigarillo as he talked with a guy at the repair shop, presumably about one of the cars. Some mechanical problem. Karlstad was genuinely interested in car repairs. He spent more time in the shop than anywhere else. Sometimes it felt like drugs were just a sideline for him. That might be how he made the big money, but it wasn't where his heart was. And half the time his mind wasn't there either. Dealers, rip-off artists, snitches, ass-kissers, wasters, and cops. Sving knew there were days when Karlstad didn't even want to think about the problems inherent in this business of his. Maybe that was why he'd been so successful. In a business like this it was important never to put in more or less than was required. People who strove too much, people who put their whole soul into it, they either got caught or croaked. Karlstad didn't like having to use excessive force either. But he was a pragmatist and knew that sometimes it was necessary. He mostly left that to Sving. It was the time he spent under the hood of a car that he lived for. And Sving liked that about him.

Right now Karlstad was grinning as he talked. His smile got even bigger when Sving came into view behind the old van.

"Sving, you're looking good!"

They shook hands. Then Karlstad turned to the young guy he'd been talking to, a promising mechanic, one of the ones he was careful to keep out of all the shit, and always would. The young mechanics were off limits. They were meant to become decent citizens.

"Call the customer and tell him we can put in the springs we've got here. They'll work like a charm. If he wants original springs, he'll have to wait a week or two. Right now I've got to talk to Sving."

The mechanic nodded and headed for the reception area, a glassed-in corner next to the doors, to speak to the customer.

Karlstad and Sving went into the office at the back of the shop. It was looking less spartan than the last time Sving had been here. Karlstad had bought new chairs at IKEA, three of them in dark brown leather, much too stylish and modern for the old office with its veneer-topped table, the ugly mahogany desk in the corner, the *Penthouse* calendar on the wall, and the plastic coffee cups.

A woman was sitting in one of the chairs. She didn't look like she was very comfortable. She was thin, bordering on gaunt, and even though she had her feet tucked up, Sving could tell that she was tall. He also realized at once that she was not one of Karlstad's customers. Her gaze was sharp, almost intense; her hair was long and thick. Her clothes were neat and clean; in fact, they looked quite expensive. She wore no makeup. A plus in Sving's opinion. A little girl was playing with her dolls as she sat on the floor near the woman. She was whispering to herself as she played.

"This is Ane. Ane Fagerhus," said Karlstad. The woman in the chair unfolded her legs and put her feet on the floor, but she didn't get up. Merely held out her hand. Sving looked her in the eye as they shook hands.

"Nice to meet you."

"Let's hope so," she said.

Karlstad pointed at the girl on the floor.

"This little sweetheart is Tina."

The girl looked up when she heard her name.

Sving leaned down.

"Tina. That's a great name. How old are you?"

"Five," she told him.

"A big girl. Almost old enough to go to school," said Sving.

The girl nodded. Then she went back to playing with her dolls.

Sving looked at the mother, who was now sitting up straight. Her expression had changed. He saw an inquiring look in her eyes. It suited her.

"Ane may have a business deal for us."

"It that what you call it, Geir?" Ane laughed.

She must know Karlstad well. Nobody called him by his first name. In fact, Sving didn't think he'd ever heard anyone do that before.

"We've talked it over, Ane. If we're going to do this, it's a business transaction. Nothing more. It's for your sake that we treat it this way. You and I are friends, but when we do business together, we have to put our feelings aside. Isn't that right, Sving?"

Sving nodded solemnly.

"Did I mention that Ane and I go way back? We've known each other since sixth grade. In the eighties. Bell-bottoms and *Sesame Street*. Prince Light."

"What's wrong with Prince Light cigarettes? I still smoke them."

"I noticed."

"Nice for you to have a reunion and everything," said Sving. "But what's this deal about?"

"Her husband beats her."

"And what am I supposed to do about that?"

"He's threatened to kill her, and he means it. So she's run away from him. All she needs is a little help to defend herself."

"Are you talking about taking him out?" Sving kept his voice low so the little girl wouldn't hear what he said.

Karlstad didn't reply. Just stared at Sving impassively.

"I don't pop them. You know that. I beat them up, but that's all. Why are you talking to me about this?"

"It's an open-ended proposition, Sving."

"The answer is no."

"It's an honest job."

Sving looked at Ane Fagerhus sitting in the chair. She had again tucked up her legs. The little girl was making her dolls do a strange dance on the floor. Then Ane abruptly got up and came over to Sving, fixing her eyes on his. She radiated confidence. There was something almost unnatural about that, considering the situation, her personal story, and what they'd just asked him to do.

"I'm desperate. If you're in, then I want you to be in for more reasons than just the money."

She placed her hand on his shoulder and came closer. He could smell her breath, sweet and attractive.

"Think about it. It's my only hope. I'll be at Geir's party tomorrow night. Maybe I'll see you there."

Shit. Sving silently cursed himself. He liked her.

Karlstad's car repair shop was located near the dock. Sving lived in Strindheim, a part of town not far away. He crossed Lilleby on foot and headed past the chapel and cemetery in Lademoen.

His thoughts were whirling, which was unusual for him. Sving was a smart guy, but he normally didn't spend much time brooding over things. Right now he felt like he was standing at a crossroads. The choice he had to make was simple. A no-brainer, actually. Anyone like him who was involved in this sideline business, and at this level, didn't kill people. That was just asking to get caught. Norway was too small. A murder attracted too much attention. Besides, he didn't know if he had it in him to kill someone. But he couldn't get the thought of her out of his head. Ane and her little girl. Was it right for somebody to threaten their lives? There was no indication that the man was bluffing, and misogynistic men killed their women all the time.

One of the busiest streets in Trondheim was Innherredsveien, and the four-plex where he lived was situated at a spot where a gap in the noise-abatement barrier allowed the traffic sounds from the bypass road to fill his yard and shake the glass of his bedroom window. He had complained to the city, but so far it was in vain. Sometimes he wondered if the traffic noise might be the cause of his son's problems. But his room was in the basement with the window facing away from the road, and he never came upstairs. There were other reasons. Maybe it was all the gaming he did. Maybe it was because he'd lost his mother so young. Sondre hadn't come up from the basement in nearly two years now. It all started after his first year in secondary school. Sving could hardly even remember what his son looked like in daylight. He saw him only when the boy was asleep, in the dim glow of that special lamp he'd installed down there. And he no longer went into his room very often.

Sving made dinner when he got home. Store-bought curried chicken. That would have to do. Two portions, heated up in the microwave. He carried one plate down to the basement and set it on the floor outside his son's bedroom door. The other he took with him into the living room and sat down on the sofa. He picked up his iPad from the coffee table to check Facebook—what his son called the book of life and death—mostly to see if there was any news from the depths of the basement. But his son hadn't posted anything today, or messaged him either, which he sometimes did on good days. On occasion he might send his father a personal message to ask a question, the way he used to when he was younger. Often he asked about completely innocent things, such as whether the stars were visible that night, or whether his father could see the full moon, whether he'd noticed the smoke from a fire he'd read about on the Web, whether he'd had a good day at work. His son's sense of curiosity was still intact, just well hidden in the dark.

Sometimes Sving wondered whether he was the only one Sondre kept at arm's length. Had he treated him so badly?

He checked the news online. The headlines were mostly about the young woman who'd been found with her throat slashed and a music box on her chest. It was a horrible case that had shaken the whole city. Given the current atmosphere, it might be possible to get away with a murder, thought Sving. But no. That was not going to happen.

Then he fell asleep.

"Let's forget about it for tonight," she said.

"Forget about what?" He gave her a crooked smile.

"You know what I mean. What we asked you about at Geir's shop."

"Nobody calls him Geir. Everyone calls him Karlstad."

"Not me. I call him Geir. But I haven't been in touch with him since we left Rosenborg Junior High. That was a long time ago. But back then we were good friends. The sort of friendship that can survive long years of absence. I've followed his life from a distance. I don't know everything he's mixed up with, but I do know he has contacts. I knew he was the only person who could help me. And I still believe that. But let's forget about it tonight. I want to think about other things. What kind of work do you do? I mean, when you're not helping Geir with his problems."

"I think you know."

"Why do you say that?"

"Karlstad wouldn't have introduced us unless he'd told you a little about me in advance. I know him."

"Isn't silence important for people who do what you two do?"

"Karlstad knows what to say and what not to say."

"I see. And you're right. He told me you're a demolition expert. That you work with explosives."

"That's right. For the next three years I'll be working on a tunnel right under the building where I live in Strindheim. The Strindheim tunnel will be finished soon. A big advantage with this job is that I mostly won't be home when the worst of the shaking is going on under the foundation. And when the tunnel is done, all the traffic on the road outside my house will be gone. So for me, the job seems meaningful."

She put her hand on his arm.

"I like explosive types," she said with a laugh.

He gave her a surprised look.

"Isn't that the kind of man you're running away from?"

"My husband?" she said, pausing to consider. "He's not explosive. Everything he's done to me, he's done without anger."

A cold type, thought Sving. *That's the most dangerous kind*.

For a while neither of them spoke. They were sitting together on the sofa. Karlstad's living room was packed. It was his wife Karen's fiftieth birthday, and he had a wide circle of friends. He was not only good at repairing cars, he was also good at socializing, and with all sorts of people. There were lawyers at the party, as well as businessmen, realtors, people who occasionally lived on the streets, half-wits, and students. Inviting students was something new. Sving knew that Karlstad was trying to get into that market and had started cultivating contacts. Two law students were sitting against one wall, bellowing at each other. Sving had seen one of them before. Karlstad had dealt to them once or twice before.

Sving downed the rest of his beer. Then he glanced at Ane Fagerhus. He didn't drink very often. He was afraid of what he might do. Most of the things he regretted in life had been done when he was drunk.

"Want to go out for a walk?" she said.

"Out? Where?"

"I don't know. Just out."

That was not a good idea. Karlstad had stepped out. There was a lot of cocaine under the bed in one of the bedrooms. It wasn't like Sving to give in to this sort of thing. But there was something about

Ane. She'd already gotten him to drink too much. He'd even been out on the balcony to try some of Karlstad's cigarillos this evening.

"How do I know I can trust you?" he said, teasing her.

"I just need some fresh air."

"Karlstad asked me to look out for things here."

"It seems nice and peaceful, and Geir will be right back. Besides, everybody here knows not to mess with him."

Karlstad lived in a huge apartment on Lademoen. If they'd wanted to go into town, it was only a short walk. But they headed in the opposite direction. Toward Strindheim.

He remembered seeing the plate outside the door in the hallway leading to the basement. He'd noticed it when he came home that night. It had almost made him lose focus. But she soon got his mind back on track. Now he just hoped that Sondre hadn't heard them.

He got up and then leaned down to give her a kiss between the shoulder blades. It was too intimate a gesture, too romantic, too early, but he did it anyway. She mumbled something, still half-asleep, and turned onto her side, facing away from him and tucking the duvet between her legs. He turned on his heel and headed for the basement door in the hall. There it was, just as he remembered. A plate with the remains of a serving of curried chicken. This was something new. Sondre had walked up the stairs. Had his son come looking for him, or had he merely turned around in the doorway and gone back to his silent, dark world?

Sving's iPad was under one of the sofa cushions. Facebook was still open, so he checked his messages. There was a new one from Sondre. He seldom received much else. Just a lot of bullshit from his colleagues at work and a rare message from his son. He had almost no presence on the Web. The things he did with the baseball bat could not be recorded electronically. Not anywhere. He opened the message.

A smiley face. That was all.

He sent three smiley faces back.

"Where's Tina?"

Sving was frying bacon.

"You've had all night to ask me that, after drinking till we were both shit-faced and then luring me home with you—but only now you wonder where my daughter is?"

"Oh, come on, who exactly lured who?" He laughed, and for once the laugh sounded genuine. "I realize somebody must be babysitting her. Just wondered who it was."

"She's on Hitra with my sister. Want to go over there with me to pick her up? We're going to stay with Geir for a few days. It's safer."

"A Sunday drive?"

"Something like that." Her dimples showed.

"Have we already reached that stage?"

"We're both adults. We can do whatever we want."

"Do I make you feel safer?"

"A little."

He set a plate of bacon and eggs on the table in the hall next to the basement door. Then he opened Facebook and wrote a new message to his son: *Breakfast at the top of the mountain you climbed yesterday.*

The plate was still there when they left. He wondered if he ought to take it downstairs, but decided not to.

In the car she asked him about the food.

"Who was that for?"

"Just my son. He sleeps late in the morning."

Which was true.

"I didn't know you have a son. Don't tell me you also have a wife you forgot to mention."

"No," he said. "I don't."

"Divorced?"

"Widower."

"Oh, sorry. Never get involved with a widower. Isn't that the conventional wisdom? Too much baggage."

"It was a long time ago. Years ago."

"How old is your boy?"

"Nineteen."

"A great age. That's when everything begins. Everything is wide open. When you have no clue what's going to happen. That's probably why everyone is so happy at that age. They don't know how wrong everything can go."

"I think my son already has some idea," said Sving.

"Do you know Pappa?"

Tina looked up from the mirror-smooth water under the dock. Her mother and aunt had gone back to the house to make salted fish and mashed potatoes. Suddenly Sving found himself alone with the girl. Between them stood a bucket half-filled with crabs.

"No, I don't," he said. Then a thought occurred to him, and he asked:

"Is your father nice?"

"Yes," replied Tina. "He sings to me."

"He sings?"

"Yes. But it doesn't sound pretty. When Pappa sings, it sounds like when other people talk."

Sving had to laugh.

"So how does it sound when he talks?"

"It sounds like when he's sleeping."

"Sleeping?"

"Like he's talking in his sleep."

"Is your father nice to your mother?"

"I think so. Pappa never gets mad."

Sving got to his feet and picked up the bucket. What was he getting himself mixed up in? He was not a killer. He beat up people, that was all. But would he be able to say no?

"Maybe we should let the crabs go," he said.

Tina looked skeptical.

"They live in the sea, you know."

She nodded.

Sving dumped the crabs back in the water.

Together they walked toward the house. Halfway there she took his hand, as if it were the most natural thing in the world. He had to pause between steps to hold back his tears.

The plate of bacon and eggs was now empty. It was in exactly the same place he'd put it before they left.

Sving was alone. After the drive to Hitra, he'd dropped Ane and Tina off outside Karlstad's shop. He hadn't gone in with them. He was worn out, and too many thoughts swirled through his mind.

There was a new message on Facebook. *It seemed steeper today.*

He was disappointed. He'd hoped this was a sign of progress. He'd already eaten on Hitra. The boy would have to settle for another TV dinner.

His phone rang.

"Sving, we need to talk." It was Karlstad.

"Is it urgent?"

"Be at the shop in fifteen minutes."

"Where are Ane and her daughter?" Sving asked, attempting small talk.

"Sit down, Sving."

Karlstad was seated behind the beat-up desk in his office. He pointed to one of the IKEA chairs.

Sving did as he was told.

"I asked you to look after things at the party for a few minutes."

"I did. For more than just a few minutes."

"But not until I came back."

"You were gone a long time."

"I hadn't come back when you left. What were you thinking?"

"What's this all about, Karlstad? What's with the tone? That's not how we talk to each other. Never have."

"You knew there was product under the bed in the bedroom."

"Sure. I thought it was safe there."

"You thought wrong."

"Fuck! Are you messing with me?"

"Am I known for messing around, Sving? Am I?"

"Not when it comes to product, no."

"Half a kilo is missing."

"Somebody made off with half a kilo from your place? Who the hell would have the nerve to steal from Karlstad?"

"That appears to be the big mystery right now. And nobody should be more interested in finding out than you."

Karlstad leaned back in his chair and lit a cigarillo.

"We're friends, Sving. I'm no shithead. I'm giving you a chance to clear up this matter. Either I get back the dope or I get the cash for its full value. And that'll be the end of it. But I expect nothing less."

"What do I have to go on?"

"There were more than fifty guests at the party yesterday. I don't want you to touch most of them unless you find out something concrete. It's highly unlikely any of them would have taken the stuff. If they did, then we might have to drop the matter. And then I'm afraid the payment would have to come from another source." Karlstad paused and fixed his eyes on the desk.

Sving knew full well what he meant. If he didn't get back what Karlstad had lost, he'd have to pay up himself, either with his own money or it would cost him his friendship with Karlstad. The latter would be the costliest form of payment.

Karlstad went on:

"But there were others there, people who have less to lose, people who don't understand what it means to steal from me. And as it happens, I'm not afraid of offending those kinds of people."

"So that's where I should start?"

"They're your best hope, Sving. If you can pound something out of them, the matter might be solved."

"Do you have any idea who they are?"

"I have a list of fourteen names. Junkies, students, welfare cheats, Web poker players, tradesmen, small-time dealers, porn-addicted losers—my best friends."

Sving couldn't help smiling. He wondered where he belonged in Karlstad's catalogue of friends.

"I'm working a lot of hours at my job right now. I can manage one a day."

"I hear you've got some leisure-time activities going on too."

"Have you talked to her?"

"She told me you two had a cozy drive, and that you played with her daughter. She and Tina have gone over to my place to have dinner tonight. I don't mind, Sving. If there's anyone who could use a little happiness in life, it's you. And by the way, if you don't manage to pound anything out of those fools, if you end up in my debt, I understand that she's prepared to pay you well for the job she proposed."

"I think I'll try the list first."

Karlstad opened a desk drawer and gave him a handwritten list of names and addresses.

"One a day," said Sving. "That's all I can manage."

"It's up to you. But the more time you take, the more time they have to squander my product, and the more expense you'll have to cover."

"Then let's hope I start at the right end of the list." Sving got up to leave.

"Break a leg," said Karlstad, smiling as he left the room. He wasn't wishing him good luck or issuing a command. It was simply a credible prediction.

She came to him that evening after Tina had gone to bed. They made love everywhere in his bedroom, tumbling off the bed, squirming across the floor. He pulled her by the arms over to the wall, grabbed her thighs and pressed her against the wallpaper his wife had once put up. She twisted out of his grip and shoved him so he landed on his back on the carpet. Then she threw herself at him, dripping with sweat. Now she did everything as he lay there, his body rubbing against the floor. She moved as if they were fighting, a wild and furious dance. There was a madness about her that he didn't understand. It had been so long since he'd been with a woman. Afterward they slept on the floor, and he dreamed that they were still making love. This time against the wall and on the ceiling, their bodies intertwined like spiders.

"This job you have. Does it mean you have access to explosives?"

They got into bed when they woke up early in the morning. He had to go to work, and she needed to go back to her daughter. But they had time for coffee in bed.

"I work as a blaster, but that doesn't mean I can just fill up a bag with C-4 before I go home in the afternoon."

"What about dynamite?"

"Nobody uses dynamite anymore. Too unstable."

"Exactly. I've heard that old dynamite is supposed to be especially bad news. Causes accidents."

Sving gave her a long look. Took a sip of his coffee.

"It's not all that easy for me to get hold of dynamite."

That wasn't true. He had a box at the cabin. Much too old and dangerous. He should have turned it in long ago.

"My sister has a house on Hitra that she never uses. There could be old explosives stored in the house. We could get him to go there. An accident might happen."

"Why are you talking about your husband now? Why not enjoy your coffee and this nice, quiet morning?"

She rested her head on his shoulder.

"I'm not going to do it," he said. "I refuse to kill anyone. I've never done that before, and I'm afraid it might destroy me."

"A pacifist? You? Don't make me laugh."

"I mean it, Ane."

"Do you like me?"

He had an urge to tell her that he loved her. But it was much too early to say that, let alone feel it.

"You're unique," he said.

"Your son. Does he go to school?"

"No."

"You don't want to talk about it?"

"No."

"See you tonight?"

"There's something I have to do after work. Could you come over late tonight?"

Sving knew people who could help him. They weren't stable, but they were cheap, and they knew how to keep their mouths shut. They were called the Lars Brothers. Both of them were named Lars, but they weren't really brothers. Lars #1 was nearly six foot six. Lars #2 was shorter than Sving, which meant under five foot nine. In the summer they both rode motorcycles. Neither of them had been allowed to join the Hells Angels at Trolla. Apparently they were too crazy. But they weren't known to blab. Everything they said was pure bullshit, but nothing that could ever get them in trouble.

Sving watched as they tied Said to the coffee table with his arms crossed underneath and his feet bound to the table legs at one end.

"The table doesn't look very sturdy. The legs are rickety."

The Lars Brothers turned to Sving. They always got frustrated when he used words they weren't used to.

"Turn it upside down!"

They did as he said.

Said was now lying on his stomach on the carpet with the table on top of him. He tried to kick and flail, but the table stopped him from rolling onto his side. The knots were tied tight. The Lars Brothers were good with their hands.

"Go fill up the bathtub!"

They both left, as if it would take at least two to fill the tub. After they left, Sving stood on what was the underside of the table. It was made of teak. A flea market find from the '70s. He jumped up and down. The wood creaked. Said whimpered. That was a sound Sving couldn't stand, to tell the truth. Whimpering infuriated him. He leaned down and peered under the table. Said stared at him, his eyes looking like those of a newly caught deep-sea fish.

"Are you sure you don't have anything else to tell me?"

Sweat spurted from his brow as he shook his head.

"You need a bath," said Sving, and he hopped onto the floor.

Said gasped for breath.

The Lars Brothers came back to get him. They picked up the table by the legs and carried him into the bathroom. There they set him down on the tiles. They probably looked quite comical as they stood there, three guys wearing winter coats, crowded into the cramped space of the bathroom with a table between them.

"Hope it's cold enough for him," said Sving as they watched the tub filling with water. He was sweating inside his wool coat.

"We're saving on hot water," said Tall Lars, pointing at the tap.

"Very sensible," said Sving.

When the tub was full, they lifted the table and lowered him into the water. The tabletop fit perfectly between the sides of the tub. Some water splashed over the sides as he struggled.

When they lifted the table again, he gasped and vomited water.

"He doesn't look clean enough yet," Sving decided.

They lowered him into the tub again. Held him there a little longer this time, but not too long. When they brought him up, there seemed to be more life in him than ever.

"Feel like talking?" said Sving, leaning down to the table.

Said spat out water, his words mixed with gurgling sounds.

"What do you want me to say? Just tell me. I'll say whatever you want. But I don't think it will help you. I was just at the party. I didn't see anything. I didn't do anything."

Sving sighed and straightened up.

"Nothing for us here, boys. Put him back in the tub. Maybe he'll have more to say the next time we come here."

The Lars Brothers exchanged glances.

"Do what I said," Sving told them.

They put the table back in the tub. Screaming, Said disappeared into the ice-cold water.

Sving took off his coat and rolled up his sleeve. Then he leaned down and stuck his arm in the water.

"You guys could have added a tad more hot water," he said resignedly as he fumbled for the plug. He found it, pulled it out, and tossed it on the floor.

"Time to go."

On his way out, Sving wrote a note that he left on the kitchen table: *You have a week to get the money.*

He didn't have much faith in Said. But he planned to leave the same message for all of them. As he saw it, it didn't matter whether he got the money from the one who was guilty or from someone else on the list, as long as he got the money.

She came to him that night, and their lovemaking was even rougher than the night before. In the morning she asked him:

"Can you watch Tina for me this afternoon?"

"I'm busy."

"You're busy a lot."

"I have something to do every afternoon this week, and probably next week too."

"Can't you take this afternoon off? There's something I need to do. And Geir is busy."

"How well do you know Karlstad?"

"We dated in junior high."

He sighed.

"Does it matter? That was a long time ago. Another lifetime. Another body. Another face. That wasn't me back then. We were just kids."

He nodded.

"It's just that I feel like I know a little more about your exes than I really want to know."

"You have nothing to fear from either of them. Geir and I are good friends. And my husband? Well, you know how I feel about him."

"You're scared of him?" said Sving, though he wasn't sure. She hadn't come right out and said as much.

"He's a shithead. That's all there is to say about that."

It occurred to him that Ane Fagerhus was not someone who showed much fear. Again he wondered what he'd gotten himself into.

They were hitting him with pillows. He lay curled up on the floor, whimpering as if they were wielding sledgehammers and not pillows from the bed. But truth be told, there was a certain vigor to their blows.

Sving let the Lars Brothers keep at it for several more minutes before he told them to stop. A strange silence settled over the place. The junkie lay on the floor, blubbering like a baby. Sving noticed there were red stripes on his bare back, as if he'd actually been whipped. Feathers drifted through the air, looking like they'd come from imploded angels.

Then Sving used the bat on the man for a while until they finally left the filthy dump, not having learned anything new.

"What were all of you doing in there?"

Tina was sitting in the car. Sving had relented and brought her along. Having her here made him feel like shit, and that had affected his performance inside. He'd been too soft on the bastard, and hadn't put enough power into the blows he delivered with the Slugger.

"We had a pillow fight," he said.

"Grown-ups don't have pillow fights."

"Grown-ups do everything that kids do, with one big difference."

She looked confused.

"We're not playing when we do it," Sving said.

"But you play with me. Pappa plays with me too."

He gave her a surprised look.

"Oh, right. What about your mother? Does she play with you?"

"No, not Mamma. She doesn't like to play."

"Shall we go over to the playground?"

Sving watched the Lars Brothers disappear around the side of the building.

"There's too much snow. And it's too cold. I don't want to play outside."

"What about Pirbadet, the indoor water park? Do you like to swim?"

The little girl nodded.

"Fucking brat!"

Sving gave a start. It was so unexpected. Out of the blue like that. The afternoon spent at Pirbadet had been so much fun. Tina had made him forget himself, taking him along to all the different pools. He'd even gone on the waterslides. It almost felt like when Sondre was small. When they both lived in the light.

"It's just an ordinary glass," he said now.

"I've told her a hundred times. No, a thousand times before. How hard can it be to hold a glass to drink?"

Ane's voice sounded like the screeching of brakes.

"She's five years old."

"About time she learned, damn it."

Ane picked up the biggest piece of broken glass from the floor and then threw it down again. He'd never seen that look on her face, not even during the wildest of their lovemaking. Tina stood there, howling, so Sving took her by the hand and led her into the living room. Told her to sit on the sofa.

"Wait here. I'll take care of this. It's just a glass," he said, and he went back in the kitchen.

Tina smiled as if she wanted to apologize. But why should she need to apologize for anything?

Ane was still standing in the same place. Her face was white. She shook her head when he came back into the room.

"You don't need to stand up for her," she said.

"She's five. It's my glass. And I don't care about it breaking."

"She needs to learn to pay attention. Sometimes I get so mad at her."

Then the tears came.

"I'm sorry. Things have just been so awful lately."

She gave him a quick look before she buried her face in her hands and sank down onto a chair at the kitchen table.

"I shouldn't have lost my temper. It's all the stress."

"You mean it's him. You're thinking about him all the time, aren't you?"

"It's hard not to when I know he's out there."

They put Tina to bed in Sondre's old room.

After the child fell asleep, Ane went to work on him. That was the only way he could describe it. She threw herself at Sving the minute they closed the bedroom door behind them. She pushed him down on the bed and tore off his clothes. After they were done, he wanted to hold her in his arms as they fell asleep, but she wouldn't let him. It made him feel so lonely. A crazy thought passed through his mind. *If I do it for her, if I help her get rid of her husband, will she hold me then?* He knew it was too early to have such foolish ideas. He shouldn't have such strong feelings for her. But he did.

He called in sick, explaining that he'd hurt his back.

Then he got in the car and drove all the way out to the cabin in Lierne. It had actually belonged to his wife. He'd inherited it from his in-laws, but he'd kept it after she died, mostly for Sondre's sake, or so he told himself. He liked the drive. All the evergreen trees. It was best in the summertime, when it never got completely dark up there, and the ground wasn't covered with big snowdrifts, like now.

The last part of the drive passed through a ravine where with a little patience it was possible to find gold in the river. He'd gone there on many summer days with Sondre to pan for bits of gold, which were precious treasures for the boy. All those tiny little pieces they had collected were stored in a tin box in a shed near the cabin.

Since it was winter, Sving had to park near the main road and put on his skis. Like most people who hadn't learned to ski until adulthood, he didn't feel entirely steady. He'd grown up in Gdańsk, Poland, which really wasn't that far away, but he still regarded skiing as somewhat exotic. In his uncle's big, ramshackle house, where the kids had been allowed to run as free as stray dogs, they'd hardly even known that skis existed. Even so, it took Sving only half an hour and three falls to reach the cabin, which stood among the last of the birch trees before the bare rock slopes of Storfloa began.

There he took a shovel out of the sack he'd brought and dug through the snow in front of the shed. When he'd cleared enough away to open the door, he went in and found an old sled, which he dragged outside. Then he made his way over to a crate that stood between the shelves of tools and the woodpile. He picked it up cautiously. It weighed over twenty pounds, and he was glad that he hadn't actually hurt his back. A man suffering from back pain shouldn't be lifting twenty pounds of dynamite. He set the crate on the sled.

Then he went inside the shed one last time. He took down the tin box that held the bits of gold from where it hung on the wall. When he peered inside, he saw the tiny glittering flakes. The color reminded him of summer nights up here. He put the box in his knapsack, climbed out of the shed, closed the door, and fastened the strap of the sled around his waist. Then he stood still and listened. It was almost like he could hear the earth rotating. When he closed his eyes for a moment, he felt outer space ruffling his hair.

To think we were once so free, he thought, looking at the sun, which was at its zenith right now at midday. It wasn't very high in the sky, not this far north.

Then he looked at the dynamite on the sled. *This doesn't mean I've decided to do it,* he told himself, registering again how reluctant he was to take on this assignment. But he could use the money. And it was a way of protecting Ane. Her husband could be dangerous to her. And of course Sving would rather see a stranger die than risk that same man killing Ane. There were plenty of reasons for him to do it, but he still felt hesitant.

No matter what, it's good to have the dynamite, he thought. *If I decide to do it, this would be the only way. Then I won't have to look him in the eye. He'll still be a stranger to me.*

But would that make it easier for him to live with what he'd done?

He had no answer to that as he headed back.

The flickering blue light made it seem like he was dreaming.

"Turn that shit off!"

Tall Lars let go of the poor guy and did what he was told. He turned off all the grow lights.

Short Lars was still holding on to the guy's other arm.

Darkness settled over the room. Only the desk lamp was on. The marijuana plants looked like the shadows of dead trees.

"Cut them down!"

"No! Don't do it, damn it!"

The guy growing dope at home tried to squirm out of Short Lars's grip.

Tall Lars had a Sami knife. It looked newly sharpened. He worked quickly, gathering the hemp plants in a sort of rack above the headboard of the bed that was covered with a brown quilt. After finishing the job, he wiped his knife on the thigh of the grower. That made the idiot stop moving.

"Okay, let's bake," said Sving.

For over an hour they went at it with a crummy electric mixer and an even worse oven. But the result was usable. Cannabis brownies. Sving had tasted them before. His uncle had made them a few times back in Gdańsk. All the crazy kids he was trying to take care of had sampled the baked goods.

But today Sving wasn't planning to eat any of them.

He told the Lars Brothers to start feeding the stupid jerk, who was number three on their list. After four brownies, they had to threaten him with the knife to make him keep eating. At the seventh brownie, Sving had to get out the baseball bat. The poor guy started spitting up blood as he chewed on the eighth one. After twelve, Sving handed him the telephone.

"Here. You should be glad cannabis is only slowly absorbed into the intestines. You can still formulate your words clearly enough to explain that you need your stomach pumped ASAP. But if you tell anybody about all this, you're dead. The next time we come here, I want to see half a kilo of snow or twenty-five hundred hundred-krone bills. Do we understand each other?"

The guy nodded, his mouth full of brownies and the pupils of his eyes huge.

As Sving drove home, he was lost in his own thoughts, lending only half an ear to the conversation in the backseat.

Tall Lars seemed to be feeling philosophical. A few times Sving couldn't figure out what he was going on about.

"Evil, right?"

"What now?"

Short Lars groaned.

"Take that guy Höss, for example."

"What did you call that piece of shit?"

"Höss. Rudolf Höss. One of the evilest fuckers those Nazi maniacs ever produced."

"Never heard of him."

"That just shows how fucking little you know about history, bro."

"Lars. I need to ask you this. You know we're not really brothers, right?"

"Shut up. This is serious. That guy Höss. He was in charge of Auschwitz during the war. A real monster. Built up the whole system. A merciless guy. Did you see the movie *Schindler's List*?"

"Was that one they were showing last year?"

"Sometimes I don't know why I even bother talking to you. It's an old movie. Fucking old. We're talking last century. But maybe you've never heard of that either."

"I don't watch old movies."

"So forget I even asked. But in any case, in that film you see him standing on the porch, picking off people in the camp. Just choosing his victims at random and shooting them because he likes killing."

"What a sick fuck."

"That's my point. It's evil, right? There's no other word for it."

"You've got a point there."

"Afterward the guy goes inside to be with his family. He's married. He's got five children. Five fucking children."

"Poor kids."

"No, that's my point. He's a good father. He's nice to them, see? After the war all his kids remember him as a loving and playful father. So that makes you wonder. What is evil, really?"

"The guy's no good. It doesn't matter what you say."

"I'm not defending him. No fucking way. But it makes you think. What are we made of, in reality?"

"Are you trying to say that this has something to do with us?"

"I'm not saying anything. I'm just thinking. Maybe it has something to do with everybody."

"You think too much. That's what's wrong with you."

After dropping off the Lars Brothers at their place, Sving drove over to Jonsvatnet. He parked the car near a run-down farm that Karlstad owned, using it as a sort of warehouse for old junked cars that he thought still had some promise. Then Sving took the bus home. With twenty-two pounds of dynamite in the trunk, he wanted to leave the car as far away from his home as possible. On the way he thought to himself that he'd never see that dynamite again. It could just stay where it was.

Tina was sitting in the kitchen eating yogurt.

"Where's your mother?"

"She went out."

"And you're here all alone?"

He noticed her cheek. There was a red mark under her eye.

"What happened to you?"

"Mamma got mad at me."

He picked her up and held her close. Then he carried her into the living room. She sat on his lap as he watched the news on TV. There was a short report on the Music Box case. Nothing about his rampages among the scum of Trondheim. He closed his eyes and listened to the little girl's breathing as she slept.

After this, I'm done. The Lars Brothers can take over, he thought.

Since Tina was sleeping so soundly, Sving put her to bed. Then he made dinner for Sondre and himself. Again he carried the food all the way down to the basement. He set the plate outside his son's door, along with the tin box containing the bits of gold.

Back upstairs in the living room, Sving sat and stared at Facebook while he waited for Ane to come home. After half an hour he got a message from Sondre: *I'd almost forgotten what the stars looked like.*

For his part, Sving had forgotten that they had called the old tin box the star box.

Ane arrived a few minutes later. Her eyes were red.

"Where have you been?"

"I just went out for walk."

"How are you doing?"

"Not good, Sving. Not good at all."

She let him put his arms around her. They sat on the sofa until late at night, like a married couple. When they made love, she was calmer than she'd ever been before, but she held on to him tight, as if she never wanted to let go.

He got up early and took the other car, an old VW Polo that had once belonged to his wife. He'd kept it for Sondre. At the Obs! Coop in Lade he bought a pair of skates. Figure skates, the smallest size they had, though he still worried they were going to be too big.

"I've never done this before."

"You haven't?"

"Pappa likes to go skiing. Pappa likes being in the woods," Tina explained.

Sving nodded. He tied the laces on her skates. She was wearing two pairs of woolen socks that used to be Sondre's. He'd found them in a box up in the attic. With those extra layers, the skates fit her pretty well. He helped her up from the bench and gave her a little push. She slid forward a short way on the newly sprayed ice of the Leangen skating rink. The next second she fell on her behind. She landed softly, as only kids can, then turned around to give him a smile.

"Aren't you going to try it?"

He looked at the old skates he'd bought back before she was even born, when he was trying to teach his son the joys of winter sports.

"It's easier for me to teach you if I'm wearing my regular shoes," he told the little girl.

"But then you won't have any fun."

She tried to stand up but slipped and fell again. On her second try she managed to stay upright. This time she took several steps forward before falling.

He saw that she was doing fine on her own, so he put on his skates.

Then he wobbled around her as she got more and more steady.

It was his turn to work the late shift. They had an early dinner, the three of them together. Afterward, Tina went into the living room.

Sving put some food on a plate for Sondre.

"What's wrong with him?" asked Ane, giving Sving a concerned look.

"Chronic fatigue syndrome—CFS, also called ME, myalgic encephalomyelitis," he said. "Or at least that's what we think. The doctor refused to give a diagnosis."

"When was the last time he went to the doctor?"

"He hasn't come up from the basement in several months."

"And you haven't seen him in all this time?"

"Just in the dark. Mostly when he's sleeping."

"That's awful."

Sving picked up the plate and looked at her, fumbling for something to say, but not finding the right words.

Then he went downstairs to the basement. Today he opened the door and went into his son's bedroom. Sondre was asleep in the dim light from a single lamp. But no matter how much he slept, he wouldn't wake up refreshed, and it wouldn't give him any energy or help him get through another day.

Sving set the food on the nightstand and ruffled his son's hair.

"Could you please wake up soon?" he said. "Then we can start over."

When he went back upstairs, Tina had drawn him a picture. Two plump people on skates. One big and one small. The small one was him. The big one was her.

There were two demolitions to handle on the job that night, plus a lot of dead time spent with his co-workers who were aware of only about a third of what went on in his life.

At 11:00 P.M. he left work. More tasks awaited him. The Lars Brothers met him outside the agreed-upon address in the city center. Sving barged in first to find a man around forty years old. He grabbed him by the hair.

"What's a man in a suit doing in a dump like this?" said Sving.

He looked around the apartment. The drywall on the walls was ripped down in lots of places, revealing the studs underneath. None of the walls in the living room were painted the same color. Old movie posters were sagging from the thumbtacks barely holding them up on the walls. Sving dragged the man into the kitchen, which, strangely enough, had been newly remodeled.

"Very stylish," he said without letting go of the man's curly hair. The Lars Brothers had followed him into the kitchen. "You've been in a real remodeling frenzy, I can see. Things like that cost money. Where'd you get the cash?"

"What do you want from me?"

"I don't want anything. But I have a friend who wants back what you stole from him."

"What are you talking about?"

"You know what I'm talking about."

Sving turned to look at the brothers while he kept his hold on the man's hair.

"Turn on the stove," he told the brothers.

"But—" one of them said.

"But? But what? Do it!"

Lars switched on the stove, turning the dial all the way up to nine on the display for one of the burners.

"All of them!"

"But, but—"

"Have you started to stammer? Just do it!"

Soon all four burners showed nine on the display.

"Let's see if a nice, thin seared steak might refresh your memory. Sorry I don't have time to chop up any garlic."

Sving hauled the man's head over to the stove and pressed one side of his face against the biggest burner. The scream he was expecting didn't come.

"Not warm enough for you? I guess it takes a little while for the burner to heat up. But I'm a patient man. I can hold you here for a very long time."

"Sving," said a voice behind him. It was Short Lars.

"What the fuck do you want?"

"The burner. I tried to tell you. It's an induction stove. I have one just like it."

"What the hell are you talking about?"

"An induction burner doesn't produce direct heat. It reacts with the metal of the pot, so the pot heats up while the burner stays cool. You can't hurt him like that."

Sving stared wild-eyed at the Lars Brothers. He felt like an idiot. Of course he knew what an induction stove was. But the one he had was the normal ceramic kind. He hadn't even thought about this possibility. Now he was standing here with both hands around the neck of this jerk, pressing his face to a cold glass surface.

"Are you saying I can't hurt him like this?" said Sving sarcastically. "Watch this."

He lifted up the man's head and held it for a second at the level of his own heart. Then he slammed it against the stove with all his might. The glass shattered instantly. Sparks flew out of the display. He did it several more times, pounding and hammering the poor guy's head against the stove until it was so covered in blood that his face was nearly hidden. Broken glass was scattered all over the counter.

Sving slammed the man's face one last time against the pulverized glass, rubbing it around like a dishrag. Then he lifted up the limp body, flung him over the counter, and tore open his shirt. He yanked out the entire stove top, shook loose the cord that was plugged into the wall socket, and stuck the cord on the man's chest. There was still some life left in him. He jerked like a shameful puppy, moaning loudly. Sving took two steps back. The man sank to his knees on the floor.

"Is that enough damage for you two fucking imbeciles?" he said to the Lars Brothers. Only now did he notice the tears running down his face.

"Shit, Sving, you've killed him!" said Tall Lars.

"No, he's still alive. He's got a pulse. But I think you might have gone a little too far, boss," said Short Lars.

Sving got up and brushed off the microscopic pieces of glass from his coat. He bent down to the man on the counter. Using a clean handkerchief, he wiped the blood from the man's face. He still had a face, sliced up and horrible, but still human. And he was breathing.

"We'll be back. And you'd better have the cocaine you took from Karlstad or two hundred and fifty grand in cash for me," he grunted.

The man nodded, breathing heavily.

Back in the car, they watched a woman walk past with a boy around ten years old. They went into the same stairwell leading to the apartment the three of them had just left.

But the Lars Brothers didn't seem to be paying much attention. They were busy arguing.

"Trondheim is a fucking gloomy town," said Tall Lars.

"What are you talking about? I like this town. It has soul."

"There's too much soul. Nothing but soul. That's what makes it so gloomy. Do you realize this place was built on death and decay?"

"Shit. Don't start on all that stupid crap of yours again. Not when the rest of us just want to relax."

"I'm serious! Have you forgotten about Olav Tryggvason? If St. Olav hadn't got himself killed somewhere up in North Trøndelag and then been buried here in town, right underneath the cathedral, Trondheim wouldn't be the big place that it is today. Not at all. That's a historical fact. It's no use denying it."

"So what? It happened."

"Yeah, it happened. But don't you get what it means?"

"It doesn't mean shit. That's what it means."

"It means the whole town is built on death."

"Shut up!"

"They built a church on top of a dead guy. The church means pilgrims, income, an archbishop's seat, all the years of a long and lifeless Middle Ages, the cathedral school, education, scholarship. Trondheim as a cathedral city and a scholarly city. The whole thing built on top of a rotting corpse."

"What a load of bullshit!"

"It's creepy. Admit it! Hair that never stops growing. Shit, somebody should make a horror movie about it. *The Return of St. Olav.*"

A report of the incident appeared in the online edition of *Adresseavisen*:

> *Man attacked by three intruders in his own home. There are no indications that anything was stolen. No explanation for the assault has been given. The victim's wife and son found him bleeding and barely conscious.*

Sving shook his head. The man's name didn't match any on his list. Farther down in the article it said that the family had moved into the apartment only a week ago and had just started remodeling. Apparently the man Sving was looking for had recently moved out. Why had he blindly relied on Karlstad's list? That was sloppy. He needed to do better advance work.

Right now Sving was sitting alone on the sofa. Tina and Ane were both asleep. Downstairs in the basement Sondre lay in bed, his breathing as steady as a metronome. On the screen of his iPad, Sving was looking at a picture of the boy from the newspaper article. The mother and son had arrived home late from visiting the grandparents because the men remodeling the boy's room had worked overtime. The carpenters had probably just left the building when Sving and the Lars Brothers showed up.

Sving sipped his beer and wept.

His tears couldn't transform him into a different kind of person. All they could do was fall onto the table and eventually evaporate—molecules of water that turned into vapor and later became water again in some entirely different context. Sving had shed tears before. And he would again. But he couldn't make any more mistakes like this one.

———

After he finished his beer, he went into the bedroom to Ane. He lay down on the bed without getting undressed and stared at the silhouette of her body in the dim light. Then he put his hand on her hip. She smacked her lips, still half-asleep.

"What time is it?"

"Twelve thirty."

"You're late."

He didn't answer as he stroked her thigh.

"He was never late. I always knew when he'd be home."

"Who are you talking about?" He felt his throat constrict.

"I'm tired," she said. "I was sound asleep."

"Do you think about him often?"

"As little as possible."

"Do you still have feelings for him?"

"You know what I feel. He's a shithead."

"'Shithead' is not a feeling. What sort of feelings do you have for him?"

She propped herself up in bed.

"Is this an interrogation? I'm tired. I want to sleep."

"If we're going to do this, I need to make sure you're telling me the truth."

The words just slipped out, but he knew the second he said them that there was no going back. He'd stopped thinking rationally. He was in love. And he was lost.

"Do what?"

"You know what I'm talking about."

"Will you do it? Have you changed your mind?"

"I haven't decided. Do you still have feelings for him?"

"You know how I feel. I've already told you."

"No, you haven't. I want to hear you say that he hit you. That you're afraid of him. That you think he wants to kill you."

"Calm down. You know what I asked you to do. Do you think I would do that for no reason?"

"No. Do you love him?"

"Let's drop it."

"Do you hit Tina?"

"What the hell does that have to do with anything? I don't like all these fucking questions."

"She's just a kid. She doesn't have anybody except you."

"You're a sick fucker. I know what you do for Geir. I know about a lot of the twisted things you've done. You're sick in the head. And then you come here asking me whether I give my kid a swat once in a while? You've got some fucking nerve!"

Then the slap came, the palm of her hand striking his cheek. He wasn't prepared for that. A feeling of shame followed instantly. Then another slap. She was sobbing.

"Fuck you!"

Sving got up and left the bedroom. He went into the bathroom and sat down on the toilet. *It's her husband's fault. It's this thing she wants me to do that's ruining it all,* he thought. There was no hope for the two of them if he didn't do it. But would there be any hope afterward? Would they finally be able to find some peace?

When he went back to bed an hour later, Ane was sleeping as if nothing had happened. Her hair hid her face. He didn't fall asleep until after dawn.

Then he left for work without waking her.

The fifth man on the list lived in a building in Malvikmarka. They stripped off his clothes and chased him through the woods. In the moonlight Sving watched him run, jumping and wading through the snow across the frozen lake outside the building like a plaster cast of a human being that had come alive, whiter than the snow, a reflection of humanity that no man could express in words.

One of the Lars Brothers found the man's shotgun and fired a shot after him.

Then they locked his door and headed home.

Sving walked behind the Lars Brothers. They were dashing

around, having a snowball fight, goofing off and tumbling into the snow like characters in a silent movie.

"We might be pushing the limits here, boys," said Tall Lars pensively after they were back in the car.

"Don't worry," said Short Lars, sticking a wad of snuff under his lip. "He's not going to freeze to death. He'll turn around. He knows these woods better than we do. All he has to do is break a window to get back inside his house. We scared him. That was the whole point. Our job is to push the limits at all times."

Sving started the car, letting the Lars Brothers go on with their discussion.

"Do you think we ever go too far?"

"Hell, where do you think we are? In the House of Literature in Oslo, or something? We're supposed to scare them. We go as far as we have to."

"I'm just thinking that sometimes—"

"Well, cut it out!"

Both laughed.

"Turn up the radio. I like this song," said Tall Lars.

Sving complied, but instantly regretted it.

"What kind of shit is this?"

"Raga Rockers. 'Somebody to Hate.'"

"Fuck. Not more of that shit of yours."

"Just listen, man!"

All three of them sat there listening.

Tall Lars wanted to roll a joint in the car, but Sving wouldn't let him.

"I didn't mean what I said last night."

She was first to apologize. He didn't think she'd be there when he returned from work, but she was in the front hall, waiting for him. Her nipples were visible through the cotton top she had on. He could hear Tina watching cartoons in the living room.

"What about you?" she asked.

"I didn't mean it either."

"I want you to mean it."

"What are you saying?"

"That you're considering it. That you're giving it serious thought. That you might do it. That's what I want."

"I need to know I can trust you."

"If that's what you need to hear, then the answer is yes. I'm scared of him. He's not like you. He's very calculating. He plans things out. He can say things that never go away. Things that eat me up inside."

"Is it just psychological?"

"What do you mean?"

"Does he just abuse you psychologically, or does he hit you too?"

She lowered her eyes.

"There's been physical abuse."

"Is he capable of killing?"

"I have no doubt about it."

20

Two weeks before it happened . . .

The sixth man on the list got a nail through his tongue early the next morning. One of the Lars Brothers hammered the guy onto the doorframe of his bathroom. That didn't make him any more talkative. Actually, it was a bad idea. They considered pulling out the nail, but that proved rather difficult.

Tall Lars began giggling in that girlish way of his.

"What's with you?" said Short Lars.

"I just happened to think up a new term."

"A new term? What's the matter with you?"

"Gastronomic crucifixion." Tall Lars was overcome with laughter.

Short Lars merely stared at him, shaking his head. As if his colleague had gone completely bonkers, as if there was no hope for him.

When Tall Lars finally stopped laughing, they decided to leave.

They left the guy hanging there, warning him that they'd be back.

Out in the car Tall Lars started laughing again.

"Could you please just shut up? We didn't nail him to a cross. We nailed him to the doorframe. Your so-called new term is stupid. And it's definitely not funny."

"The Romans didn't just use the traditional Christian form of crucifixion. There were a whole bunch of variations. Bet you didn't know that. How can you talk about anything when you never read? In Roman times, most crucifixions used only a single upright pole. Some people even think that Jesus was nailed to a pole. But that sort of design wouldn't work as a logo for a whole fucking world religion, would it?"

"Shut the fuck up, Lars! Please just shut up."

After that Sving finally had a day off. He and Tina went over to the film club to see the movie *Up*. They laughed themselves silly over the dogs. The filmmakers had really nailed it with the dogs. Whenever Sving watched a movie about dogs, he had an urge to get a dog for himself.

Afterward they went out to Hitra to plan the murder of Rolf Fagerhus, Ane's husband.

For once it was good weather. As they drove, they heard on the radio a lot of talk about a young girl who had disappeared from her home in Rosenborg. The reporter interviewed a policeman named Odd Singsaker, asking whether the incident might be related to the Music Box case. No mention was made of all the violent things Sving had done lately. The story about the poor innocent guy whose face Sving had battered was no longer news.

Ane's sister arrived by boat to pick up Tina, taking her back to where she lived out in the islands.

Then Sving and Ane were alone.

Ane showed him around the house. It was run-down and falling apart and needed all sorts of repairs. Even that might not be enough. But the place still had charm, and the view out to sea was fantastic.

Sving sat on top of the big table in the living room.

"This is where we'll put the explosives."

"In here? I thought it was supposed to be an accident. Who keeps dynamite in the living room?"

"The thing is, he needs to get really close. And there's no guarantee that he'd go down in the basement."

"But won't it look suspicious?"

"I've thought it through. Has your sister agreed to this?"

She nodded.

"Are you sure?"

"She knows what he's capable of. She agreed to the plan because she knows it's the only way to make us safe."

"Good. I've worked with a guy who was in touch with the sheriff out here. He once called me to order some dynamite. Exactly the kind we have, old and dangerous. It took almost a month before the sheriff came over to pick it up."

"He's not the speediest kind of guy."

"It's a calculated risk. But I suggest that when everything is ready, when you've put out the bait and we can count on your husband showing up soon, then you should call the sheriff. Pretend to be your sister and tell him that you want to turn in some explosives that were left in this unoccupied house. So in that case, it would seem careless but not entirely unusual for her to have brought the dynamite up from the basement and put it here."

"What if the sheriff shows up too soon, before Rolf gets here?"

"Give him a phone number and ask him to call before he comes out. Say that you're not living in the house, so you need to make arrangements to meet. Then we'll need to stall him as long as we can. If he doesn't go along, then we'll just have to turn in the dynamite and think up a plan B. But as I mentioned, he's not usually in a hurry."

"Sounds like a pretty good idea. If he dawdles, he'll feel responsible for the explosion. And that would probably mean a less thorough investigation. It seems right, psychologically."

"Yeah. The trouble is that I need to use a lot of equipment to trigger the explosion at the exact moment your husband is inside. We can't stand guard 24-7, and we have no idea when he'll arrive. We need an automatic detonator. And the equipment has to be removed after the explosion. The problem is that the parts of the actual bomb will break into thousands of pieces. I know how to clean up after myself, but there's no guarantee that the police won't find something that could arouse suspicion."

"Is that a risk we just have to live with?"

"I'm afraid so. But the risk of being discovered is very low. The most important thing is to make the explosion look like an accident from the very beginning. Does your sister have an insurance policy on this house?"

"I don't know."

"If she does, ask her to cancel it. Insurance companies are often more suspicious than the police in such matters."

"How do we explain why he was in the house?"

"How many people know about your breakup?"

"Only my sister. Everybody thinks we're on vacation. I know Rolf. He wouldn't tell anybody. There's no one he would confide in."

"Okay. You'll say that you had agreed to meet him here, that he was going to join you at a later date for vacation. Your sister had forgotten to tell anyone about the dynamite in the living room. That's all."

"Do you think the story will hold up?"

"Are there many people who know about your marital problems? Who know how dangerous he is? Who think you have good reason to kill him?"

"Only those few I've already mentioned. Outwardly we had a perfect relationship. We traveled. He pampered me. He had the drollest sense of humor whenever we were in social situations. It makes me sick to think about all the people who like him, who see him as a quiet, calm, and patient man."

"I think your story will sound plausible. There's no apparent motive for murder. A tragic accident would seem like the most likely explanation. The police will be satisfied with that. As long as nothing unexpected happens, it should work."

"What do you mean by 'unexpected'?"

"We wouldn't want anyone else to show up. It's not good to have witnesses. Luckily the place can't be seen from any of the farms around here. The big boulders are perfectly placed. The worst that could happen is that he survives."

"Is that a possibility?"

"Twenty-two pounds of dynamite in a room this size? A small possibility. Very small."

"But it could happen?"

"There's always a risk with anything you do. If you want to kill him, you might get caught. That's just how it is. The question you need to ask yourself is: Are you prepared to take that risk? Is it important enough to you to try? Do you want it badly enough?"

Ane Fagerhus looked at him with those big, intense eyes of hers, and he realized that the question was superfluous.

She sat on the table. Unbuttoned her coat and let it fall around her.

"Take me right here," she said.

"Now? After all this?"

"Now!" She lay back and wriggled out of the heavy gray wool dress she had on. Underneath she wore only pantyhose. "Rip them off me!"

He did, and then lay on top of her on the table. The air in the room was ice cold, but they were hot. The table creaked ominously as they got going.

"Fuck me!" she howled.

He stopped. Couldn't make himself do it.

"Fuck me!"

"I can't."

She ended up hitting him. Multiple times before it was over.

"Did you ever hit him?"

"Do we have to talk about him?"

"When did you start being afraid of him?"

"Are you jealous?"

"I'm just asking."

"In the past there were plenty of times when I felt sorry for him. It seemed like he wanted to have feelings about things, but that he couldn't. He used to tell me about his father, who disappeared on a hunting trip when Rolf was a boy. He never came back. No one ever found out what happened to him. His father used to hunt in remote areas. Maybe he had an accident. Maybe a bear got him. Or maybe he got shot by another hunter. But every time Rolf told me about it, I had a definite feeling that he knew what happened. He never said anything, but I'm positive he thought his father committed suicide. And I think that destroyed something inside of him."

"Are you sure you don't still have feelings for him?"

"Could you stop asking me that? You're driving me crazy!"

"It's just that when you talk about him like that, it sounds like you still care about him."

"Would you please shut up! You're a sick bastard. Why would I care about him? He's a shithead. I want him dead."

Ane slid off the table and got dressed.

"Sorry," she said. "You make me so mad when you talk like that. You can stop being jealous. I don't care about him anymore. He's a danger to us. That's all. It'll be a relief when he's gone. Then it'll just be us."

He got up and smiled.

"I can drive out here with the equipment next week. I have most of what I need at home in the basement, but I have to get a few things from work. You can send the letter when I've got it rigged up and ready. Do you think he'll take the bait fast?"

"He's just waiting to get some clue about where I am. I know him. He'll come the minute he gets wind of where to find me."

"Don't make it too difficult for him."

"The trick will be not to make it too easy. He's a suspicious man. But I think I know how to create a plausible chain of coincidences that he'll be able to follow."

Sving looked at Ane. Her intelligence scared him.

"Good. But it's important that he doesn't take too many days. I have to take off from work during that time, so we can stay here on the island. Then I'll come in right after the explosion and clean up."

She led him into the kitchen and pointed out the window at a grove of spruce trees between two boulders.

"You could back your car into that space between the trees. Nobody would be able to see us from any direction. It's a good place for a stakeout." She laughed.

"What are you laughing at?"

"Nothing. Just something I happened to think of."

There were still a few names on the list when Sving came back from Hitra.

They chopped off a finger from number seven. Sving thought it was the guy's little finger, but he wasn't really paying attention. He sat at the back of the room, lost in his own thoughts, while Short Lars used the severed finger to write something on the wall.

Pay up! it said in bloodred letters on the white wall.

They tied the guy to a chair so he could sit and look at what it said. He stared at the words as if staring at the red numbers in the account books of his life.

They took care of the eighth person that same day. It was the only woman on the list.

Sving didn't want to go in with the Lars Brothers. At first Tall Lars refused to do it, but they persuaded him.

Afterward he was more keyed up and boisterous than the other Lars.

"She had one of those fridges with a lock. The bolt is on the side. You know?"

"I guess," said Sving.

"Practically no food inside, but we had to pull out the shelves. Then we stuffed her in there and threw the bolt."

"Is she in there now?"

"Yeah."

"Use your heads, boys. We don't want to kill anybody."

"No, but this is so brilliant. The bolt is a little loose, so the door doesn't close tight. Plus we gave her a hacksaw so she can work at the crack. You know how the ladies are with tools. It's going to take a while, but she should have cut through part of the bolt already. Then it's just a matter of whether she dares come out. Lars gave her a good punch in the nose before we locked her in."

"Good job. What about her apartment? Did you find anything?"

"Empty. Just like all the other places."

"Shit! This is taking a long time. Tomorrow we'll start revisiting guys on the list. Maybe somebody's ready to pay up. And we'll keep working on the rest of the list. We're going to be busy."

"At least we have work," said Short Lars.

"Do you remember when we were locked up, Lars?" Tall Lars suddenly asked.

"How could I forget?"

"The weirdest thing is the way you change in there. Even your voice is different. Remember? That friendly voice? People like us, with tats on our necks and steroid chins don't have such fucking nice voices, like some sort of kindergarten teacher, right? No, they make us sound like the worst druggies, right? The kind that wander around the streets pretending to be so pitiful because they need money for the bus. After a while in the pen, you start to say things like you 'realize your behavior was offensive.' Shit, man! I mean, behavior? Who uses words like that? *Behavior?!* You can't talk about life that way, as if it's just a little behavior here, and a little behavior there. See what I'm getting at?"

"Sure, I get it," said Sving. "I know exactly what you mean, Lars."

The Lars Brothers looked at Sving in surprise.

"I mean it," he merely said and turned on the engine. "I promise that you're not going to be out of work, and you won't have to worry too much about your own behavior until this is over."

Neither of them replied. They weren't used to him talking to them that way, about something that was semi-personal.

Sving put the car in gear, and they drove out of town toward Charlottenlund. None of them said much for a while.

"Fucking social democratic piss," muttered Lars halfway there.

Apparently he wasn't quite done with the topic of behavior and the prison system, but he might also have been thinking about something else.

"A clock? Why do you want a clock? That'll just make things less certain," said Sving.

"I want a countdown that he can see. I want him to have enough time to understand that it's over, but not enough time to do anything about it."

"But don't you see that's exactly what you're giving him? Time to do something. It increases the uncertainty."

"I want him to know that I've won," said Ane.

"But why? I thought it was enough for you to know he was gone. Don't you just want to get rid of him so we can live our lives in peace?"

They were sitting in Sving's kitchen discussing the details of the planned explosion. It was evening. Tina was asleep. They had made love and then got up again. Ane had on her nightgown. Sving wore boxers. They were eating peanuts and drinking water. He studied the tattoo on his right arm. It was supposed to be Mars, the god of war. It was the first tattoo he ever got, back when he was still in the Polish military. These days he hated the sight of that tattoo. The figure looked too much like a devil.

"I do want to get rid of him," said Ane, tossing back her hair. "But I also want him to realize what's happening."

"Why?"

"I don't know."

"But why does it matter whether he knows or doesn't know?"

"I just want a clock."

"That's stupid. Even if we give him only a few seconds, it makes the whole business less certain."

"I'm willing to take that chance."

"There'll be more to clean up afterward."

"You said they won't do a very thorough investigation. They'll think it was an accident."

"Not if they find pieces of a clock."

"But can't you get it out of there?"

"Maybe."

"I want to take that chance. I want him to know what's going on."

Sving didn't reply, but he was aware of the doubt that had refused to let go of him after he'd made the decision. Was he doing the right thing? Did he really have any say in the matter anymore?

He woke up at night and heard voices in the living room. There was no one there. The window stood open, banging back and forth, but he wasn't the one who'd left it unlatched. Then he heard the door to the basement slam.

Sving dashed as fast as he could to the basement door. He opened it and listened. Was that footsteps he was hearing? He stood there a long time, listening, but all was quiet. Had Sondre come upstairs in the night? Was it really him, or had Sving just imagined the whole thing? He considered going downstairs to check on his son. But he didn't. If Sondre had come up here, that was a huge step forward. It would be wrong to put any pressure on him. Slowly Sving went back to the living room and closed the window. Why had he opened it? Did he feel the need for fresh air? Sving remembered that ever since Sondre was a little boy, he had occasionally walked in his sleep. And then he would do the strangest things, like peeing in the potted plants. Was that what had happened now? Was he sleepwalking? Had he risen up from his state of eternal torpor to go walking?

Sving paused to think about this, but was unable to come to any conclusion. Then he crawled back in bed.

After the day shift on the following afternoon, he made two more home visits along with the Lars Brothers.

First they went to see the guy they'd put in the bathtub.

He had actually scraped together twenty-five thousand kroner. He still swore that he'd had nothing to do with the matter, but he would give them the money if they agreed to leave him alone. Sving took the money. He believed the guy, but still promised to come back for more.

Then it was time for number nine on the list.

After ransacking the guy's apartment, which was in a high-rise on Lade with a wonderful view of the sea, they stripped off his clothes and wrapped his whole body in duct tape. Right up until the moment they reached his head and taped his mouth shut, the guy alternated between cursing them and begging for mercy. He swore that he hadn't even gone to the party in question. When the Lars Brothers were done, he looked like a gleaming silver mummy.

Short Lars found a pair of nail scissors and cut a neat hole for his nostrils. Then he cut the guy's right hand free and put the scissors in his palm.

"We'll be back," said Sving, stepping over him as he lay on the kitchen floor like a sprawling gray cocoon.

21

One week before it happened . . .

A *few days later* they drove to Hitra to talk to Ane's sister. It was important to fill her in on some of the details of their plan so that she'd know what to say if the police questioned her.

Ane and her sister sat in the kitchen all afternoon while Sving and Tina made a snow fort outside. There was rarely any snow out near the open sea, but at the foot of a hill behind the house enough snow had collected to build an entire defensive barrier.

Sving followed the little girl's instructions. He was impressed by how detailed her plans were. Emerging from her imagination were doors, tunnels, various-sized rooms, defensive walls, and towers. It was the most beautiful snow fort Sving had ever seen, and the biggest. When they were finally finished, his knees and arms ached, like after a long work day down in the tunnel underneath Trondheim.

"We could move in here," she said.

It was getting dark. They were sitting on either side of a snow lantern, in the middle of the fort.

"We could be happy here. Nobody would bother us."

"We'd like that," said Sving.

He was thinking about how the fort must look from above,

picturing the design as seen from the air. They'd done a good job. She'd envisioned the right sort of shapes. It was a well-conceived structure.

A question that often tormented him again popped into his head. Was it possible for all things to be beautiful? Were there shapes and patterns that might give meaning to any type of material? What about the work he did—the unofficial assignments? Was there a right and a wrong way to carry them out, or was it an ugly business, no matter what? That was the crux of his dilemma. He did the job better than anyone he knew, but he never felt any sense of pride. He was always trying not to think about what he did for Karlstad, but every time he did, it ate him up inside, like flesh-eating bacteria inside his thoughts. But could he really say that what he did had no redeeming qualities from an aesthetic standpoint? The job was carefully thought out and meticulously done. There was a definite pattern to it. And it served the intended purpose. Maybe it was the latter that bothered him the most, the fear of failure, of not being able to do the assignment properly. This fear was worse than the memories of all the bad deeds he'd carried out. For him, nothing was uglier than a failed assignment, an accident, a misplaced blow with the baseball bat. There was never anything moral about what he did, but there was an art to it, a display of craftsmanship and skill and design. The thought of losing that sometimes made him sick.

It's only when someone actually fails that things get truly ugly, he thought. *That's why the human being is the most anxious creature on earth. We are the only species that can fail at what we do. And that makes us the sole owners of what is most hideous. Everything except human failure is beautiful. And everything beautiful has something good inside. Isn't that true?*

Sving had a tendency to be bombastic at times.

It's the girl, he thought. *She's making me philosophical.*

"Are we going to sleep here tonight?" asked Tina. "We should have brought sleeping bags."

He was roused from his thoughts.

"Your mother and I probably need to go back home tonight. But you can stay here with your aunt," he said.

It was late by the time they got back to Trondheim, but there's no rest for the wicked, as the saying goes. He dropped Ane off at his apartment.

The Lars Brothers had taken the bus into town, and they were waiting for him near Rosenborg Junior High. They looked like schoolkids, only twice the size, and with contorted and unnatural features. Both of them had broken noses and tattoos that seemed to slide down their faces like charred and sagging skin. They looked like cartoon characters, animated sacks of shit, planned and designed by some outside force.

One of them grinned as Sving pulled up to the curb next to them. The other wore a serious expression. They got in, and Sving drove a few hundred yards to the parking lot at the REMA 1000 supermarket on Stadsingeniør Dahls Gate.

Sving grabbed the baseball bat and followed the Lars Brothers between the buildings of Rosenborg Park.

They were on their way to visit number ten on the list. A young law student named Jonas Fredly Holm.

Sving had softened him up with multiple blows. But all they'd been able to get out of him so far was that he'd been at the party. And he'd brought along a classmate named Knut Andersen Stang. The name wasn't on the list, but Sving wrote it down in his notebook. Maybe he was somebody Karlstad had overlooked. It'd be worth checking him out if they ended up leaving here empty-handed.

"Hey, look what I found!" Tall Lars grinned as he held up a pet rat. "Can I keep it?"

"No. You need to make yourself useful here," said Sving.

"Okay, here's something we can use," said Tall Lars. He put the rat on the coffee table and took out something from behind the bookcase. A strange contraption made from a piece of garden hose attached to a big container made from a plastic jug split in two.

"What the hell is that?"

Short Lars sounded annoyed. He was in the process of tying the student to a chair. It was hard work. The guy refused to stay upright because he was so dazed after Sving had worked him over with the bat.

"It's a beer bong."

"A what?"

"A *beer bong*. Real popular in the US. Essential for any respectable college party."

"How do you use it?"

Short Lars finished tying the last knot.

"Put a piece of tape over his mouth and I'll show you."

Short Lars did as he was told. Then Tall Lars got out his switchblade and cut a small opening in the tape. He stuck the end of the hose in the hole.

"Hold this. I'll be right back."

He handed the contraption to Short Lars and went into the kitchen.

"All I could find in the fridge was Paulaner. German wheat beer. It'll have to do."

Then he picked up the homemade bong, holding it lower than the student's head, and filled it with beer.

"There's no faster way to empty a half liter," he said as he raised the bong.

All of them watched as the beer disappeared through the semitransparent hose. The poor student desperately coughed and gagged, but in the end the only thing he could do was swallow.

"Shit. Those Americans sure think up some stupid things," said Short Lars.

"You've gotta love 'em," said Tall Lars.

The beer in the hose quickly disappeared, and they felt sure the student had swallowed all of it. So they were surprised when he suddenly started gasping and coughing violently behind the tape. He threw his head back and forth, and his eyes began to bulge. Then his whole face turned red. His neck muscles went rigid.

"Take off the tape!" said Sving.

Tall Lars complied.

The student was foaming at the mouth. A mixture of saliva, beer, and vomit ran down his chin. He started to shake violently, first just his head, then his whole body. He was gasping for air, making shrill gurgling sounds. He might have been trying to say something, but he managed only to gasp and squeal.

Short Lars took out his Sami knife and cut the rope binding him to the chair. The student toppled forward onto the floor. There he stayed, shaking as if having an epileptic fit. Sving and the Lars Brothers exchanged glances, stunned and confused. It was over in less than a minute. The violent spasms gradually ceased. The labored breathing stopped. Now he wasn't breathing at all. He lay there, lifeless, at their feet.

None of them spoke. They just stood there. The student's eyes were wide open, staring past them, his gaze unwavering.

Finally, Sving leaned down to feel for a pulse. The guy's throat was soft and motionless. There was no sign of life inside.

"Is he dead?" asked Tall Lars quietly.

Sving nodded.

"Fuck! We weren't supposed to kill anybody."

"What happened?" asked Short Lars.

"Anaphylaxis," said Sving.

"Ana what?" said Short Lars.

"Allergic shock," said Sving. "There must have been something in the beer that he couldn't tolerate."

"Then why the hell was it in his fridge?"

"Hard to say. But it doesn't matter. We've finished him off."

"What'll we do now?"

"We get the hell out of here," said Sving. "Not much else we can do."

"We'll put him out on the balcony," said Tall Lars.

"Why the hell would we do that?" said Short Lars.

"Because he's going to stink pretty soon."

"What does that have to do with anything?"

"Corpse stench. It settles in the walls. There's practically no way to get rid of it. Nobody's going to buy this apartment if it stinks of death."

"Lars, look at him. Does he look like he needs a Realtor?"

"No, but somebody's going to have to sell this place. Maybe his parents."

"Oh, right, his parents. And they'll be so grateful if we don't leave him here to stink up the whole apartment after we killed him. Is that what you're thinking?"

"Okay, never mind. I just thought that . . ."

"I told you not to think, you idiot!"

Sving couldn't believe what he was listening to as he stood there. Then he happened to notice a torn piece of plastic on the floor. Apparently something that had fallen out of one of the cupboards when they were ransacking the apartment.

He bent down and picked it up. He studied it carefully, then licked it. A piece of tape was attached to the plastic.

"I think we've actually found something," he murmured.

Unless he was terribly mistaken, this was a piece of plastic from the packaging Karlstad had used for the dope. He'd seen the package, and this was the same kind of plastic and tape. And unless his tongue was deceiving him, he had tasted traces of cocaine.

He got out his notebook and looked at the name he'd written down:

Knut Andersen Stang.

"Boys," he said calmly. "I think we need to change the order around a bit. And one more thing. The body? Lars is right." He pointed to Tall Lars. "It'd be better to put him outdoors. But we're not going to leave him on the balcony. We're going to chuck him over the side."

"Why's that?"

"Because we want to send a signal. Somebody's going to find him sooner or later anyway. There'll be an investigation. There's really nothing we can do about that. But the way things now stand, I think it would be advantageous for young Jonas Fredly Holm to be in the headlines."

"Is there somebody you want to send a message to?"

Sving looked again at the name he'd written down. He nodded.

"Let's get going, boys," he said.

"Here's how we're going to do it. The two of you go in and render him harmless. Then you exit and leave the rest of the job to me. I don't want any more fuckups. No more accidents."

The Lars Brothers nodded.

Sving started the car, and they drove off from Karlstad's farm at Jonsvatnet. They'd used the main building to regroup, finalize their plans, and take a quick nap. Short Lars had Googled Knut Andersen Stang, and they'd found an address for him in Trondheim, posted in connection with a page regarding orientation for new students. The post was only six months old, so they assumed the address was still valid.

It was early morning. They stopped at the Exxon gas station in Moholt. Sving went inside to buy a newspaper. Just as he'd thought, the headlines were all about the student from last night.

Did I lose control? he asked himself. He wasn't sure of the answer. But there had to be a way out of the whole mess. And if he found it, he promised himself that he was going to quit this shit. He was going to be the man he once thought he'd be.

"Have you noticed that movies are getting more and more violent?" said Tall Lars from the backseat as Sving took his place behind the wheel again.

"Not now," said Short Lars, sounding resigned.

"There's more violence everywhere."

"So are you going to lecture me on the harmful effects of violence in movies?"

"No, just the opposite," said Tall Lars. "I was going to say that I don't think it's harmful. And I don't think we enjoy watching those kinds of things because we're evil people, or because we all have a dark side, and stuff like that. I think we just plain need those kinds of movies because they remind us of our own mortality. They tell us how vulnerable our bodies are, how thin our skin is, literally, and how little it takes to turn us into nothing but gushing blood."

"And why is it good for us to be reminded of all that?"

"It think it makes us better human beings. I think it's cleansing."

"Cleansing? Christ, I can't believe the stupid things that come out of your mouth. It's tragic."

"Life is a tragedy," said Tall Lars.

"What you need to get cleansed out of you is the meth you smoked earlier."

Then they drove off to make a house call.

A couple of days later, Sving went out to Hitra to rig up the equipment. After giving Knut Andersen Stang his best performance that morning, he was positive he was their man. It was just a matter of time before he cracked. And Sving had given him a week. Just to make sure, he'd loaned out another baseball bat he owned. This one was made of aluminum, a present Karlstad had once given him. Sving hadn't had the heart to tell his friend that he preferred wooden bats. But now he didn't mind lending the practically new bat to the Lars Brothers so they could give this Stang guy a gentle reminder. Sving wasn't very pleased when they reported back from the assignment, telling him about using the rat that Tall Lars had taken from the student.

Now he was in Hitra alone, setting up things as quickly as he could. In either end of the living room he placed the laser sensors and the remote detonator for the bomb, so they would suffer the least amount of damage during the explosion. That would make it easier to remove them afterward. There wouldn't be much left of the blasting cap and timer. He hoped the police wouldn't find any leftover fragments. The success of the whole operation depended on the police quickly deciding that the old dynamite, which had been recently reported, had exploded accidentally.

After completing the work, he gathered up all the extra wires, packaging, and trash. The last time they were out here, Ane had shown him where her sister used to throw junk down a dried-out old well some distance from the house. And on that occasion they had helped her get rid of a moldy old mattress from upstairs. But Sving thought it would be too risky to leave any evidence so close to the explosion, so he put all the remaining items in a black garbage bag that he would take back with him. Then he paused to look out at the sea.

They hadn't yet seen any of the stormy weather that had been forecast for the south. But apparently it was headed north.

He took out his cell and called Ane.

Tina was crying in the background when she answered. Sving couldn't tell if it was defiance or desperation he heard in her voice.

"Okay, you can start the process now," he said.

"I laid the trail today. I met with a mutual friend of ours and mentioned exactly what he needed to know. So now I'll go out and send the letter."

"Remember to call the sheriff."

"Are you sure that's a good idea?"

"Trust me. He's a real slowpoke. And it's important."

22

The day before it happened . . .

"Do *you think* he'll come in the night or in the daytime?"

"It seems more likely he'd arrive at night so he could surprise me when I'm asleep. But we can't think like that when it comes to Rolf. You can't assume anything when it comes to him. He's always calculating. Probably he'll decide that I'd be less on my guard during the day, so that's when he'll get here."

"It's starting to get dark," said Sving.

They had backed the car in among the boulders and spruce trees, just as Ane had suggested. It was a good hiding place. Sving had suggested that they sit and wait in the boat that belonged to Ane's sister. They had borrowed the boat after taking Tina out to stay with her. It was an "archipelago jeep," a speedboat intended mostly for transport, though it did have a tarp that could be pulled up like a roof over the stern, if needed. But they had quickly dismissed the boat idea. The storm had now reached them, even though it wasn't as fierce as when it had raged over the southern and southwestern regions of the country. The boats were all safely moored inside the breakwater, but the water was anything but calm. In among the rocks, where the car was parked, they were protected from the squalls. It was cold outside, and every once in a while they had to turn on the car to stay warm. But it was the safest place to wait, and they also had a good view. They could see the road as it curved around the boulders on the other side of the property. And they had an adequate view of both sides of the house.

As soon as the dynamite exploded and they made sure that everything had gone as planned, Ane was going to get in the boat and head straight across the water to where her sister lived. The key was already waiting in the ignition. Sving would stay behind and clean up as fast as possible before any neighbors showed up after hearing the explosion. Then he would get in the car and drive to Trondheim. They had agreed not to meet again for several weeks. Not until everything had settled down and all suspicion had faded from the case.

"It's impossible to know when he might arrive," she said now.

"He'll probably get here sometime tomorrow," said Sving. "The only question is how long it'll take him to track you out here."

"He's efficient. That's all I can say."

She put her hand on Sving's thigh. He responded. They tore off their clothes and made love in the ice-cold car while steam poured off their bodies like dread.

Afterward they put their clothes back on, zipped their sleeping bags together, and snuggled next to each other. That was how they kept warm through the night, occasionally dozing off, with dreams that lasted only seconds, flaring up and then vanishing. In his dream, Sving caught a glimpse of his son, sleeping with his eyes open. He saw the young student they'd killed a few nights before, gasping and slobbering in the throes of death. He saw himself as a tattoo on Ane's skin. He saw a lot of other images in the tension between fear and hope, budding dreams that died with each restless movement next to him.

23

The day before it happened . . .

I*n the early morning hours,* they drove off to get coffee. It felt good to keep the heater on inside the car. Then they went back to resume their watch. Later in the day an old Mercedes appeared and parked down by the marina. An overweight young guy and a very old man transferred a lot of gear into one of the boats and then headed out to sea. Not long after that, Fagerhus finally showed up. Ane had fallen asleep and was snoring with her head resting on Sving's shoulder.

"Wake up," he said, giving her a cautious poke in the arm.

"What's happening?"

He pointed at the car as it pulled in behind the house and then reappeared in the driveway leading to the porch.

"We've got a nibble," she said, her voice so tense it sounded electrified.

They sat and watched without speaking.

Fagerhus got out of the car and immediately headed for the front door. Then they couldn't see him anymore. They didn't know whether he was waiting outside or had gone right in. All they could do was breathe heavily and wait.

"That's not his car," Ane said suddenly.

Sving didn't reply.

Inside him the clock was ticking. He pictured Rolf Fagerhus moving about inside the house. Where would he go first? How fast would he get to the dining table in the main room?

"He's been inside there forever," she said.

"No, it just feels like that," he told her.

Then came the explosion. The boom was more violent than even he could have imagined. The whole house seemed to expand. Boards were ripped off the walls and went flying in every direction. The windowpanes were pulverized by the shock wave and shot through the air like glitter.

Sving fixed his gaze on what was happening at the front of the house. The top of the table, under which he'd set the dynamite, now came flying through the big picture window. In front of the tabletop dove a dark-clad figure. Rolf Fagerhus. He had launched himself on top of the table just before the explosion, and now he'd been hurled through the window, with the table serving as a shield. He turned a somersault in the air and landed on the ground where it sloped down to the sea. There he rolled over several times before coming to a halt.

"Is he alive?"

Ane was whispering, as if there was a risk he might hear her from where he lay, stretched out in the snow, his body motionless and smoking. The tabletop lay below him, like a big ashtray from which he'd tumbled.

Then he moved. He put the palm of his hand on the ground and pushed himself up. Then he was on his knees, and finally standing upright, swaying.

"Shit! He's alive!" said Ane.

"I told you we shouldn't give him any time," said Sving. "That fucking countdown of yours. Give me the binoculars!"

Ane Fagerhus didn't move. Sving had to reach over her to get the binoculars out of the glove compartment. When he raised them to his eyes, he got a better look.

Rolf Fagerhus was standing there picking pieces of glass out of his face. A big shard had pierced his cheek, leaving an ugly gash. A big splinter was sticking out of one eye. Displaying a strange calm, he slowly pulled it out. Blood gushed out over his whole face. That eye had clearly been destroyed. Almost as if he were sleepy, Fagerhus rubbed his good eye. Then he looked down at himself. His pants hung in tatters around his legs, and a flesh wound marred one thigh. But his jacket seemed to be intact. He took a few tentative steps as he flexed his wrists. They had probably been badly sprained as he tried to break his fall after being hurled through the air. Sving couldn't even imagine the pain he must be feeling. He was amazed the man could stay on his feet at all.

"What do we do now?" Sving was thinking aloud.

"The baseball bat. You have to go after him with the bat."

"No. Then it's guaranteed to be a homicide case."

"I don't give a fuck!"

"Who else but you has a motive for wanting him dead? Do you know how fast they'd come after us if we kill him here in the yard?"

They sat there staring at Fagerhus. He had started walking around the house to the car he'd parked in the driveway. They saw him open the door and take out a bag from the passenger seat. Then he closed the door and sank down onto the ground. He sat there, leaning against the front tire as he took out something that looked like a toiletry kit.

"A syringe, rubber tubing, a spoon, a little cylinder. He's pouring something out of it into the spoon." Sving was still looking through the binoculars as he recounted what he saw.

"Christ, I think he's going to shoot up."

"Rolf? Not on your life. He'd never do anything that might impede his thinking."

"It's for the pain," said Sving. "He can't keep going unless he does something about the pain."

"What do you think it is?"

"Heroin."

"Will that help with the pain?"

"Heroin helps with just about anything."

Sving moved the binoculars over the scene as Rolf Fagerhus got ready to shoot up.

"Wait a minute," he said suddenly. "I can see a face in the back window. There's somebody else in the car."

"Are you kidding? Give me those!" Ane grabbed the binoculars from Sving. "You're right. There's a woman in there."

Now Fagerhus stood up and tossed away the syringe. He was moving in slow motion. Like a sleepwalker, he opened the back door and hauled out the woman. She fell to the ground because her wrists and feet were bound. Then he took out a knife.

"Shit, that's the knife he bought on Crete last summer. Do you know how much it cost? What a fucking idiot!"

Sving looked at Ane Fagerhus. How could she be thinking about the cost of the knife right now? Again he sensed something that had been nagging him for a while. A thought that he didn't want to consider popped into his mind. Did she have other reasons for wanting her husband dead?

Even without the binoculars he could see what was happening. Slowly Fagerhus leaned down and cut the plastic ties around the woman's wrists and ankles. He was setting her free. Quickly she got to her feet and took three steps away from him. Sving was all too familiar with her body language. She was afraid.

But it turned out she had nothing to fear from Fagerhus. As soon as she was free, he turned on his heel and set off running. He dashed around the house to where they couldn't see him and then reappeared on the path leading to the dock.

"Shit, Sving! You have to stop him!" cried Ane.

But Sving didn't move.

They watched as Fagerhus jumped into the speedboat. The key was in the ignition, so he turned on the engine and then untied the mooring lines. The next second he was heading out to sea.

Sving took back the binoculars and watched him go.

Ane kept on howling.

"Tina! He knows that she's out there with my sister! That's where he's going! He's going to get her!"

Sving didn't move as he studied the motorboat. Fagerhus was steering in a drug-induced haze. He was going much too fast for the huge waves left by the storm that had raged during the night. His reflexes were dulled by the heroin. He was having a hard time setting a straight course.

All of a sudden it happened. The boat slammed right into a high wave and was thrown violently into the air so it almost tipped over and capsized. It miraculously came back down with the rudder in the water, but Fagerhus was thrown overboard. Since he was so out of it when he commandeered the boat, he hadn't fastened the wire to the dead-man's switch, so the boat continued on without him. But it didn't get far. Only now did Sving notice the smaller boat, which was directly in the speedboat's path. Moving at an insane speed, it headed for the small vessel. Just before the collision, he saw somebody jump into the sea.

"That's got to be the end of him," said Sving.

"Did he fall in?" asked Ane as if she couldn't quite believe it. She grabbed the binoculars from him. "He won't live long in such cold water. Looks like we've had better luck than we expected. Maybe we'll get out of this after all."

"Except that we're forgetting one thing."

"What's that?"

"We have a witness."

Sving pointed to the yard where the woman from the car—a brunette around thirty or forty—was now sitting on the backseat with her legs sticking out as she bent forward with her head resting on her knees.

"How are we going to clean up after ourselves now?"

"You need to take care of her."

"She's an innocent bystander. Plus, we don't know anything about her. She could be anyone. If we kill her, we don't know whether that might lead the police to us."

"Fuck, Sving! This doesn't fit with what I've heard about you. Innocent bystander? Don't you get that she's a fucking whore?"

"Ane, what are you talking about? He had her tied up. There's something strange about all this. Something very strange, if you ask me."

"A fucking whore!"

Now Ane got out of the car and slammed the door behind her. She opened the back door and took out the baseball bat, which was lying on the backseat.

Sving saw her fury erupt like a trembling frenzy in every move she made. Where did that kind of anger come from? *It's not fear,* he thought. *It's not the terrified thought of getting caught for doing something bad out of necessity.* This was something altogether different.

Silently he watched as Ane began hammering the woman with the bat. She hit her again and again, until there was no sign of resistance left in her, until she could no longer protect her bloodied face with her hands. Even then Ane didn't stop. Finally, she tossed aside the bat and sank down on the slushy driveway.

She stayed there for a moment, huddled up and looking almost like she was praying. Then she stood up and grabbed the arm of the woman she had practically beaten to death. She dragged her over to the well at the edge of the property, toward the boulders.

Sving still didn't move. He merely raised the binoculars to his eyes, as if they might protect him from what he was seeing, a way of filtering out the madness.

Ane dragged the thin, lifeless body to the well and pushed it over the side. But her hand must have got caught on something, maybe a cord from the woman's jacket, because she ended up being pulled partway in before she managed to get loose and straighten up.

On her way back, Ane stopped at the car and rummaged around inside. She took out a bag before retrieving the baseball bat from the driveway.

Then she came back and got in beside Sving. She tossed the bat and the bag in the backseat.

"Shit! I dropped my cell phone in the well!"

"Christ!" said Sving. That's all he managed to say.

"I took his bag. Maybe there's something inside we can use. I think there's more heroin inside."

"Do you realize what you've done?" Sving glared at her, furious and in despair.

"That's what I hired you for, you shithead!" she said.

She seemed exhilarated and confused. Her eyes flitted around, unable to settled on any fixed point. Ane Fagerhus was shivering like a freezing dog.

"You didn't hire me," said Sving. "I went along with this to protect you."

"Some protection! What fucking bullshit! You're nothing but a fuckup. Shit! I don't know what to say. Protection? You? You utter fuck!"

She wasn't making any sense. She turned to face Sving and began hitting him. First the same kind of slaps that she'd given him that time in bed back at his place in Strindheim. And he instantly felt the same sort of shame that had come over him afterward as he sat on the toilet for over an hour. But once again he didn't have it in him to strike a woman.

She kept on hitting, now using her fists. Finally, he grabbed her wrists and managed to push her, flailing and cursing, back in the passenger seat. He put both arms around her and held on tight. He felt the rage in her body ebbing and flowing spasmodically. At last she calmed down, breathing hard.

"It was you who hit *him*," said Sving as he sank back in the driver's seat.

Then he turned pensive. "In ten percent of domestic violence cases, it's the woman who's the abuser, but people don't want to believe it. You said there was physical abuse involved, but you never said he was the one doing the beating."

"He's a shithead!"

"It was you who hit him."

"He used psychological terror. He kept on talking about his fucking father the whole time. His father, who disappeared into the woods and had words of wisdom for everything. You have no idea how horrible it is to feel like you're never right about anything, like you're worthless. That man didn't have a single feeling in his whole body. I hit him to make him react. And one thing I told you was true."

"What's that?"

"He was capable of murder. There's no doubt about it."

"You loved him," said Sving. "This rage of yours? It's jealousy. The way you attacked that woman. It can only be jealousy. You loved him. Why did you want me to kill him?"

"I told you. He was impossible to live with."

"But you loved him."

"Love dies."

"But why murder? You could have left him."

"I didn't want him to destroy Tina. That's what he does. He destroys everyone around him. Just look what he did to me."

"There's some other motive here."

All sorts of things were whirling through Sving's mind. He thought back to the planning they'd done.

"I asked your sister to cancel the insurance on the house," he said. "But I forgot to ask about any other kind of insurance."

"Do you really think it's that simple, you idiot?"

"No, but that's part of the picture. How much was he worth?"

"More than you'll ever be," said Ane Fagerhus.

Then she opened the door on her side and got out, heading back to the other car. Sving watched as she reached in through the door, which was still open. Had she seen something else when she went over there? A moment later she stood up. And in her hands was a sawed-off shotgun.

Sving instantly started up the car. He got it moving, following the same tracks in the thin layer of snow that they'd made when they'd backed the car into position.

Up ahead he could see that she was now standing between the house and the parked car. She was aiming at him.

He stomped on the gas and drove straight for her. The shotgun went off when he was no more than ten yards away. Instinctively he ducked below the dashboard. The buckshot struck the windshield, which exploded over him. He couldn't see where he was going, but he felt the car veer and start to skid. It came to an abrupt halt with the driver's side pressed against the wall of the house. When he sat up, he saw that she was right in front of the car. She'd thrown herself to the side to avoid the swerving vehicle, and now she lay on her stomach on the ground. In a flash Sving put the car in reverse and backed in an arc away from the house. He gave the other car a slight nudge with his bumper before he shifted into first and raced down the driveway toward the road. Behind him, Ane Fagerhus, his lover, was now back on her feet. In the rearview mirror he saw her take aim and fire again, but this time she missed completely. Sving eventually came out onto the highway. Driving without a windshield, he headed for Trondheim. He was hoping to leave this whole episode behind him for good.

24

Three days after it happened . . .

Look at the boy. Look at the way his mother is looking at him now. He's sitting on the floor in the living room, on the rug that came from his grandfather's house in the south. On the TV a news clip is showing a house on Hitra with all the windows blown out. Shards of glass and pieces of the building are scattered over the dried, brown tufts of grass and traces of snow. A reporter with wind ruffling his hair stares somberly at the boy, almost as if they're together in the same scene, on either side of the TV screen.

Then the picture cuts to a photo of a woman in her thirties, with dark, shoulder-length hair. In the photo she is wearing a police uniform from the state of Virginia in the United States.

The mother, who is standing in the doorway behind the TV, sees something in the boy that she has never seen before. Something that has to do with the woods.

Frost has settled inside of him, she thinks. And it may never let go of him again. This is a dangerous country. Not everyone can stand as much silence as they have here.

She wants to move back south, taking along only the boy and his siblings and move away from this land that killed their father.

As she stands there, she is holding a book in her hand. It was his. A souvenir of the man she loved. She doesn't read. But now that he's gone, she takes comfort in holding his books, rubbing her fingertips over the leather, lovingly, as if he now lived inside these books.

25

When it happened . . .

J*ensen had been talking* on his cell almost the whole drive. After he reported to Trondheim about the man who'd run away from the doctor's clinic, his phone hadn't stopped ringing. The police were at a loss about what to do. It wasn't clear who exactly they were dealing with. When the man was brought into the clinic, he'd had no ID on him, and the name he gave had quickly turned out to be phony. Jensen and the sheriff's deputy had agreed to meet at the sheriff's office on Hitra to discuss the matter further.

It was on their way out to the cars that Singsaker's cell had rung. It took a moment for him to realize it was his phone. After he went on sick leave and Felicia disappeared, he could go an entire day without getting a call. But he managed to pick up before it stopped ringing.

"Odd Singsaker."

At first no one spoke on the other end. All he could hear was someone breathing heavily.

"Who is this?"

A voice said something. It was garbled, incoherent, sounding like the person was ill and barely able to speak.

"Who?"

"It's me."

Now he managed to hear the words over all the traffic noise, the wheezing and gurgling.

He recognized something in the voice that had initially sounded so foreign.

"It's me, sweetheart."

Even though every word was so contorted as to be nearly incomprehensible, the accent was still audible.

"Felicia? Is that you?"

He had stopped halfway between the clinic and the cars. Up ahead he saw Jensen and the sheriff's deputy. They were discussing something. But Odd felt as if he was in some other reality.

"It's me."

"Good Lord, what's wrong with you? What's happened to your voice?"

"You have to find me, Odd. You have to come and find me now. Please."

"Where are you?"

"I don't know."

Her voice was getting weaker, as if it had taken all her strength to speak. Now she was barely whispering.

"You need to tell me where you are. Are you locked in somewhere?"

"I heard an explosion. That was a long time ago." That's what he thought she said, but he could hardly hear her anymore.

He heard some clattering sounds on the line.

"Are you still there? Where you heard the explosion?"

"Not far away."

She was clearly straining to make an effort.

"Please come, Odd! Just come. You have to get me out of here. We . . ."

She was breathing hard. Then he heard another clattering sound, as if she'd dropped the phone, as if it fell to the ground and she was trying to pick it up.

He stood there, shouting to her on his cell. But either she was gone, or she couldn't say anything more. Soon the line went dead.

He rushed over to Jensen.

"I need to take your car," he said.

"Why?"

"Felicia. She just called me. I think she's near the site of the explosion. I know that you have to go to the sheriff's office and try to track down the man who fled. That's your job. But I need to go and find her."

Jensen gave Singsaker a long look. Then he nodded.

"I'll catch a ride with him," he said, nodding toward the sheriff's deputy. Then he handed his car keys to Singsaker.

Singsaker jumped into the driver's seat. As he backed out of the parking lot and raced toward the highway, Jensen and the deputy were still standing next to their vehicle. Jensen looked worried. By that point he'd probably realized that he'd just done something he was going to regret.

The site of the explosion had already been logged into the GPS in Jensen's car, so it didn't take Singsaker long to find it. The last part of the way he drove on a narrow country road that hadn't been properly plowed, but a number of other cars had already made a track in the snow. He came around two boulders, and there it was. Dusk was starting to settle in, but even from a distance the damage to the house was still visible. All the windows on the ground floor had been blown out, and some of the panes upstairs had also shattered. A lot of the siding had fallen off the walls, and in some places there were holes all the way through. It must have been a big explosion. In the driveway Singsaker saw a rental car parked behind the local doctor's vehicle. The rental was the car that had been traced to Felicia.

She was at Gardermoen Airport, he thought. She was on her way home, for the second time, and she ended up here. Why? And why hadn't she come back the first time she was booked on a flight? Then none of this would have happened. Then both of them would be sitting at home, and she wouldn't be lying injured somewhere, waiting for him to find her.

He approached the driveway in front of the house.

Then he stomped on the brakes. A figure came running toward his car from some trees that stood between the road and what looked like a well over by the rocks nearby. He heard a shot and noticed that one of his tires exploded. Another shot struck the window behind him on the driver's side, shattering the glass. Bits of glass rained down on him. Then the door was yanked open. He saw only half a figure—an arm, one side of the face, short dark hair. The rest was behind the door. The man was dressed in white. On his chest it said in blue letters: *Health Services*.

The man who escaped from the clinic, thought Singsaker. *What's he doing here?* Now he caught a glimpse of his whole face, a bandage covering one eye. Then a gun struck him in the face and night fell instantly.

When Singsaker came to, he was lying on a dock. His face was pressed down into the snow, but he was able to breathe through a crack between the planks. He heard the sea underneath him. The waves were still high, and a strong wind was blowing through his gray hair. He turned his head to one side and caught sight of feet. Wearing slippers. Bare calves covered in cuts and gashes. A white gown, like the ones given to hospital patients, reached past the man's knees.

Then Singsaker realized that his wrists and ankles were bound. The man who had attacked him in the car now grabbed the plastic ties around his wrists and began tugging at him.

Then Singsaker's phone rang. He felt fingers rummaging in his right-hand pocket to get out his cell, which was then held out so he could see the display. The hands holding the phone had the same injuries as the man's legs. Some of the cuts looked deep, and one of them had been bandaged, most likely at the clinic.

Singsaker could no longer trust his memory, yet he was positive the number he saw was the same one that Felicia had called from less than half an hour ago. It wasn't Felicia's number. He had that one stored on his contact list, and her name would have shown up if she was using it to call him. He wondered how she'd gotten access to this number. Was somebody helping her to call? That didn't seem likely. She had sounded so alone.

"Anybody you know?" asked the voice above him, sounding eerily calm.

He didn't reply.

"Well, I'm afraid you're not going to take the call."

The display went dark. The ringtone died away. Then the cell disappeared from view. Singsaker saw the slippers move across the dock. Desperately he tried to raise his head to see what was going on, but he couldn't lift his gaze higher than the man's waist. The man stopped at the end of the dock. Singsaker could hear what happened next. A loud splash as the phone hit the water.

Then the man came back and grabbed him again. This time he didn't hesitate. He dragged Singsaker over to the very edge of the dock and pushed him far enough that his own weight pulled him down into the water.

Was Singsaker scared? Was he consumed by an intense and paralyzing fear of death? He'd always been the type of person who could never imagine his own death. The thought seemed somehow irrelevant. Maybe that was why he'd never fully considered any other consequences of his illness other than that it made him forgetful and put him behind at work.

But right now it was difficult to imagine any outcome other than death. He drifted down in the water. It was only a few degrees above freezing, but as an enthusiastic ice bather, he was used to this kind of temperature. He could stand it for a while, but not forever. And it wasn't very deep at this spot. Maybe six or seven feet. Enough that his head was underwater when he stood on the bottom. He kicked with all his might and managed to get his face above the waves for a short time before sinking down again.

The first time he came to the surface, he saw the man standing on the dock. And for the first time he saw all of him, not just arms and feet. A tall figure wearing hospital garb. He'd turned around and was on his way back toward shore, moving calmly, as if he had no worries, was in no hurry, indifferent to what had just happened behind him, as if Singsaker no longer existed.

Then he was gone. Singsaker sank down again, touched bottom, and kicked his way back up to the surface.

By then the perpetrator had reached shore. His white clothing made him nearly invisible against the snow on the slope leading up to the house. It almost looked as if his dark head were hovering all by itself in the dim light.

Singsaker repeated his kicking maneuver on the bottom several more times. But each time he sank down, the current pulled him a little farther out, and the sea got deeper. On his sixth and seventh attempts, he didn't make it to the surface before going down again. This time he thought:

Now she's going to die.

That much he understood. If he didn't manage to get to Felicia, it would be over. She was badly injured and had lost all strength. He'd heard that in her voice. If there were other people near her, they weren't there to help. And now both of them were going to die.

What were you doing out here, Felicia? he thought. *How did you end up here of all places?*

When he touched bottom again, he lay down.

Normally he was good at holding his breath. He also knew that the low temperature of the water had set off a diving reflex that is common to all mammals when they land in cold water. This reflex moves the blood from the extremities to the body's most important organs, the brain and the area behind the rib cage, which supports the lungs. So it's possible to survive longer without oxygen than under normal circumstances. Singsaker estimated that he had about a minute left before panic would take over. Then he'd start straining his arms and legs, which would quickly increase his need for oxygen. Sooner or later he'd open his mouth and water would enter his respiratory passages. That in turn would cause a so-called larynx spasm, an automatic constriction of the vocal cords to prevent water from seeping all the way down into his lungs. But it wouldn't give him more oxygen. Soon afterward he would lose consciousness, the spasm in his throat would cease, and luckily he'd be blacked out and unable to notice his blood vessels bursting before his heart stopped beating and his brain slowly died. Without oxygen it might take six or seven minutes at this temperature before he was totally brain dead. Drowning was a slow and brutal way to die. If some miracle didn't occur, drowning was all he had left in this life.

Even so, he lay on the sea bottom, thinking.

Then something occurred to him that almost gave him hope. He started tugging at his coat with his fingers, bound behind his back. He pulled and scratched until he managed to get hold of his left pocket. After more fumbling, he reached one hand inside. Then he pulled out the plastic bag that he'd put there in the clinic. From the bag he fished out the item he'd seized as evidence. It was the scalpel that Knut Andersen Stang had used to kill himself. Singsaker held it firmly with his fingers and directed it toward the plastic ties binding him.

After cutting his wrists and ankles free, Singsaker rose to the surface and gulped in air that tasted both sour and sweet. He didn't just inhale, he swallowed the air, drinking it in. It felt like something brightened inside of him, and he could have laughed. If he hadn't been about to be carried beyond the breakwater, wearing heavy clothes and boots, and if he hadn't known that he'd lost way too much valuable time, he might have howled and bellowed with glee. But as things stood, this moment of joy and relief could only be short-lived.

Quickly he shed his coat and boots and began swimming toward shore. In the harbor, within the breakwater, the water was thankfully calm and made for easy swimming.

When Singsaker finally clambered up onto the dock, he couldn't see his attacker, but he realized he knew far too little about the man. What was he doing out here? Had he come here with Felicia? Could he possibly be the man the Oslo police were looking for? Had he caused the explosion? Or was the tentative official theory correct, that old dynamite had exploded accidentally? And why had the man crashed his boat out there at sea? There were too many loose ends. Nothing made sense. And what Singsaker most wanted to know about this man was: Did he know where Felicia was? Was he the person holding her captive?

Singsaker took off all his clothes and wrung out as much water as he could before he put them back on. The temperature in the air was well above freezing now that the storm had passed. His clothes weren't going to freeze on his body, but they also weren't going to dry anytime soon. It was important for him to keep moving.

There were too many footprints leading up the slope from the dock for him to know which way the man had gone, but he followed the tracks toward the house. Halfway there, he stopped abruptly. A sharp bang came from the open windows of the house. A shot fired from a medium-sized weapon, he determined. And with that he started running toward the front entrance.

The moment he reached it, he saw that the police tape the fire department had put up to cordon off the front door had been broken. The ends of the tape fluttered in the drifts still surrounding the house. The front door had been blown off its hinges and stood leaning against the wall next to the opening.

Singsaker ran up the stairs to the porch and went inside. The main room had been totally wrecked by the explosion. The wind blowing in from the sea was sharp with damp and salt. The whole place smelled scorched. The walls were black with soot. Several gaps in the ceiling revealed the upstairs, and a big hole in the floor opened into the basement.

Singsaker moved cautiously around the hole on the rickety floorboards. In the middle of the room a person lay on the floor. The white hospital garb told Singsaker that the man who had attacked him was dead. A big red patch was spreading over the white back. He'd probably been shot in the chest. That meant the blood on his shirt was pouring out of an exit hole in his back. A shotgun lay next to him.

Then he caught sight of her. She was sitting on a burned sofa in front of a window with no glass. Her smile was calm, very, very calm, as if none of what had just happened was real.

"I prefer a pistol," she said, holding up a weapon.

Singsaker looked at her, uncomprehending.

She laughed.

"He had a pistol when he came in. It was loaded. He was going to shoot me. But I shot him with the shotgun that I found in his car. The pistol must have been in the car the whole time too, but I didn't see it. That's where he must have gotten it. His car is still out there. Shouldn't the police have come to get it long ago?"

"Up until now this has been considered an accident. The police don't have the manpower out here, and their priority was what happened out at sea," said Singsaker. "But backup is on the way from Trondheim," he added, mostly in an attempt to worry her.

"I wonder where he got this gun from. It's not a service weapon, is it?" she said.

Singsaker looked at it. A Glock 19, nine millimeter. Used by PST's security service, among others, but not standard issue for a police officer. The gun was also popular among criminals. But for both policeman and crook, the gun worked the same. It didn't discriminate.

"Is the man lying on the floor a police officer?"

She nodded, casually motioning with the gun.

"Do you know him?"

"He's my husband. He came here to kill me."

"So you shot him in self-defense?"

She didn't reply.

"I'm looking for a woman," said Singsaker. "Dark hair, brown eyes, in her thirties, with an American accent."

She still didn't speak.

"Why don't you give me the gun?" He held out his hand.

"Are you from the police?"

Singsaker nodded.

"What are you doing here alone?"

"I came to inspect the site."

"Alone? Just you? You're not telling me the whole truth, are you?"

Singsaker looked at her. The sweat on her face, the makeup that was smeared all over, her hair sticking out in all directions, her intense gaze fixed on a spot somewhere above his head.

"You know her personally," she said then.

Singsaker didn't answer. Now she lowered her gaze and looked him in the eye. The gun was still aimed at him.

"It's love, isn't it?"

"Why don't you give me the gun and we can go outside and talk about it. It's not safe in here. The floor could collapse at any minute."

"I was once in love too," she said, pointing the gun at the dead man on the floor. It looked like she was pointing at the patch of blood and the heart that had stopped beating.

"Why don't you tell me about it outside?"

"I'll tell you everything. But we have to stay in here."

Then she aimed the gun at Singsaker before lowering it again.

"I was the one who killed her."

"Killed who?"

"You'll find out sooner or later. I know that now. But this really shouldn't end with prison time."

"Who? Who did you kill?"

"The person you just asked me about."

"Felicia?"

"Was that her name?"

"What have you done?"

"I beat her to death with a baseball bat."

"When did you do that?"

"Hours ago. Since then I've been sitting in here waiting. Except when the fire department was here. I went for a walk then. I've had time to think about what I did."

She laughed, a strange, hollow-sounding laughter, as if she'd said something funny far away outside the windows, something that had nothing to do with them.

"I've been sitting here holding the shotgun." She pointed at the floor. "Stuck the muzzle in my mouth several times. This shouldn't end with prison time. Why couldn't I stay calm? I could have learned a lot from that shithead."

Singsaker didn't understand what she was talking about, but he wanted to get back to the only thing that mattered.

"I talked to her less than an hour ago," he said.

"Who?"

"Felicia."

"Impossible. I beat the living daylights out of her."

"But she didn't die. Did she have a phone on her?"

"I tried to pull the trigger," she said, ignoring Singsaker. "I tried, but I couldn't do it. I stuck the muzzle in my mouth, but my fingers were shaking so badly. There was no strength in them. No matter what I've done up to now, I can't finish it."

"I don't know half of what's gone on here. The only thing I need to know is where she is. You don't have to tell me anything else. What did you do with her after you hit her with the bat?"

Singsaker gave her a fierce look. He didn't know whether to believe her or not. Did she kill her husband in self-defense? Had he come out here to kill her? Why was she confessing to murdering Felicia?

"You think this is some sort of mystery?" she said as if she could read his mind. "This is no a mystery. It's a thriller. I don't watch thrillers. I like mysteries. They have such a meditative calm about them. But this has been too much of a thriller. Don't you agree?"

The gun in her hand was still not pointed directly at Singsaker as she talked, but more or less in his direction. The whole time he kept glancing at the floor between them, at the shotgun and the man's body. He was surprised at how cold and calm she sounded, talking about what had happened as if it were all images in a movie. How was it possible for her to distance herself like that?

"I know you want to shoot me, but as a police officer there are certain rules you have to follow. So let me make it easy for you: Pick up the shotgun!"

Singsaker didn't move. Now he was looking straight down the barrel of the gun, which was twenty-five or thirty feet away.

"Pick up the shotgun, or I'll shoot you!" The voice didn't waver. The tone remained flat.

He took two steps forward, still not sure what he was going to do. Now he was standing with the shotgun between his feet. His heart was pounding. He didn't know what he was feeling. Was it hate? Was this what hate felt like? No, more like sorrow or anger, rage, but also hope.

Then he picked up the shotgun and took aim.

"You know I'm never going to kill you. Not as long as you haven't told me where Felicia is and what you've done with her," he said.

"Shoot!" she said. "I killed your girlfriend with a baseball bat. Shoot me! That's what you want to do."

He was breathing hard. He realized he needed to change tactics.

"Why do you want me to shoot you? Why don't you want to live anymore?"

"What do I have to live for? I've killed someone. I'll end up in prison. Tina."

"Tina?"

"My daughter."

"Where is she now?"

"She's staying with my sister."

"It's not certain that you'll get prison time for this," said Singsaker. "It was self-defense. Was he the one who blew up the house?"

She nodded.

"And Felicia. I don't know what you've done with her. But she can be saved."

"No, she can't. You said so yourself. You don't know what I've done." For the first time a hint of vulnerability appeared in her voice.

He saw her finger beginning to curl around the trigger of the gun. He saw it in her eyes. A deathly calm came over her. He knew from experience that he couldn't wait any longer.

"Do it before I do!" she said.

Those were her last words. There was nothing more to say. And he pulled the trigger.

The buckshot sprayed into her right thigh. She fell to the floor with a shriek. The gun fell out of her hand as she grabbed her thigh. In a flash, Singsaker ran over to her and picked up the gun, took out the magazine, and stuck it under his belt. She lay on the floor, squirming. When she realized that he hadn't shot to kill, rage took over.

"You fucking bastard, you motherfucker!" she howled.

Singsaker looked at her. Some part of him might have felt sorry for her, but mostly he was furious. And in a hurry. Now that he'd started on this path, there was no going back. He was under the command of the sweat pouring out of him, urged on by his own nerves, with a flickering, wild feeling all over his body, as if his brain were vibrating at a totally unfamiliar frequency.

With his bare right foot, he rolled her over onto her back. Then he planted his heel on her thigh.

She screamed.

He pointed the muzzle of the shotgun at her head.

"Where is she?"

"Just shoot me, you bastard!"

"Tell me where she is and I'll shoot you if that's what you really want." He'd never heard himself talk like this before.

She fell quiet, lay there for a long time with her eyes closed and breathing hard. Her hair was soaked with sweat.

Then she screamed again, and now it felt like they were both part of the same pain. As if pain were everywhere.

They were breathing in time. Then she spoke.

"In the well."

"What well?" Singsaker racked his memory.

"The one outside. You must have seen it."

He crossed the room in one bound.

Behind him he could hear her screaming, but he didn't know what she was saying. He was relieved that he'd resisted the temptation to fill her head with buckshot. It had scared him. That dark impulse coming from somewhere inside of him, a place that he hadn't known existed. He could have killed her. He'd been very close to doing it, very close.

When he reached the well, he looked down over a high edge that was walled up with granite. He was still wearing his wet clothes and had neither a flashlight nor phone to give him any light. At first he saw nothing but darkness down there. But after a moment his eyes adjusted to the dark and he could make out a figure against a lighter backdrop, with slender limbs stretched out to either side, looking like dark cracks in the bottom of the well.

"Felicia!" he shouted.

But there was no answer.

He yelled her name over and over, as if that might be enough to keep her alive. But he didn't hear a sound. The figure down there didn't move. So there was nothing else to do. He dropped over the side of the well and hung from his hands. A smell of mold and decay rose up from the well. Because of the dark, it was impossible to judge the distance. He'd just have to chance it. He let go, hoping he wouldn't hit her when he fell.

About ten feet down his feet landed on a mattress. He deliberately turned his body toward the stone wall so as not fall on her. Luckily he managed to use his hands to break his fall so the only injury he suffered was bruised wrists. Crouching down, he turned to face her.

The dry well was full of trash. Paint cans, broken furniture, boards. A lot of discarded electronics piled on top of each other. For a moment his gaze rested on a twisted piece of gray plastic that didn't look like anything else. But he couldn't say why it had caught his eye.

Felicia lay on the rough, gray mattress.

She almost looked like she was asleep. But if so, it was a deep sleep. Now he could clearly see her face, her fair skin, her closed lips. There were dark stains on the mattress under her head. He reached out to touch them, then sniffed at his fingers. It was blood. Behind her lay a cell phone. He grabbed it and saw that it was turned on. The display lit up. He punched in the number of police headquarters in Trondheim.

"This is Chief Inspector Odd Singsaker. I'm at the site of the explosion on Hitra. Are you familiar with the case?"

A female officer answered in the affirmative.

"There's a woman with gunshot wounds inside the house. Another woman with unknown injuries is down in the well. A man has been killed. Send an ambulance and a helicopter! Now!"

As soon as he was certain that his colleague on the phone had grasped the seriousness of the situation, he ended the call.

Then he gathered his courage and held his hand to Felicia's lips. He stayed like that until he was sure about what he felt, until he could determine that there was in fact a faint, rhythmic puff of warm air coming from her mouth. She was breathing.

He felt for her pulse to confirm what he almost didn't dare believe. It was there. She was alive.

He shouldn't move her head. That much he knew about head trauma. But he needed to revive her. He began blowing air into Felicia's face at the same time as he massaged her hands. Her fingers were ice cold.

He kept it up for a long time as he listened for the sounds of the rescue team. Suddenly she opened her eyes. Blinked several times. Her gaze was dazed and damp, like a child with fever.

"Felicia?" he said calmly.

She heard him. That was immediately apparent in her face, although it took her a moment for her eyes to find his in the dark.

"Odd?"

Her voice still sounded as garbled as it had on the phone. He saw why she was having trouble talking. Her jaw was swollen from a violent blow. It was probably broken. Blood was still trickling out of her mouth.

"It's me," he said.

"Where are we?"

"Inside a well on Hitra."

Unexpectedly she smiled, as if he'd said something funny.

"What are we doing here?"

"Somebody threw you down here."

"I remember a woman with a baseball bat. Where is she?"

"You saw her? You know that it was a woman who did this?"

"I think that's what I remember. I'm not sure."

"It's not important. We're safe now."

"Everything hurts, Odd," she said.

"I know. It's going to be all right, sweetie. Everything's going to be fine."

"Really? I'm so cold."

"The ambulance is on its way. They're sending a helicopter."

She smiled again. She seemed more lucid.

"I can't be rescued by helicopter every six months."

She was talking about something that had happened when they first met, and she'd been wounded by the perpetrator in a homicide case out on Fosen.

They both smiled.

"This is the last time. You just have to get through this too."

He put his hand on her hair.

"Odd," she said, suddenly serious. "I don't know if I can make it. It doesn't feel like I will this time."

"Of course you're going to make it. The helicopter is on the way. They'll be here any second. They have equipment to get you out of here quickly. You'll be at St. Olav Hospital in less than an hour."

"I need to tell you something, Odd."

"You can tell me tomorrow, when you're feeling better."

"I've done something."

"Tomorrow, I said."

"Something that you won't be able to forgive."

"Do you love me?"

"I can't lie to you, Odd. Not now. I had doubts. I've had doubts."

"About us?"

She nodded, very cautiously.

"It's natural to have doubts."

"I don't have doubts anymore. I know what I did was wrong."

"What?"

"It was me. I don't know what it is. But I panicked. I fell in love with you, and then I panicked. I didn't think I could handle it, that it would all be too much. You know. Us. This whole life."

"And now?"

"Now I know better. I could have handled it. You're the one, Odd. It can't be anyone else. But I need you to forgive me for something."

"We'll talk more about it tomorrow."

"Odd, look at me. There's not going to be any tomorrow. All we have is now."

"Only now?"

"Only now, sweetheart. That's all."

She was crying. Wasn't she? He thought it sounded like crying.

"You can't give up."

"It's not a matter of giving up, Odd. This is bigger than us. It's not something I can control. I want you to hold me."

"Felicia. I can hear them now. The sirens. They're coming."

"Please hold me, Odd."

He lay down next to her. Put his arm around her waist and pressed close.

"Felicia?" he whispered into her ear. "Felicia, can you hear me?"

He thought she nodded. A gurgling sound came from her throat.

"Sweetie. It doesn't matter, whatever it is. I forgive you. But you can't die. We'll make it through together. I can hear them coming."

"I don't want to leave you, Odd," she said. "Not now. Not now that I'm finally sure."

"You're not going to leave. I love you. You know that?"

Neither of them said a word for a while. The sound of the sirens got louder. Then she spoke, so faintly that he almost couldn't hear what she said.

"I love you too, Odd."

Then she took a breath that seemed to go on forever.

"Good-bye, my love," said the weary voice of Felicia.

Then the silence seemed different, a silence that was no longer anything but silence, the silence that was left behind. She suddenly felt heavy in his arms. Singsaker sat up and looked at her. Her face was unmarked from that angle. It seemed clean and freshly washed, as if she were suddenly surfacing from the water in a bathtub. She was smiling. The way she smiled when she teased him.

He raised her head, felt for her breath, her pulse, tried to breathe life back into her, massaged her, wept on her breast, listened to the calm inside. Her heart didn't beat again. Life didn't return.

Finally, he lay down beside her and looked up. The sky had turned pitch dark while he was inside the well. It was night. The sun had set, and the eternal night of space had settled over the earth.

Overhead he could hear the sound of sirens from the vehicles screeching into the yard, and then came the whirring of the helicopter's blades.

26

Two weeks after it happened . . .

O*dd Singsaker threw up* into the toilet. After flushing, he sat down on the toilet seat and sucked on a Fisherman's Friend lozenge.

They'd been at it for hours now. He'd told Melhus everything that had happened, without embellishing. The only thing he'd kept to himself was the part about stepping on her thigh and grinding his heel in the wound when he was desperate for an answer. Nor had he said anything about wanting to kill her. That was a feeling that had only grown stronger as he sat on the ground next to the well and watched as Felicia's lifeless body was hoisted into the helicopter and flown up toward the dark, starless sky.

Ane Fagerhus had tried to get up after he ran out of the house to find the well. Then she had fallen through the floor, which collapsed as she was about to leave, and she'd ended up in the basement. It took so long to saw through all the building materials and get her safely out of there that Felicia had long ago been transported away by the time Ane was carried off on a stretcher, right past Singsaker. He now remembered how he'd wanted to strangle her then and there. He wasn't proud of that, but in many ways it was the simple, brutal truth—he had wanted revenge. And that urge hadn't entirely faded over the past two weeks. It had diminished and taken on a more dreamlike quality, most prevalent in the evening and morning, but it was still there. The thought, the fantasy of killing her. If only he could understand why she'd done it, why Felicia had been made to suffer for something that was between Ane and her husband.

There was no doubt that Rolf Fagerhus had intended to kill his wife. Why else would he have taken the trouble to get rid of Singsaker first? Maybe he didn't want any witnesses, but Singsaker thought there was another, simpler reason. He no longer cared whether or not he got caught. The only reason he threw Singsaker into the water was because otherwise the detective might have reached Ane before he did. At that point, of course, he didn't know that she was sitting inside the blown-up house. Singsaker had tormented himself with the thought that she must have seen everything from the window. Fagerhus had probably been on his way to steal another small boat from the marina so he could go out to where Ane's sister lived. In his eyes, that must have been the most natural place to look for his wife. And presumably he was worried that Singsaker had had the same idea when he arrived, so he decided to get rid of him first. The fact that Fagerhus went back to check the house before leaving had to be because, as a policeman, he'd been trained to be thorough. The main thing was that he hadn't wanted anyone or anything to stop him from killing his wife. That was the only thing of importance. By then, it was most likely that the murder of Ane Fagerhus was the very last thing Rolf Fagerhus intended to do in his life. Unfortunately for him, she was more than capable of defending herself.

Singsaker went back to the interview room.

Kurt Melhus was still there, but Attorney Gregersen had left. The session was over, and Singsaker had no obligation to tell Melhus anything more. Plenty of people would have advised him to refrain from saying another word. But he wanted to say a proper good-bye. He no longer feared Melhus or the interview process. Not the way he had when it began. He now realized that it had done him good to go through the entire course of events with a man who was such a lucid thinker, someone from whom he couldn't hide. It had been a form of therapy for him.

"How much do you have left to do?" asked Singsaker.

Melhus looked up. He was busy packing up his briefcase.

"I'm done with my part. But I'm only concerned with the role of the police in the case. The actual investigation is far from finished."

"I'm aware of that."

"Singsaker," said Melhus, standing up. "I'm really sorry about what happened. No matter what conclusion we come to, I'm really sorry."

"Melhus," said Singsaker, "do you ever feel the effects of what we do?"

"What do you mean?"

"All the brutality."

"Sometimes."

"Things have gotten a lot worse in a very short time, haven't they?"

Melhus nodded.

"A lot of people still say that we're spoiled, that Norway is so peaceful, that we live in a peaceful time. I know what the murder rate was in Norway during the Viking period, and I know what it is in the slums of Rio, but it's gotten worse here too. I think it gets worse every year. And it's happening so fast. It feels like something is about to happen soon that will really shake us up."

"You've just been through a terrible experience. You need to get your mind off it."

"I suppose it's too early to say anything about your findings?"

"It's not solely up to me, Singsaker. You'll hear from us soon if there's any question of filing charges."

Melhus's handshake was as firm as Singsaker remembered from

Horten. Then the brilliant investigator, who once might have been a friend, picked up his briefcase and left.

Singsaker remained sitting in the interview room, giving himself time to think before Jensen came to join him.

"How'd it go?"

"Fine, I think. You know what, Thorvald? It feels good."

"I hope you're right. They can't get us for breaking any specific law. Melhus knows that. But I should never have taken you along."

"I know. But I shot a witness in the thigh. It was self-defense, but I can't deny doing it. The question is whether they believe that I had to shoot, that I had no choice. And that my actions weren't prompted by some other motive, or based on emotion. I had a sense that Melhus left here in a different frame of mind than when he arrived. I think that's significant for both of us, but only time will tell. What about Brattberg? Is she in a better mood now?"

"Improving, I think. As you know, the case is now being handled by Kripo. So she's not about to let me anywhere near it. Right now I'm working on a different case. A father was severely beaten by three men in his own home in the center of town. All indications are that two men living in Charlottenlund were involved. We've dealt with them before. And we're convinced that they know who the third man is. Unfortunately, the victim changed his story over the last few days, and now he claims he can't recall what any of the intruders looked like."

"Shit. How do they manage to do that?"

"Your guess is as good as mine. But we're working with the technical evidence and hope to make some progress in the case. Some of the physical evidence as well as accounts from witnesses point to a connection with the Rosenborg Park case. That student who was beat up and, according to the autopsy report, most likely died from allergic shock after drinking beer. There's also something about the MO in each case that links them together."

"So we're suddenly back to Knut Andersen Stang, that young man in the boat."

"Right. He was a witness in the Rosenborg Park case. By the way, they've dismissed any consideration of possible criminal actions on his part in connection with the boating accident and the break-in at Guttorm Gjessing's house. Because of the state of the evidence."

"So Melhus was onto something," murmured Singsaker.

"What did you say?"

"It's strange how there seems to be a connection between all these cases that the police are working on."

"I agree."

"What do you know about Ane Fagerhus?"

Finally, Singsaker had gotten around to what he really wanted to talk about.

"You may not have heard, but she's still in the hospital. She broke her back when she fell through the floor, and she's paralyzed from the waist down. She's probably never going to walk again."

"Is there enough evidence to indict her?"

"All we have is the confession that she made to you. The weapon, the alleged baseball bat, is gone. And she's no longer cooperating with the police."

"Felicia thought it was a woman who attacked her."

"Felicia was badly injured. And . . ."

Jensen stopped himself. Singsaker knew why. It was too hard for him to say it out loud. Felicia could not be used as a witness in the case.

"What about everything else?" said Singsaker to keep the conversation going.

"As far as I know, we're working on the theory that everything can be ascribed to Rolf Fagerhus."

"Everything?"

"Now listen here, Singsaker. Rolf Fagerhus killed a drug dealer in Oslo, a man named Isaac Casaubon that he was actually supposed to be investigating. We assume that Fagerhus took a large amount of cash from the man, but the money hasn't been found."

"Do we actually know that he killed Casaubon?"

"The man died from an overdose of heroin. Yet there are no indications that he ever used the stuff. We also interviewed his son. He said that he watched Fagerhus force his father to shoot up the heroin. After that he kidnapped the son and tried to kill him out in the woods. We assume it was in that connection that Fagerhus came in contact with Felicia. We know that she rented a car at Gardermoen Airport and was planning to drive to Trondheim. We have to assume that for some reason she ended up witnessing Fagerhus's attempt to kill the boy. The boy says that she rescued him by hiding him in a cabin. Blood tests have also shown that Felicia had heroin in her bloodstream. Fagerhus most likely subjected her to the same treatment as Casaubon, but this time he didn't manage to give her as big a dose. Felicia survived, but Fagerhus still had a motive for killing her.

"Yet everything that happened up to that point was just preparation for Fagerhus's real plan. He wanted to kill his wife and daughter. We're talking here about a classic case of wiping out a whole family. One theory is that he blew up the house believing that his wife and daughter were inside. The idea was to take them with him when he killed himself. The autopsy report confirms that he most likely had survived an extreme explosive event before he got into the boat. We don't know what went wrong. We have no good answer for why he survived the explosion, but such things do happen. Hitler survived the assassination attempt on July 20, 1944, in his bunker because the bomb was placed underneath a table. The theory is that Fagerhus had not intended to survive. His wild maneuvering of the speedboat and the subsequent collision with the other boat can be seen as another suicide attempt. We also don't know why he blew up the house when his family was not in fact inside. It shouldn't have taken much effort for him to find out where his wife and daughter were. But traces of heroin were also found in his blood. He may have been acting under the influence of the drug. Maybe he just happened to find the dynamite, which his sister-in-law had left to be picked up by the sheriff. Maybe he convinced himself that his wife and daughter were asleep upstairs. And then he decided to blow the house to smithereens."

"That doesn't really mesh with what I've heard about his personality."

"It's true that everyone has described him as an extremely calm and rational person. But there's no doubt he had a dark side that no one knew about. He hid behind a mask, concealing what was really going on inside. You know as well as I do that even the most peaceful person can have a dark side. And besides, from what I heard, Fagerhus never got over the loss of his father when he was a kid. So his cold demeanor may have been an unhealthy defense mechanism against the grief that was never resolved."

"Do you believe that?"

"Nothing else seems plausible, Odd."

"But what about Felicia?"

"Most likely he beat her nearly half to death before they reached Hitra. Maybe he saw the well and thought it would be a good place to get rid of her."

"But he had a gun with him. She wasn't dead when he threw her into the well."

"He felt sure that she wouldn't survive. And he didn't want anybody to hear the sound of a gunshot."

Singsaker got up.

"Is this the direction the investigation is taking?"

"Think about it, Odd. I know it's not easy, but we have a story line that makes sense. How far from the truth could it be?"

"I don't know, Thorvald. Maybe you're right. Or maybe we're just looking for what's most plausible and neglecting other possibilities."

"It's the nature of an investigation to search for the truth. And in almost all instances, we do get very close to the truth."

Jensen looked at Singsaker. He knew him better than most.

"I don't know whether it will give you any peace of mind," he said. "But it's no longer our case. We have to let it go."

"But you realize that if the police allow this theory about Ane Fagerhus to stand, then my credibility is undercut. Who will believe that I shot her in self-defense? Who will believe that she aimed a gun at me and threatened to pull the trigger?"

"No one here at the station has any doubt about that part of the story."

"But Melhus doesn't work here."

"I know what you're getting at. But there could have been other reasons why Ane Fagerhus aimed a gun at you. She had just shot her husband. Maybe she was afraid he had accomplices. You weren't wearing a uniform, after all."

"I saw her. There was no fear in her eyes. By the way, Melhus said something interesting during the interview."

"What's that?"

"He said something about the connection between things. What we were just talking about. The link between all these different cases. Melhus has a theory, or something like it, that the solution can be found in the unknown, in what he called the fifth element. And there are things here that don't add up. You know that yourself."

"Maybe, Odd. Maybe. But as I said, it's no longer our case. All I want is for you to find peace."

Peace, thought Singsaker. He'd forgotten how that felt. He had no idea how he'd ever find peace again.

During the drive out to Hitra that night he definitely didn't find it.

He'd gone out there after receiving a text message from Melhus a short time after he left the police station. He wondered why his old colleague had sent it to him. It couldn't be regarded as merely an expression of concern. Even if Internal Affairs hadn't yet decided what to do about him and Jensen, Melhus knew how much it meant to Singsaker that the case involving Felicia shouldn't get stuck on the track that the police had settled on. As usual, Melhus had put his finger on a crucial point, something that didn't mesh. But why his concern? *Maybe*, thought Singsaker, *Melhus is more biased than we expected*. They'd shared something back then in Horten. Hadn't they? When it came right down to it, were they actually friends, after all?

For the first time in two weeks Singsaker returned to where it all happened. Everything still looked the same. Because of the ongoing investigation, the house hadn't yet been torn down. It was still standing, threatening to collapse all on its own.

He parked his car in the driveway and went straight to the well. The police had covered it with a plank and then placed a rock on top of the board. Singsaker removed them, and shone his flashlight down inside. The well hadn't yet been cleaned up. Presumably the crime techs had done a number of inspections down there, looking for organic evidence and fingerprints. But since the police had settled on the theory that the well was important only because Felicia had been thrown into it, nothing had been cleared away. Nor had the police done a thorough examination of all the trash inside.

This time Singsaker took the trouble to get a ladder that he'd seen lying next to the wall of the house. He lowered it down to the mattress, which was still in the well, and climbed down.

Then he began rummaging through all the garbage. Among some rusty junk he found what he was looking for, something that he'd seen the last time he was down there. The police hadn't separated it out from the other useless trash, probably because they hadn't had any reason to look for something like that. It was a gray box that was cracked in several places and look half-melted. It was not normal household garbage, that much was clear. Singsaker shone his flashlight on what he'd found and then used his cell to take a picture of the battered object.

On his way back to town he phoned Jensen.

He asked him the exact same question that Melhus had asked in his brief text message:

"How did she know that Felicia was in the well?" he said as soon as Jensen picked up.

"Odd? Is that you?"

"Ane Fagerhus was the one who told me that Felicia was in the well. If Rolf Fagerhus had thrown her in before he blew up the house, how did his wife know about Felicia? Ane wasn't there at the time."

"Odd, what are you getting at?"

"The well. You need to ask the crime scene investigators to take a closer look at the well."

"I think they've planned to do a thorough inspection. But there's just a bunch of old junk down there. It's a time-consuming job, and the house has to be their first priority."

"The junk isn't all old," said Singsaker. "I've just been out there to take a look."

"What did you find?"

"It's something that CSI will have to look at. But ask them to look at a broken gray box that's partially melted. No labels on it, but it contains a lot of electronics. Reminds me of some sort of sensor, like a laser, or maybe a detonator of some kind. Looks much too sophisticated to be normal household trash. If I'm not mistaken, this is going to knock the wind out of the theory that Rolf Fagerhus blew up the house in a state of emotional agitation. We may be talking about a carefully staged 'accident.' Something that took a lot longer to rig up than the time Fagerhus had at his disposal."

It was past midnight by the time he got home. She was standing at the kitchen counter, right where she was when he got up in the morning, as if she hadn't gone anywhere in the meantime. She handed him a cup of coffee again, though not in a paper cup this time.

He felt like he'd been away for weeks, as if everything he'd recounted during the interview had been played out again in real time.

Singsaker went past her into the laundry room. In a box on top of the washing machine he found what he was looking for. The cell phone from the well. He'd stuck it in his pocket before they'd pulled him out. The phone had stayed in his filthy pants until he washed them a few days ago. Then he'd put it in the box. All along he'd intended to hand the phone over to the police, but he'd had other things on his mind lately. He had no idea how it had ended up in the well, but he was positive now he knew who it belonged to. He also realized how out of it he'd been over the past few weeks, and how far he was from being able to return to work as a police detective. He should have done this long ago. Now he put the cell in a plastic bag he found in the drawer under the washing machine, and then he took it with him to the kitchen. The lab needed to take a closer look at it. *Yet another item that linked Ane Fagerhus to the well and to Felicia,* he thought.

Singsaker put the cell on the kitchen counter and looked at her.

Her red hair was pulled back into a ponytail. She held her head tilted slightly to one side, as usual. She looked at him with those green eyes of hers.

"How did it go?"

"Hard to say. But I don't think I'm going to be charged with anything."

"That wasn't exactly what I meant. How did it go having to talk about everything? It must have been hell."

Siri Holm had spent a lot of time with him after it happened. She'd truly been a huge support. In many ways they'd felt as if they were sharing this fate, especially the same feeling of guilt. This was something neither of them could escape. It was a fact that Felicia had gone to Oslo because of them. It was irrelevant that they couldn't have known what the consequences would be, or that it would have been impossible to undo what they'd done. Their feeling of guilt had nothing to do with rational thought. But it eased the burden a bit that they shared it.

"You know how sorry I am about everything," she said.

He wasn't listening to her. From the cupboard he got out two glasses and a bottle of Red Aalborg.

"Let's have a drink before bed," he said. "There's not much else we can do at the moment except drink and hope."

No sooner did he say those words than his phone rang. It was late. There weren't many who would call at this hour. He stared at the number on the display.

"I have to take this," he said and went into the bedroom.

He was gone for quite a while, carrying on a lengthy conversation. When he came back into the kitchen, he felt as if he was floating on warm air. He filled the glasses that were still on the counter, and handed one of them to Siri. Then he raised his glass, and broke into a tentative smile, as if his face had forgotten how to smile and needed practice.

"Felicia woke up," he said.

Siri Holm shrieked like a teenager.

"Really? Did she really?"

"Yes. That was the hospital. She woke up!"

"They said it was next to impossible."

"I know, but she woke up."

"So how's her condition now?"

Singsaker turned serious.

"Of course she's very weak. But they say that she's able to answer their questions. She's conscious, and she has mobility and feeling in every part of her body. It seems very likely that she's going to be okay."

"What were the chances of that happening?"

"I don't remember what they told us. But what difference does it make now?"

"It's a miracle," said Siri Holm.

No, he thought, sending a warm thank-you to Kurt Melhus, *it's the fifth element*.

"Shall we drink a toast?"

"No," he said. "Actually, I think I'm giving up Red Aalborg."

"That's probably wise," she said with a somber expression. "For her sake."

"For her sake," he said, noticing how amazing it felt to talk about Felicia like that, as if she was once again part of his future.

"I want to give you a present to take to her," said Siri. She rummaged through her bag.

Singsaker waited impatiently, wanting to go out the door.

"A book?" he said when he saw what she was holding.

"It's old."

"I can see that. Latin?"

"Some Latin and some English, from the 1600s."

"Not exactly easy reading."

"No, but if you guys don't like it, you can always sell it. I think you'd get a pretty sizable amount for it, if you sold it to the right antiquarian bookseller in London. Actually, that's what you should do. Sell it and take Felicia on a long trip when she's back on her feet. That's what you both need right now."

"Maybe. But where did you get this book?"

"From somebody who can't appreciate it anymore."

"Did you borrow it?"

"Trust me. The person who owned this book doesn't need it anymore. That's for sure. It's mine now, a souvenir from him. But I'm giving it to you and Felicia."

"This seems a little weird."

"Odd, do you always have to act like a policeman? Can't you just take the book? I don't know exactly how much you can get for it, but I think it'll be enough for a nice vacation. Treat yourselves. Let your hair down. Life is short."

Singsaker looked at her. He was used to regarding this young woman as smarter than himself.

"Maybe we do need to live a little more, to say what the hell and do something wild when all this is over," he said. "Thanks for the book."

He put it in his leather briefcase. Then he gave Siri a hug.

27

Four weeks after it happened . . .

O*dd, do you remember* the well?"

"Do you think I'll ever forget it?"

It was their second night home together. They'd turned in early.

"I lay there for a long time. It felt like I died several times, and I was dreaming. I dreamed about his eyes. They were totally white. That's how I remember them, anyway. They probably had some color, but I remember them as completely white out there in the woods. He could have just shot me. Why didn't he?"

"He found a less bloody way to render you harmless. Either he was sure that he'd given you an overdose, or else he didn't want another murder added to the charges unless it was necessary."

"But he fired at me on the road. He could have killed me then."

"Sure, but at that time he wasn't in control of the situation. He needed to stop you. Maybe he didn't shoot to kill. Maybe he just wanted to scare you and throw you off guard. He was a policeman, you know. Don't you think he would have shot you if he really meant to?"

"But why do you think he decided to set me free on Hitra, even though I might be a threat to him as a witness?"

"I don't know. At that point he'd suffered serious injuries. Things hadn't gone as planned. Maybe he thought one more witness wasn't going to make any difference. He'd already burned all his bridges. I think the whole time he was planning to flee. I think he was going to take his daughter and leave the country. If that didn't work out, then plan B was to put an end to it all, maybe after killing both Ane and Tina. I don't think he pictured himself ever being brought to trial. But you shouldn't let all this keep bothering you, Felicia."

"Don't ask me to forget. I'm never going to forget. And I'm never going to understand it either. But I don't think he was capable of pulling the trigger. He might have shot me when I was on the move, when I was running away from him. But when I sat there, motionless, right in front of him, he couldn't do it. And I think you're right about it being a matter of control. At that moment he did have control, and if he shot me, he would have felt like he'd lost it. I think Rolf Fagerhus was all about being in control."

"Control." Singsaker thought about that word. "Do you think that's why he took you along in his car instead of leaving you behind in Østerdalen?"

"He probably realized that I wasn't going to die of a heroin overdose, but I'd still been put out of commission, so he had total control over me. It was safer to take me with him."

Felicia put her hand on Singsaker's shoulder. They lay in bed, facing each other, breathing in the same air. Both of them knew they would spend weeks, maybe months, going over all these events. So they were discussing only small details at a time. They were both happy when they got into bed. That afternoon he'd received a letter informing him that all charges against him had been dropped.

"Do you remember me saying that I needed you to forgive me for something?"

He nodded.

"I slept with someone else."

He turned onto his back and stared up at the ceiling.

"Aren't you going to say anything?" she said.

"I don't know what to say."

"You should get mad. That's the least you can do."

"It feels like that was a whole different lifetime. That wasn't us."

"Yes, it was. Aren't you mad?"

"No."

He wasn't sure that was true. Or if it would always be true. But right now he didn't feel angry. He felt dizzy.

"Who was it?"

"Just somebody I met in Oslo. I was drunk."

"Are you going to start drinking again?"

"All I can promise is that I'll try not to."

"I had a feeling that's what happened."

"I had a test done in the hospital. I'm not pregnant."

"Why are you telling me this?"

"I've been thinking, Odd. Thinking and thinking. I want to have a baby. With you. If you can forgive me."

He looked at her.

She was talking about forgiveness. But he still hadn't forgiven her for almost dying. He remembered holding her body, limp and lifeless. It was something he would always feel in his hands. He couldn't forget the way she was hoisted up into the helicopter, strapped onto a stretcher. Somewhere up in the air above him she had regained consciousness for a brief moment, very brief. They'd told him about that afterward. Then she had slipped away again, and they put her on the respirator that had kept her alive for almost two weeks. They said that her heart had kept beating the whole time, but her pulse had been so weak down there in the well that in the end he couldn't feel it. How would he ever get over that?

"A baby?" he said now. "I don't know how long I'm going to live."

"I think you'll live longer than you expect."

"It'll be your child."

"It'll be ours. Maybe I'll have to take over raising the child by myself in the future. But it will always be ours."

"Shouldn't we think about this some more? You've just come back."

"You can think about it," she said.

"Because you already have?"

"It feels like I thought about a lot of things while I was asleep, and somewhere in that darkness I made a decision that I don't want to change."

"But I need time to think."

"So think. Take all the time you need."

"While we're thinking, could we do something wild?" he said, hearing an echo of an old dream.

"You never want to do anything wild." Then she laughed.

Finally, she laughed. That had happened so seldom since she'd awakened from the coma. This was how he wanted to see her. He wanted her to laugh more. Then he could forgive her for anything.

"I can be wild," he said.

"What do you mean?"

"I've never been to Virginia. I hear it's nice this time of year."

"Odd," she said, bending over him so he could see her face. She was giving him a teasing smile. "You know that for me, going to Virginia isn't exactly wild."

"It is for me. I'm always dreaming about traveling, but I never go anywhere. It's been like that my whole life."

"Virginia isn't wild."

"Okay, but is it romantic?"

"Richmond? Romantic? You'll have to show me."

"So you'll go?"

"Can we afford it?"

"I have money. But maybe we'll take a trip to London first."

He thought about the book that Siri had given him. He'd decided to follow her advice. It wasn't that he didn't have the money for plane tickets. But it felt right to do it this way. He needed to do something reckless. He needed that in his life. They both needed it. They couldn't allow themselves to get mired in regret, partial forgiveness, and deadly seriousness. If they were going to bring a new life into this cruel world, as Felicia suggested, then they first had to prove that they were capable of truly living.

EPILOGUE

Six weeks after it happened . . .

There were at least a hundred reasons for Sving to be furious with her. And this was one of them: Why hadn't she told him that she was married to a cop? Karlstad had told him after the fact that even he wasn't aware of his occupation. She'd never told him either. Maybe it wasn't so strange, since they were old friends who hadn't been in contact for a long time, and because Karlstad had chosen a slightly different career than Rolf Fagerhus. Karlstad assured Sving that he would never have given him the assignment if he'd known they were dealing with a police officer. Sving believed him. But had Ane really intended for him to kill a cop without knowing who he was murdering? And would he have still done it if he'd known? There were definitely plenty of reasons to be furious. But in the end, he'd started asking himself whether there might also be some love left.

Ane had done the job that he should have done. She had removed the boxes with the sensors and remote control and most likely any other equipment she could find. And she hadn't mentioned his name during any of the interrogations. Plus she'd killed her husband all on her own. That might seem like love. Of course there were other reasons why she'd want to keep him out of the matter. Maybe she was protecting Karlstad, her childhood friend. Maybe she thought Sving might be a dangerous witness against her if the police turned the spotlight on him. But maybe that too was love. Sving noticed that, against his will, he'd begun hoping that was true. No matter what, it was to his benefit that she'd kept her mouth shut. If only she'd used her head when she got rid of all the wreckage.

If everything had gone as planned, Ane could have put all the blame on Rolf Fagerhus and claimed self-defense, even though she'd apparently been careless enough to confess to the first policeman who showed up that day. As soon as she got a lawyer, the confession had been retracted. She'd been confused and delirious after the attack by her husband, and she hadn't known what she was saying. Besides, the police officer wasn't on duty and was subsequently investigated by Internal Affairs. But then that same cop got curious and found the evidence against Ane. Now she was in real trouble. It looked as if she might get prison time. So far she still hadn't roped Sving into the whole thing. But the police hadn't put much pressure on her yet. She was still in the hospital, and the investigation was far from over. Sving did not feel safe, by any means.

And then there was Ane's sister. Karlstad had called her, and she'd agreed to keep Sving out of it, for her sister's sake, and for Tina's sake too. But she wasn't 100 percent reliable, and if the police really went after her, he had no idea how things might go.

The worst part was that they couldn't see each other. He couldn't sit next to Ane's hospital bed and comfort her. What if she was never able to walk again, which now seemed most likely? Maybe that was why she hadn't turned him in. She needed someone to push her wheelchair when she got out of prison someday. Sving noticed that in a strange way he liked that idea. He really wished he could talk to her so they could have planned what she should say when she was questioned. But it would be too risky to meet. He didn't even dare go out to Hitra to see Tina, who was still staying with her aunt.

But he'd promised himself to do that when this was over, provided he managed to stay out of it all.

Right now Sving was driving his VW Polo from Karlstad's car repair shop to an address in Byåsen. He was playing music in the car, Polish tunes by the Norwegian-Polish band Karuzela. He was singing along. He was in such a good mood that he was singing sad ballads from his native country.

He and Karlstad were on good terms again. Even though that Stang guy had slit his wrists in a clinic out on Hitra, the money Sving had found in Rolf Fagerhus's fanny pack—which Ane had tossed onto the backseat before they'd parted—had been more than enough to cover the debt. He even had some money left over. Now things were mostly back to the way they'd always been.

That fanny pack had been useful in other ways too. Inside Sving had found confirmation of what he'd been hoping. Rolf Fagerhus really had been planning to kill Ane. How else was he supposed to interpret the documents he'd found? It was true that it didn't look like Tina's life had ever been in danger, since there were phony passports and plane tickets for both Rolf and his daughter.

As Sving saw it, that was enough proof that Ane had plenty of reason to fear her husband. She was a complicated woman, not easy to understand, and her motives for wanting Rolf dead were also complex. Yet it seemed as if there was also a kernel of truth in what she'd told Sving the first time they'd met. Rolf Fagerhus had definitely presented a danger to her.

When it came to Ane hitting him, he'd overreacted. He realized that now. It was only a few slaps to his cheek. Okay, maybe a few punches too, but he'd let her do it. He hadn't tried to stop her. None of that would have happened if he'd grabbed her immediately and held her tight. And besides, it wouldn't happen again, whether she was able to walk or not. She'd been in a horribly stressful situation. He understood that now. That's what had caused her to act that way.

Sving had decided to keep the promise he'd made to himself and get out of the business. And he needed to do it now, before he ended up feeling completely dead inside. That's why he was interested in checking out this one last job. It might be his ticket out.

This wasn't something that Karlstad was personally involved with. He'd just found out about the job through his network of contacts, and now he was passing along the information to Sving. Meaning that Sving could do whatever he liked with it, no strings attached. If he chose to take the job, it was his, with no restrictions, no quid pro quo. And it was supposed to be a straightforward job, a simple assignment, and a lot of money. *If I pull it off,* he thought, *then I'm going to retire.* With the rest of the money from Rolf Fagerhus's fanny pack and what he earned from this job, he'd be a free man. Maybe he'd be able to get his son out of bed so he could move out of Norway. Find himself a place in the sun and wait for Ane. Or maybe move back to Poland, where the money would go much further. He could take Sondre there. A change of scene would do the boy good.

"I hear you're good with a baseball bat," said the man who introduced himself as Roger Gjessing.

"That's not widely known. I assume you heard about it from people you can trust," replied Sving.

"Karlstad and I are old friends."

"How do you know each other?"

Did this man know Ane too? Sving felt an irrational twinge of jealousy.

"That's not important. The point is that when Karlstad tells me something about his colleagues, he knows I'll keep my mouth shut. And when he sends me somebody to do a job, I know he's the right man for that job."

Sving studied him carefully. A short, slightly chubby man with a shuffling gait, around fifty or sixty, a dangerous age. He wore a corduroy jacket and glasses that kept sliding down his nose. Rather professorial and shabby looking, but with a nervous intensity about him that might be a substitute for his lack of authority. A man who knew what he wanted but could never trust that he'd get what he asked for. The house he lived in spoke of money. And Sving guessed it was old money.

After parking in the driveway outside the house and ringing the bell, he'd been shown into a room filled with bookcases and art that even Sving could tell had cost big bucks.

Now they were sitting on plain-looking designer chairs, slightly worn, with a coffee table between them. Sving had been offered something to drink, and he'd said yes to a bottle of water. Gjessing was sipping a whiskey that was called something Sving couldn't even pronounce.

"A book has gone missing," said Gjessing. His voice was sharp and urgent, like chalk on a blackboard.

"A book. Is that the job? To find a book?"

"It's not just any book. It's worth a lot of money."

"One book? A lot of money?"

"Not many people think that books are valuable. But the truth is that books are among the most valuable of collectibles in the marketplace. A single book can sell for millions."

"And it's that kind of book?"

Gjessing sipped his whiskey almost anxiously, the way a hunted deer might graze in open countryside.

"Maybe not millions, but it's definitely valuable. It's a Burton. A first edition."

"A what?"

"We'll go over the details once you agree to take the job. The thing is that I inherited a number of valuable books from my uncle. But one of the books, apparently the most valuable of the lot, has disappeared from his estate."

"I assume you had an accurate list of your uncle's books?"

"I've known for a long time what I would inherit. The book we're talking about has suddenly popped up in London. I have contacts in the book world, and I know that someone went there to inquire about the book's value. Somebody wants to put it on the market."

"And do you know who this person is?"

"I have a picture of him. It was taken by my contact in London."

Gjessing showed Sving a picture on his cell phone. Sving didn't recognize the man until he heard his name.

"The man in the photo is Odd Singsaker, a police officer from Trondheim. There was a break-in at my uncle's place right before he died. The police investigated. I assume that's when he must have made off with it."

"This country is going to the dogs. We can't even trust the police anymore," said Sving, smiling.

"Personally, I don't trust anybody. I want the book back, and at the same time I want to send a clear message to this policeman."

"Excuse me for asking," said Sving and then paused for effect. "But if I take this job, we need to have all the cards on the table. Why don't you just go to the police and tell them that something was stolen from you?"

The man gave him a long look, took a sip of his whiskey, and said:

"What do you think?"

"I think there's something in what you said at the very beginning. Not everyone realizes the value of old books. And since we're talking about your uncle, that means there must be other heirs to his estate."

"There are five cousins. He had no children of his own and no living siblings. We divided up the estate among us. The biggest rivalry was for the artwork and crystal glasses, plus some cash found inside a mattress from his boat. I was happy to settle for the old 'worthless' books. No one, not even the estate's executor, had any idea what they might be worth."

"I see," said Sving. "You don't like to share. Not to mention the inheritance taxes you won't have to pay. It's understandable that you wouldn't want to get the police involved. Just get the book back and deliver a slap on the hand. What do I get in return?"

"It's impossible to say what a book like this might go for. The copy was in first-class condition. But we're talking about close to fifty or sixty thousand pounds. You get 50 percent as a finder's fee. The money isn't that important to me. It's the book I want. It may be one of the best preserved copies in the whole world."

Sving packed his bag. The plane to London left in three hours. He'd decided to take the airport bus and needed to get over to the bus stop. He needed to leave early because he wanted to check his baggage. Passengers were not allowed to carry on things like baseball bats.

He hadn't tried to jack up the price of the job. He'd made up his mind to take it the minute he heard the name of the cop. Odd Singsaker. He was the shithead who'd shot Ane and later found the evidence that could put her in prison.

Sving had been looking for some way to repay her for not implicating him after she was arrested. Now he didn't need to look any further.

He closed up the suitcase and lifted it off the bed where they had made love so roughly. Then he went through the kitchen to the living room.

And there he was, standing in the middle of the room. He was fully dressed, wearing pants and a sweater. His hair had grown long after so many months in the basement, but it looked clean and neat.

"Sondre?"

"Pappa!"

They just stood there, staring at each other.

"It's time for me to get up," said Sondre after a moment.

"You're going to get out of bed now?"

"Yes. Aren't you proud of me?"

Sving nodded pensively.

"What's with the suitcase? Are you going somewhere?"

"I've phoned your grandmother. She's going to come over and cook for you. I didn't know you'd be up. If I'd known . . ."

"You can't leave now. I've spent weeks getting ready. I think I can do it now."

Sving looked down at the floor, not daring to meet his son's eye.

"This trip is important for both of us."

"Pappa, are you serious?"

"I'll be on Facebook," said Sving, walking past him. The only sound was the creaking of the wheels on his roller bag as it moved across the floor.

At the front door he turned around and called:

"I'll be gone a week, tops. Then we'll make a fresh start."

He didn't begin to shake until he was sitting in the airport bus.